D0937486

CIRCLES IN SAPPHIRE

Donna Tregear

Believe that you can
and you will –

Donna Tregear

*I would like to thank my family and friends for their support
and encouragement throughout this process.*

*Margaret and Richard Addario -
I owe you a debt I can never repay. I have never forgotten all
you did for me when I needed you the most.*

*This book is dedicated to everyone who has loved and lost,
but wasn't afraid to love again - the dreamers of this world!*

Learn to let go of the hurt others
may have chosen to cause you;
learn to forgive yourself, for the
things you chose to do.

forgiveness

Forgiving is not easy, but when
you choose that path you'll see,
to unlock the door to your happiness,
forgiveness is the key.

CHAPTER 1

Maggie stepped onto her front porch in jeans and a long-sleeved thermal shirt. She closed her eyes, raised her face to the sun and inhaled salty ocean air. Halloween was two weeks away, but it was an Indian summer and the days were still warm. She froze. An eerie chill crawled up her arms that told her she was not alone on her quiet, tree-lined street. Absently, she rubbed the goose-bumps away and bounced down the steps. She scrutinized the handful of cars parked nearby. "Get a grip," she said to the empty street and headed toward the shops in the center of her new hometown.

The town she'd stumbled into four years earlier. The town that embraced her with open arms and offered her a chance at the fresh start she had desperately needed. Unable to shake off the sensation of being watched, Maggie looked behind her one last time before she turned the corner.

Kevin crept low in the seat of the Cherokee when Maggie stood in front of her house. He watched her look left, then right, then left again. He'd waited a good five minutes before he sat back up.

"Why are you here?" He asked himself for the thousandth time. Kevin knew he was the last person Maggie would want to see. *Well, second to last person* he thought. He rubbed his face and felt the one-day stubble, and reminded himself that *his son* was the last person Maggie would want to see. "Then again, if I know Maggie, she's probably forgiven Tommy", he said out loud. Kevin rolled down the window and lit a cigarette. Again, he thought that *he* probably was the last person Maggie would want to see. Before he could stop them, memories of those couple of weeks assaulted him in rapid-fire succession.

True to form, March had "come in like a lion". The rain had been off and on for two days, but that night it was steady with gale-like winds. Kevin had just finished his shift at Philly International and had pulled into his driveway when he heard the call come over the radio. A hit-and-run at 30th and Market. The suspect had been able to jump on the Schuylkill. "Yeah, keep going idiot." Kevin said as he lit a cigarette. As he leashed Duke, his K-9 partner, the song Bad Boys popped into his head. He sang out loud and took Duke for a walk. One look at his watch reminded him that it was daylight savings. "Let's go Duke" he said, "it's later than I thought."

As he approached his house, he saw his son's car, then noticed Tommy on the porch. He unhooked Duke's leash and watched him run up to Tommy and try to climb up on him. "Get off me" Tommy yelled and pushed him away.

"Yo," Kevin threatened, "don't talk to him like that. What happened? You and Darlene break up again?" Kevin stopped when he saw his son's face. "Tommy." He demanded. "What happened?"

Silence hung between them as Tommy stared past Kevin at the Explorer parked by the curb. "I screwed up dad. Bad." Kevin started to ask him what, but Tommy cut him off. "I think I hit someone." He looked up at his dad and let the tears fall.

Kevin took a long swig of the Coors' Light he'd grabbed from the fridge. "What do you mean you think you hit" but stopped as he felt the kick in his gut. "Aww Tommy. No. The hit and run."

Tommy snapped his head up to ask his dad how he knew. Then figured the car radio must've told him. But Kevin was already up. He moved towards Tommy's car to check for any damage. Kevin grabbed Tommy's keys. He pulled the K-9 car out of the driveway, opened the garage and pulled the Explorer in; he reparked his squad car and told Tommy to go inside and go to bed, they'd talk in the morning.

Kevin shook his head and came back to the present, but that didn't stop that week from replaying in his mind. The day after the accident, Kevin was able to find out that the vic was D.O.A. when he got to the ER. A friend of Kevin's worked the precinct that included the Hospital of University of Pennsylvania. He found out that witnesses only saw a dark colored SUV – either Jeep or Explorer – leave the scene; but the weather prevented anyone from getting the license plate. Kevin had a friend who could chop the Explorer, that wasn't an issue. He was torn though.

As a cop, he knew he had a duty; but as a dad, he couldn't let his son have his life thrown away on an accident. Screw that. Maybe the vic stepped out in front of the SUV and Tommy couldn't stop in time. Kevin thought about this over and over til he convinced himself the guy had committed suicide. The next day, he got gut-kicked again.

When Kevin saw Maggie's name pop up on his cell, he almost didn't answer. Then he thought that if there was one person he could talk to about this without judgement, it was her. They'd been best friends since the third grade. She'd seen him through two divorces and used to babysit Tommy when Kevin had to work nights. Outside his mom and sister, she was the one female in his life who he hadn't managed to drive away. So, he answered the phone.

"Hey Mag, I'm glad you called. You free for dinner tonight? I really need to talk to you." There was a pause before Maggie replied.

"Kev," she said and cleared her throat. "I guess you haven't heard."

He didn't know why fear had settled in his stomach, but asked if he'd heard what. Maggie was too quiet. "Mag, what's wrong. Is your mom okay?"

Maggie told him her mom was fine. "It's Jase. He. Um. He." *She stuttered.*

Kevin didn't want to know what Jase um was, but braced for what he knew she was gonna say. Almost like she was in a tunnel, he faintly heard her tell him that her fiancé had been involved in a hit and run two nights earlier and that he didn't make it.

"They still can't find the driver. But who does that Kev? Who is that horrible? How can someone hit another human being and just take off?" Maggie stopped her rant. She told Kevin that she was okay for now. "You know me, gotta be strong for everyone else. My family has been in and out, but they don't know what to do for me. Hell, I don't know what to do for me."

Then she whispered to him. "I finally found love Kev. Ya know. It took me almost 40 years, but I'd found someone. And now he's gone. Why?"

Kevin was speechless but knew he had to say something. "I'm sorry Mag, I".

But Maggie stopped him. "I know Kev. I sort of hoped that you could maybe find out some information for me. But I don't want you to get into any trouble. You know how you sometimes like to cross the line to help a friend."

Kevin told her he was sorry and that he'd call her later. They never spoke again.

At Tommy's hearing, Maggie refused to make eye contact with Kevin. Not that he'd had the guts to look her in the eye. Almost two years later, she sold her house and moved to Lantern Light Cove. *And now here I sit, again. Still don't have the guts to actually try and talk to her.*

Kevin decided he'd messed with Maggie's emotions enough. She didn't need to know that Tommy would be paroled next week. She didn't need to know that Tommy would be able to move to Florida with Kevin; where he ran away to when he was forced into early retirement. Maggie wouldn't care that Kevin's younger son had changed his name and wanted nothing to do with Kevin or his half-brother.

One accident – so much damage. With a loud sigh, Kevin started the Cherokee, and wished Maggie the happiness she deserved. He headed back to Pennsylvania, out of Maggie's life forever.

CHAPTER 2

Maggie turned onto Main Street and put the jitters behind her. She smiled to herself. *I really lucked out when I wandered into this place.* As she walked into the diner, she saw the owner behind the counter deep in conversation with Arty, the Cove's mechanic. Joe looked up at the bell that announced her arrival.

"Mornin Mag," Joe mouthed as he tried to break away from Arty. When he could, he grabbed the coffee pot and sauntered over to the booth she had taken by a window. He set a mug down and poured. Then loud enough for Angie to hear he asked her when she was gonna run away with him.

Before Maggie could respond, Joe's wife called out from the kitchen to wish Maggie luck with that one. Arty then joined the conversation and told Angie that *they* could finally run away together. Maggie smirked, Joe rolled his eyes and Angie came over with a perfectly toasted cinnamon raisin bagel with cream cheese.

"I just assumed when you sat you wanted breakfast this morning", she said and set the plate down.

"Thanks Angie," Maggie said. "Can I get a side of bacon too? Please." She pleaded.

"Extra crispy?" Angie asked.

Maggie felt pure contentment after she took a sip of coffee. Then replied, "is there any other way to eat bacon?"

Angie patted Maggie's shoulder and told her it would be right up. With a wink, she whispered, "I'll trade you Joe for that Luke any day of the week."

Joe snorted. "I heard that." Then he and Arty continued to discuss the Giants' chances this season. Maggie leaned back in the red leather booth and thought about the day she drove into the Cove. It amazed her how well she could still recall that day in vivid detail.

CHAPTER 3

Lantern Light Cove – just "The Cove" to locals – was one of a hundred little sleepy seaside towns along the Jersey coast. It was actually a peninsula, with the bay on one side and the ocean on the other. There was one road that led in and out. It was seven miles long and two-and-a-half miles at its widest.

One dreary Saturday, about eighteen months after her fiancé passed, Maggie woke up around 4:00 in the morning. Ever since the cops had called her *that* other morning, she found herself wide awake this same time every day. Almost always she'd jump up with a start and the hope that it had all been a horrible nightmare. Instinctively, she reached for Charlie – her three-year-old yellow lab. Then reminded herself that she had taken him to her sister's house the night before.

"Thanks for this Liz," she said as she unhooked his leash. "I know it sounds selfish."

"Stop it Mag," Lizzie said harshly. "You haven't done a single thing for yourself in the past eighteen months. Tomorrow's your birthday. If you wake up and decide you want to go somewhere for a couple of days. Then go."

Maggie knelt down in front of Charlie to hug him and remind him to be good for his Aunt Liz. She looked up at her sister with half a smile. "You're right. But I still appreciate this."

She hugged Charlie again and stood up. Charlie nodded his head first at Maggie then at Liz. When that didn't work, he pawed the air. Maggie asked him if he wanted a treat. At the sound of the "T" word, Charlie padded out to the kitchen, followed by Reggie, Liz's lab/rottweiler mix. The canine cousins sat patiently in front of the treat cabinet. They looked back at their respective moms as they waited to be rewarded.

The sisters walked to the door. Liz told Maggie that whatever she decided to do, Charlie could stay as long as Maggie needed him to. Then she hooked her arm around Maggie's waist, kissed her cheek and said, "consider it your birthday present. Because I haven't shopped for you yet." Maggie climbed into her Wrangler and with one honk of the horn, she waved, then drove home.

CHAPTER 4

Maggie walked into the house and let the quietness envelop her. It was the first time she'd been truly alone there since Jase died. For a little while, she just wandered around and watched, as if from a distance, her fingers caress objects that lay carelessly about. Jase's denim jacket that still hung on the coat rack. The framed photo of the two of them the day they brought Charlie home. The empty bottle of wine from their engagement dinner he insisted they needed to hold onto. It wasn't until she stood in front of the pine and glass curio cabinet he'd made her for their first Christmas that the tears seem to pour out of her.

It stood six feet tall and two feet wide. The sides and door had glass panels, and there were four adjustable glass shelves. It had a light at the top and a drawer at the bottom. For the door and drawer, he'd found silver knobs with Celtic knots etched into them. Maggie cherished that cabinet, but Jase always pointed out the flaws. She would ignore his criticism and tell him he should sell the things he made. Then he would tell her she was crazy. That no one in their right mind would pay for his stuff. Jase never felt good enough.

Maggie blamed his dad for that; and truth was she hated him for it. She never understood how a parent could make their child feel worthless. The only thing Jase thought he was good at was the gym. So, he became a personal trainer and decided to get a job at what he loved to do. He tried to push Maggie into what made her happy and helped her create an on-line presence with her photos and greeting cards. But Maggie never thought *she* was good enough.

"We were two peas in a pod," she said, as she took the time to look at every picture and knick-knack on each shelf. She closed the door to the cabinet and leaned her head against it. "All of this adds up to the life we had together. And the life we'll never know." She whispered to the empty room.

Before memories could swallow her, Maggie went upstairs. After a long hot shower, she turned on the TV in their bedroom and stumbled onto a Cary Grant marathon. *His Girl Friday* had just started. Maggie loved the old black and white movies. Mostly, she appreciated that they didn't need special effects, but instead, relied on really good dialogue to carry them. But God how Jase hated them.

"And yet you always snuggled up to watch them with me," she reminded his picture on her nightstand. She could almost hear him tell her that he agreed to watch them so he could try to cop a feel. The memory made her laugh. Maggie went downstairs, made some popcorn, poured a glass of wine and went back up to her bedroom.

She set the bowl of popcorn on the dresser and started to pace. So many thoughts raced through her mind. Vaguely, she listened to Cary Grant try and convince Rosalind Russell not to marry Ralph Bellamy. This particular movie was full of fast-paced, snappy dialogue and was one of Maggie's favorites. She stopped for minute, sipped her wine and stared vacantly at the screen. Then turned back to Jase's picture.

"Talk to me babe. It's so hard. I need help. I'm stuck in limbo," she said as the sadness washed over her.

Maggie let the tears fall again. She walked over to the window and watched the rain fall on Dorchester Road. The window felt cold when Maggie leaned her forehead against the glass. For a couple of minutes, she stood there in the hope that the rain could somehow wash away all the hurt. She rubbed her engagement ring and wondered what she should do with everything. The house. Their stuff. Her life.

She turned and walked into the bathroom, the wine and popcorn forgotten. She washed her face, brushed her teeth then crawled into bed and hugged Jase's pillow to her chest. As she started to fall asleep, she whispered through her tears, "please babe. Give me a sign. Help me figure out where I go from here."

So, with Charlie at her sister's, and certain she wouldn't go back to sleep, Maggie decided she really had to get away. She dragged herself out of bed, stretched and looked out the window. It was still dark, but she could see by the streetlamp that the rain had become a drizzle. As if on auto-pilot, Maggie made the bed and began to throw things into an overnight bag. She didn't have a clue where she was going, all she knew is that she had to get away.

By six o'clock, she had packed and backed the Jeep out of her drive. With no real destination in mind, all Maggie knew was that she needed the ocean, so she decided to head East.

"But first coffee," she said to the empty seat beside her. "And since it's my birthday, a vanilla crème powdered donut."

CHAPTER 5

Maggie drove over the Walt Whitman Bridge which would take her from Pennsylvania into New Jersey. There was no toll in this direction and Maggie always thought it was funny that you had to pay to get out of New Jersey. She'd driven this route thousands of times on her way to the Jersey Shore. *Not the MTV Jersey Shore*, she thought to herself with a snort as she took the Atlantic City Expressway to the Garden State Parkway.

She'd often pester Jase on these trips about why we drive on a parkway and park on a driveway. Jase would just roll his eyes whenever she pointed this out and tell her she was weird. Instead of the parkway south to Ocean City or Sea Isle, Maggie jumped on the northbound side. After about two-and-a-half hours of twists, turns and backroads she saw a sign for Lantern Light Cove and found herself on Main Street USA. Literally.

She hadn't thought about where she was when she found an open spot and parked. But when she got out of the Jeep, she looked up and smiled. A sign over a storefront read 'Cup o' Joe'. Somehow, she had managed to find a diner.

Maggie loved diners. Jase had always said it was one of the reasons he fell in love with her. She was the kind of girl who would rather go to a diner for breakfast than some fancy restaurant for dinner. Maggie had never heard of Lantern Light Cove, but as she stood there in the morning rain, an unmistakable presence of comfort started to come over her. For a brief second, Maggie believed that Jase had somehow led her here.

The sound of tap-tap-tap caused Maggie to spin around.

Behind the front window of the diner, she saw a large black man in a greasy apron. He pointed at the rain and brandished a pot of coffee. He tilted his head toward the front door. Maggie nodded, then followed his suggestion and walked in.

A bell over the front door jingled to announce her arrival, and the handful of people that had taken up space in booths or at the counter looked up, acknowledged her, then went back to their conversations, newspapers or books. Maggie felt right at home.

The owner, Joe, came over and introduced himself. With a toothpick in the right corner of his mouth, he grunted, "Philly. Huh?"

Maggie looked at him confused for a second, then remembered she had on her Eagles' hoodie. With a nod and vote of confidence, told him that she thought they had a real chance this year. "If not, the Philly sports fan motto is there's always next season." Joe chuckled and asked if she wanted counter, table or booth. Maggie looked around then hopped up on a vacant stool at the counter and asked for coffee and a menu.

CHAPTER 6

Joe Garcia had a checkered past and wasn't the least bit ashamed to talk about it. He'd gotten into some trouble in his late teens, early twenties and actually did some time. It was in prison that he learned to be a short order cook. When he was released, he worked his way down the coast til he landed in the Cove. It just so happened the owner, Sam, needed a short-order cook. Joe took the job and when Sam retired and moved South, he bought the diner and kept the name.

Maggie sat at the counter on the red vinyl 50s-style stool. She had ordered one of her diner-breakfast staples: two eggs over easy, crispy bacon, hash browns, whole wheat toast. She'd been delighted to see that the hash browns were the shredded crispy kind. As Joe stood behind the counter and recounted his story, Maggie couldn't help but wonder *why* he felt the need to share it with her. So she asked him.

He wiped his hands on his grease-stained apron and took his trademark toothpick out of his mouth. "I'm telling you", he began, "because a beautiful girl like you, sporting that" he jutted his chin at her left hand, "shouldn't be so sad."

Maggie looked away for a second and brushed away a tear before it could spill down her cheek. When she looked back, Joe had his elbows on the counter and had leaned in close enough that she could see a small scar under his left eye.

"The Cove is a place people find themselves in when they need a change. People here don't ask questions and they don't judge. They just accept. Because most of us stumbled into this town when we were in search of our own fresh start."

Maggie rested her chin on her hand and sighed. "What makes you think I'm someone who needs a fresh start?" She asked him.

Joe shrugged, then asked Maggie if she was a day-tripper. Maggie looked confused for a minute. "Oh, you mean a shoobie." As the bell over the front door rang and a group of teenagers came in, it was Joe's turn to look confused.

"A what?" Before Maggie could answer he asked, "what the heck is a shoobie?"

Maggie laughed and explained that further south along the coast, shoobies were day-trippers. Joe raised an eyebrow and Maggie continued. She told him that the name came about from the days when people who travelled to the shore for the day would pack their lunches in shoeboxes. Maggie threw out her hands and said, "shoobies."

"And no, I didn't pack a shoebox." She added with a wink. She did tell him that she had packed an overnight bag just in case. Before he turned his attention to the group of teenagers by the pinball machine, he told Maggie to take a walk around town. "The Cove just may be exactly where you want to be." He then added that if she needed a place to stay, he was sure that The Oyster Bed & Breakfast had an available room.

"The Oyster Bed. I get it," Maggie said with a chuckle. She stopped to pay the cashier, and helped herself to one of the starlight mints in a bowl, then wandered back out the front door.

Maggie stood outside Joe's and inhaled the unmistakable odor that sometimes drifted off the bay. Since the rain had stopped, Maggie decided to take Joe's advice. She looked up and down the street and loved what she saw: Ginny's Flowers.

Wicznewski's Pharmacy. The Tea Shoppe. Rosa's Boutique. Even more, she was thrilled with what she didn't see. Not a single Starbuck's, McDonald's, or any other national chain. It was the exact town she and Jase had always hoped to find. Main Street was the only non-beach-themed street in town.

As Maggie meandered around, she discovered streets with whimsical names: Seashell Way, Dolphin Court, Crab Alley. The cross streets were avenues named after bodies of water. Maggie followed the sound of gulls that pulled her to the ocean. She realized she'd never asked Joe where the B&B was, but figured she'd find it eventually. The need to be by the water consumed her. She picked up her pace and almost ran the three blocks to the beach.

CHAPTER 7

Maggie made her way up the short path between the dunes then down to the water's edge. Even with the tide on its way out, it was clear that the beach at Lantern Light Cove was very narrow. A light breeze brushed over her as she listened to the cries of seagulls that combed the shoreline in search of food. She backed up a bit and plopped down on the hard sand.

For a while, Maggie sat there, hugged her knees to her chest and let the ocean work its charm on her. No matter what her mood, or what the weather, five minutes beside the water and Maggie was soothed. Out of the corner of her eye, she caught movement. When she looked to her right, she noticed a man and a black dog headed in her general direction.

The man threw a ball into the shallow waves and the lab ran in to retrieve it. The dog seemed quite proud of himself each time he dropped the ball at his owner's feet. Maggie thought about Charlie. *He would love to run on the beach every day*, she mused as she doodled in the wet sand with her finger. When the wind shifted, the dog must have picked up her scent.

He lost all interest in the ball, sniffed the air, and turned to face her. Without warning, a mass of black fur was barreling down the beach in a beeline straight towards her. The owner was in hot pursuit, but the lab easily won that race. Maggie began to laugh as the dog tried to lick her face and almost knocked her over.

"I am so sorry," the man stammered when he finally caught up. Then he pointed to the dog. "You are in so much trouble."

Maggie told the man she was fine as the dog made himself comfortable next to Maggie. She rubbed his side and asked, "what's his name?"

"*Her* name," the man corrected, "is Molly."

Maggie apologized and said she should've known. "Cause you're so pretty", she told Molly; who had rolled over on her back and begged for a belly rub. That lasted for about three seconds as a seagull caught Molly's attention and she chased it into the water.

The man reached out and said, "I'm Luke."

Maggie took his hand to help her up. "Maggie," she said as she wiped the sand off her jeans.

This close to him, Maggie thought he smelled clean. Fresh. His light brown, sun-streaked hair hung just at his collar's edge. She also liked the casual way he carried himself. Dressed in loose jeans with a gold and green flannel that was open over a tan thermal shirt. *Which, really brings out the flecks of gold in his hazel eyes*, she thought. A pair of very worn, beat-up Vans covered his feet. His hand, when he helped her up was rough, callused. She was certain that whatever he did for a living, he worked with those hands. In a different time, she might have flirted with him. Instead, she asked him how to get to the Oyster Bed & Breakfast.

Luke knew she wasn't a local. He would never forget those blue eyes. Obviously, she had planned to spend the night here. He considered asking her out for drinks; but as the sun tried to break through the clouds, light glinted off the ring on the third finger of her left hand. *Maybe she's having second thoughts*, he considered. But that didn't matter to Luke; he didn't play those games. As long as she wore that ring, she was off limits.

"The Oyster Bed?" He asked as he whistled for Molly. "It's about two blocks north." Then he turned and pointed past the dunes. Luke told her it would be easier from the street. "It's at the corner of Atlantic Avenue and Oyster Road".

The look in her eyes caused Luke to snort and he told her he didn't name the streets. Maggie thanked him, said goodbye to Molly and made her way back up the path through the dunes. As man and dog watched her walked away, the lab whined.

Luke looked down at her. "I know girl," he said and picked up the ball at his feet. "I might've liked her too. But she's already spoken for." With that, he threw Molly's ball back the way they had come from and headed home.

Maggie stopped at the top of the dunes and watched them until they were nothing more than specks in the distance. She hadn't wanted to be rude, but she wanted a little more time to herself. Once they had disappeared beyond a jetty, Maggie sat back down in the sand. She let the sun warm her face and the sound of the waves wash over her. With another deep breath of salty air, she decided she should probably find that B&B to see if they had a room.

She walked back to the Jeep and as she turned onto Main Street, she saw it was already early afternoon. The break in rain had brought out people. Some were carrying bags; some were putting together bouquets from the barrels outside Ginny's; some seemed to be catching up with news and town gossip. Maggie overheard the word festival several times and briefly wondered what that was about. She could see that the diner was filled to capacity and noticed Luke's green and gold flannel at the same stool she'd occupied a couple hours earlier. The fact that she'd notice it startled her.

Joe was at the counter. When he saw Maggie through the window, he waved. She nodded a smile and waved back. At Joe's wave, Luke turned just in time to see Maggie jump into an army-green Wrangler. He snorted. "Of course she drives a Jeep." Then mumbled, "damn shame she's off limits."

Joe stood close enough to catch some of Luke's comments. "Something on your mind son", he asked and wiped away some hamburger grease that had pooled in drips on the counter. But when he followed Luke's gaze he asked, "or someone?" Luke just shook his head and mentioned ships that passed in the night.

CHAPTER 8

Maggie drove down Ocean Avenue to Oyster Road and turned right. She found a parking spot, but sat in the Jeep for a couple of minutes. All of a sudden, she remembered it was her birthday, *and how could I forget that?* She asked herself as she wondered why she hadn't heard from her family or friends. She picked up the phone and answered her own question. "The phone's turned off you moron." Once she turned it back on, she saw she'd missed a bunch of texts and a couple of calls. One of those missed calls was from Lizzie.

Maggie knew that if she checked voicemail, she would hear her sister's Marilyn Monroe rendition of happy birthday. Everyone Lizzie knew – friend, family, co-worker - got the same rendition every year. And everyone looked forward to it. Since she didn't want to talk to anyone; she texted her sister to let her know where she was, that she would stay at least tonight and would call her in the morning. She ended the text with hugs to Charlie.

Maggie got out and watched an older gentleman hang a sign from two hooks on the porch. It was in the shape of an oyster shell and painted in shades of pink in what is known as the ombre effect. Dark black letters announced: The Oyster Bed & Breakfast. Then in smaller letters: Established 1853. She did not want to disturb a man while he stood on a ladder – something she learned from Jase – so she leaned back against her Jeep and just took it all in.

It's beautiful, Maggie thought as she stared at the weathered Victorian house. Like most Victorians, this one had a tower, which was on the right side of the building. The railinged porch, went from the tower and around the house to the beach side. There were several sets of old-fashioned rocking chairs spaced apart for private conversations. Each pair had different colored cushions in orange, yellow, purple and green. Maggie caught the late afternoon sun that reflected golden in the two dormers. The house was blue siding with white trim.

The overall picture reminded Maggie of colors found on a beautiful October day. The kind of day where the sky was bright blue with pristine white clouds. Add in the pots of yellow and rust-colored mums – one on each step that led up to the porch – and that's exactly what this house was. A perfect Autumn day! Maggie was reminded of the beautiful Victorian homes that used to line the streets of Ocean City when she was a child. Most of those homes had been torn down and replaced with duplexes crammed on top of each other. Maggie hoped that didn't happen here. She smiled at the man who called out to her with a delightful Irish brogue to ask if she'd be needing a place to spend the night.

Maggie walked up the steps with her bag and said, "Yes, I would if there's a room available."

The man reached for her bag and introduced himself. "Paddy O'Roarke," he said with a wink. "Proprietor. General handyman. And official greeter." He opened the door. "Welcome to the Oyster Bed and Breakfast." A short gray-haired lady came from behind the counter and kissed him on the cheek. Then she turned her attention to Maggie. "He's also the teller of tall tales and blarney if you share a Guinness with him."

Maggie said she preferred Smithwick's. She extended her hand, told them her name and that she could stand there all day just to listen to the lilt in their voices.

"I'm Nell", the woman replied. "And anyone who pronounces Smitticks properly, gets a hug in this house."

From behind the desk, Paddy offered her a choice of seafoam or silver. At Maggie's confused look, they explained that each room was a different color scheme. Maggie thought that Lizzie would love this place. Then she asked if either of those rooms faced the ocean.

"Seafoam it is," Paddy said as he grabbed a key and handed Maggie a pen to sign the guest register. "So, is it just the one night you'll be here with us?" He asked and pointed to her overnight bag.

Maggie apologized and said she wasn't sure. Paddy told her that was fine, but the Oyster Bed was booked for the festival in two weeks. Maggie assured him she'd be gone before then, but did want to know more about the festival she kept hearing about.

He escorted his guest up the stairs and told her she would learn all about it at supper. "Which," he informed her, "is at six-thirty if she's interested."

They stopped in front of a white door with a seafoam-colored oyster shell painted on it. Paddy opened it for her and handed her the key. "Don't forget about dinner lass," he reminded her as he went back downstairs. Maggie dropped her bag on the bed and closed the door behind her. For a minute she leaned against it and took in her surroundings.

CHAPTER 9

Maggie wasn't sure what the silver room looked like, but she instantly fell in love with the seafoam room. The walls were indeed a soft hue of seafoam green. The queen-size bed was antiqued bronze and covered in a creamy goose down quilt. At the base of the headboard, accent pillows in various shapes and sizes decorated the bed in peach and seafoam. The hardwood floors, which appeared to be original, gleamed. There was an area rug in muted cream and peach. The color scheme carried over into the small bathroom, but as accents to the white tile. The bathroom itself was simple with a walk-in shower, toilet and pedestal sink; scalloped of course like an oyster shell.

Maggie turned back into the room, and walked to the over-sized chair in the corner. It was upholstered in thin stripes of seafoam, peach and cream. Beside the chair was a small table with a land-line phone, writing pad and pen. Maggie picked up the phone just to hear the dial tone. A small reminder of a simpler time. That time before cell phones, text messages and an automated world. She replaced the receiver, opened the French doors and stepped out onto the private balcony that overlooked the Atlantic Ocean.

Maggie looked down on the beach and appreciated the scene from the eye of a photographer. There were a couple of kids with buckets weighted down with rocks and shells. There were some joggers – one behind the other – along the line where the water met the sand. And there was an older couple, not in any hurry, as they walked hand-in-hand. It was the couple that captured Maggie's attention and made her wish she'd thought to bring her camera.

Were they reliving their past? Making plans to visit grandchildren? Or enjoying a stroll in comfortable silence the way some couples can? Maggie wondered all these things as it occurred to her for the millionth time that she and Jase would not grow old together.

A knock on her door saved her from the wallow of self-pity that threatened to smother her. As she went back inside, she noticed the two Adirondack chairs pushed up against the far railing. Laughing, she told the chairs that of course they were painted seafoam green!

Maggie opened her door to find a young woman there. If Maggie had to guess, the girl was in her late teens. There was still an air of innocence in her lively green eyes. Her deep auburn hair was carelessly thrown up in a ponytail and a few of the curly tendrils had slipped out. They stood close enough to each other so that Maggie could see a trail of freckles across the girl's cheeks and over the bridge of her nose.

"Hi," she said with a smile. "I'm Kathleen. Mum-mum sent me up with fresh towels and tonight's dinner menu." She strolled past Maggie, put the towels in the bathroom and handed Maggie the menu. "Oh," she started again, "mum-mum wanted to know if you'd like a cup of tea before dinner."

Maggie thanked her but declined the tea. "Honestly, I could go for a beer," she replied.

Kathleen looked her watch. "It's four o'clock. Mick should be about ready to open the bar for the supper crowd." At Maggie's confused look, Kathleen provided a brief history of the inn.

The Oyster Bed & Breakfast had been established as

a boarding house. For seventy cents a week, a person had their own bed, clean linens, breakfast and supper. It catered mostly to men who dredged for oysters, and the occasional drifter who passed through town on the way to somewhere else. As the town grew, and people began to build homes, the boarding house was converted to a restaurant with hotel-like accommodations. This, in turn, led to the current day bed and breakfast; which still served the oyster stew it had become famous for.

"It was my great-great grandparents who opened the boarding house," Kathleen told her. She went on to say that her family learned to change with the times. Today, the B&B does well; but the weekend supper crowd definitely helps. Since the island has one fancy restaurant, one diner and one locals' bar, my grandparents thought that another place to dine on the weekends is a good idea. "And of course, a signature dish like our oyster stew doesn't hurt." With a whisper, she told Maggie that the oyster stew was a recipe only given to blood relatives who are sworn to secrecy!

Maggie told Kathleen she was looking forward to trying it. "So, there's a bar in the dining room?" She asked still unsure she'd heard correctly.

"Yes ma'am." Kathleen replied. "Your breakfast and supper are included in your bill, but it's a cash bar. It's open from four til eleven, and there are Saturday night regulars. Sometimes, a lot of times actually, a party breaks out."

Before Kathleen had a chance to say anything else, Paddy could be heard somewhere in the house loudly singing "I'll Take You Home Again Kathleen." With exasperation, the young girl informed Maggie that was her Pop's subtle way to let her know he needed her help. Paddy continued to croon and Kathleen joined in on the next verse.

Maggie watched her make her way down the stairs, then went into the bathroom to freshen up. She opened her overnight bag and changed into the lightweight black turtleneck she'd packed, then checked herself in the mirror.

"If you're plan to spend more time here," she said to her reflection, "and you probably will, then you need to go shopping." Maggie hoped Lantern Light Cove was not one of those towns whose shops were closed on Sundays. After she applied mascara and added silver hoop earrings, but before she could talk herself out of it, Maggie headed downstairs to get that beer.

CHAPTER 10

Maggie stopped short before she walked into the dining room. Stunned, she was able to pull herself together before her mouth dropped open. *Not at all what I expected* she thought. Then reminded herself that she'd never actually stayed at a B&B, so she didn't know what to expect. There were two buffet tables up against a wall – dark oak filled with nicks from years of use. But, just like the hardwood floors they stood on, they too gleamed. Evidence that they were very well cared for. On one table there were small trays of fruit, vegetables and cheese and crackers. Beside those were small plates for the hors d'oeuvres.

On the next table were warming trays, currently empty. And if the aromas that wafted from the kitchen were any indication, those trays would be emptied again as soon as they were filled. Next to the kitchen door was a sweets table that displayed brightly colored petit fours, miniature cream puffs and eclairs. There was also a coffee urn, hot water urn, a variety of tea bags and cream and sugar.

In the center of the room, a long table sat with four mismatched chairs on each side and one on each end. This was set up for family style dining, which is how the O'Roarkes liked it. However, there were also three smaller tables set for intimate dining.

Each table was draped in a white linen tablecloth. If Maggie was a betting woman, she'd bet the farm that those linens were oyster-shell white. Maggie moved over to one table to take a closer look at the place settings that added a splash of color to each table. The china was a very pretty shade of mint green trimmed in cream. There was a small cream-colored shamrock in the center of each piece. They were quite lovely; and Maggie was certain they'd come over from the 'auld sod'. As beautiful as the tables were set, it was the bar that caught your attention.

It too, was dark wood, rounded and set inside the tower section of the dining room. There was a brass rail footrest that ran the length of the bottom of the bar. Maggie was certain that that also had come over from Ireland. Two of the four stools were occupied by men that talked loud with the bartender while their attention was riveted to the soccer game on the muted television.

The street-facing wall was all windows framed with white lace curtains that fluttered in the night breeze. Opposite the window, stood floor-to-ceiling inset shelves, again in dark wood, and lined with glasses in every size imaginable. Wine goblets, champagne flutes, cordial glasses and ones for anything "on-the-rocks". They shimmered in shades of cobalt blue, ruby red, emerald green and sunflower yellow. The shelf that was eye-level was lined with pint glasses that bore the Oyster Bed's logo. The entire unit was framed in white Christmas lights that twinkled off all those glasses and reflected in the window panes. Maggie could only imagine the image it painted to a passer-by.

The shelves behind the bar were glass. They started at counter level but ran up to the ceiling and were filled with liquor bottles – all top shelf and organized by type. The center shelf was reserved for whiskey. Irish whiskey. Mainly Jameson. Then Maggie noticed there were just three beer taps: Guinness, Smithwick's and Harp. As she took it all in, she felt completely at ease and walked over to one of the unoccupied bar stools.

When she settled herself on one, the bartender came over and set a drink napkin in front of her. He was burly, and looked like he'd be right at home working on the docks. His hair, close-cropped beard and mustache were red, streaked with gray. His blue eyes were kind, but aged with the wisdom of someone who had seen too much. Maggie imagined he'd been in his share of brawls. When he spoke, there was still a trace of a brogue. Smiling, Maggie said, "you must be Mick."

Mick wiped his hands on a bar towel, told her he was and asked what he could get for her. With a nod toward the taps, she said, "I'll have a Smithwick's please."

Mick smiled and said, "you must be the lovely lass who checked in today. Maggie, is it?"

"Yes." She replied. "I'm Maggie. Unless you're a Catholic school nun. Then I'm Margaret."

Mick laughed and went to pour her beer. The two men at the other end of the bar turned and tipped their pints toward Maggie. She nodded in reply. Mick asked what room she was in, so he could add her tab to her room bill; then turned his attention back to the soccer game and his friends. Maggie took a long sip and watched as Kathleen came into the room.

CHAPTER 11

Kathleen had changed into jeans and a loose fitting emerald green sweater. Her auburn curls hung just below her shoulders and Maggie was impressed with the air of confidence that seemed to contradict the tinge of innocence Maggie felt earlier. One of the men at the bar called out to her.

"Kathleen love, when are you going to run away with me?"

Without missing a step, she answered, "when you're about 30 years younger Mr. Donovan."

This caused Mick and the other man at the bar to roar with laughter. "It's okay lass, I believe my Connor has his eye on you," he said and tipped his pint in her direction.

"Your son has his eye on any girl who walks past him." She took the stool beside Maggie. "And I deserve a whole lot better than Connor Donovan." As if she needed confirmation, she looked at the other patron. "Isn't that right Uncle Seamus?"

Seamus agreed with a slap on his friend's back. Then ordered another pint and told his friend that Kathleen was O'Roarke through and through, and Connor didn't stand a chance.

Mick set a Guinness in front of Kathleen. After she took a sip, she looked at Maggie. "Yes, I'm only 17. But Pop and mum-mum let me have one Guinness on Saturday nights as long as I don't plan to go out."

Maggie held up her hands and assured the young woman that she didn't judge. "Irish is in my blood. When we were babies teething, it was whiskey on our gums. When we came in from the cold, there was whiskey in our tea." Then she took a sip of her beer and added, "and of course there were potatoes at every meal."

Kathleen wrinkled her nose, then swiveled on her stool to turn and face the room. She proceeded to share who was who at the B&B.

CHAPTER 12

She started with Mark, the young man who'd come up and gotten two pints. He took them back to one of the small tables where his girlfriend Chrissy had made a plate of hors d'oeuvres for them to share. They were in the coral room. Mark and Chrissy had graduated from somewhere up North back in May and had taken the summer to visit Bed and Breakfasts up and down the Eastern seaboard. Tomorrow they'd be headed to Rhode Island. From there they would go back to Massachusetts where they both had jobs waiting for them. But one day they hoped to open an inn of their own.

Then there were the two older couples who sipped dirty martinis in the sitting room. Charlotte and Abigail were sisters. Charlotte was married to Stephen, who worked on Wall Street. They always took the ocean room. Abigail and her husband Jeremy ran a small, but successful, real estate firm in Connecticut. And they always had the sunlight room. Between the two couples, there were seven children and five grandchildren with another on the way for Charlotte and Stephen. They've been coming to the Oyster Bed on this same weekend every year for the past ten years to celebrate their anniversaries.

"Wait," Maggie replied. "They got married on the same day?" She asked in surprise.

Kathleen almost spit out the Guinness she'd just taken a sip of. After she wiped her chin, she clarified that Abigail and Jeremy got married in August; and Char and Stephen got married in October. So, they split the difference and chose a weekend in September.

Maggie watched Paddy and Nell move between the dining room and sitting room to mingle with their guests. Nell was just about to head over to the bar when three more people came in from outside, so she turned her attention to them. It was then that Maggie noticed the strong resemblance between the gracious older innkeeper and her grounded, determined granddaughter. She signaled Mick for another pint and asked Kathleen how she was related to Paddy and Nell. Sadness crept into Kathleen's eyes. Maggie regretted that she asked and started to apologize.

Kathleen stopped her. "It's okay," she said but chewed on her lower lip. Then, with a deep breath and another sip of Guinness, she told Maggie her story.

Kathleen's mom, Norah, was Paddy and Nell's only daughter. They had two sons. Their oldest, John, lived in Philadelphia with his wife and their four sons. Their youngest, Emmett, was in the navy and was currently a flight instructor stationed in San Diego. When Kathleen was eleven, Norah was diagnosed with pancreatic cancer.

"It took her very quickly and that almost killed my da."

Norah and Liam Walsh were high school sweethearts. Liam worked on the fishing boats and Norah had gone to school for hospitality and business management. She knew that one day she would take over the B&B. After Norah passed, Liam tried to work on land for a full year, but he couldn't adjust.

"Do you know that song Brandy?" Norah asked Maggie.

"Sure. It's one of my favorites." Maggie replied as Kathleen fingered the silver chain she wore.

"Wait," Maggie said. Then pointed at Kathleen's necklace.

She asked if that was from the north of Spain and did it have a locket. The young girl beamed. She said she wasn't sure where it was from, but her ma never took it off. "Sometimes, I can still hear her singing about how much he loved the sea."

One day, when Kathleen was almost 13, Liam approached her grandparents and asked if she could move in with them. He didn't know how to raise a little girl on his own, and he struggled to make it on land. The night before he left, he sat Kathleen down and talked to her about everything as best he could.

"At first, I was sad. And very confused," Kathleen admitted. "Then, he slipped this chain over my head and told me to look in the locket. Instead of just his picture, like my ma carried, it was a photo of both my parents."

Liam reminded Kathleen that just like he always came home to her ma, he would always come home to her. Kathleen looked intensely at Maggie. She asked her if she ever had a feeling of calm just wash over her.

Maggie thought about her time on the beach earlier that day and told her she did. Shrugging, her shoulders, Kathleen said, "that's what happened when da put this chain on me." Then she told Maggie that her da did come home every two or three months for a week to ten days, and he spent most of that time with his daughter.

Maggie was about to say something, but the kitchen door swung open and servers had begun to bring out the warming trays filled with that night's supper choices. Kathleen slid off her stool and grabbed Maggie's hand to pull her over to the big table to eat with the family.

CHAPTER 13

Paddy and Nell took their seats at either end of the table. Kathleen sat to the left of her grandmother, with Maggie beside her. Seamus and Jimmy, Mr. Donovan, came over from the bar and took the seats on either side of Paddy. Mark and Chrissy introduced themselves to Maggie as they sat on the opposite side of the table. The two older couples who had been in the sitting room said their goodbyes and left.

They had an annual reservation for dinner at Tradewinds. With a clip in her voice, Nell explained to Maggie that was the *fancy* restaurant at the tip of the peninsula. Then she added, "the food is good; but it's the view that pulls you in and keeps you mesmerized. Every table looks out over the water in one direction or another."

Mark chimed in to inform Maggie that lanterns were placed around the property to throw light onto the water that glistened like diamonds. "They only open for dinner," he told her. "And if you get a chance, you should go. The views are definitely worth the price of admission."

Maggie thanked him and said she would look into it. Then she noticed that the three people who'd come in earlier had taken one of the small tables; and another table was occupied by a couple and their two children. The front door opened just as Nell asked everyone to close their eyes and offer up a prayer of gratitude.

"Be grateful for family – near and far. Be grateful for friends – old and new. Be grateful for blessings – big and small. And know that I'm grateful for each of you." There was a chorus of Amens around the table.

Dinner was buffet style, and Maggie stood up to make her platter. Out of the corner of her eye, she noticed someone had taken a seat at the bar and was engaged in a serious conversation with Mick.

Nell noticed him at the same time, and exclaimed, "Luke! When did you sneak in?"

Luke told her he'd come in just as she gave her blessing and that he didn't want to disturb her. He declined Nell's offer to join them for supper because he'd had a late lunch, he said he'd come in to go over some work with Mick. Nell noticed that Luke hadn't taken his eyes off Maggie, and her curiosity piqued when Maggie asked about Molly. Luke told her Molly was sulking at home because Luke had to give her a bath. Before Maggie could respond, he told her to enjoy her dinner and turned his attention back to Mick and the pint he had in front of him.

While Nell took the time to fill water glasses, Maggie walked over to the serving tables and looked over her choices. She decided on salmon with the roasted vegetables of carrots, broccoli and cauliflower. And, of course, a cup of their world-famous oyster stew! Back at the table, she noticed that Seamus and Kevin had opted for shepherd's pie. Someone had placed baskets of homemade soda bread on each of the tables, along with small bowls filled with pats of Kerrygold Irish Butter.

Maggie took her seat and let the chatter of conversations wash over her. She would answer questions when asked, but for the most part she sat and listened. Caught up in another one of Paddy's childhood stories, she leaned over towards Nell and whispered, "he certainly was blessed with the gift of gab."

Nell rolled her eyes. "Maggie lass, you have no idea."

As Mick tended to some patrons, Luke took the opportunity to look into the "Guinness is good for you" mirror that hung across from him. It was in the perfect position for him to stare at Maggie without actually looking at her.

Based on her jeans, sweater and simple earrings, Luke knew Maggie was not a high maintenance kind of girl. And Luke knew a lot about high maintenance from his ex-wife. He appreciated the way she paid attention when someone spoke to her. Maggie's dark brown hair had some red in it that you could pick up when the lights hit it a certain way. Luke allowed himself to imagine what it would feel like to run his fingers through that hair. Then the light caught the ring on her left hand and snapped him back to reality. With a shake of his head, he raised his glass towards Mick.

"Another one Luke?" Mick asked surprised.

"Like the sign says," Luke answered, "Guinness is good for you."

Mick nodded in agreement. "That it is Luke. That it is."

Luke finished his pint, told Mick he'd get him an estimate for the work he wanted done, said his good byes and left. Seamus and Kevin went back to the bar for a nightcap of Jameson; Mark and Chrissy went upstairs to pack. Nell and Kathleen helped clear the tables and Paddy went to the front desk. Maggie wasn't ready for bed yet. So, she fixed a cup of lemon tea with honey, grabbed one of the throw blankets strewn around the sitting room, and went out to the porch.

CHAPTER 14

Maggie walked around to the beach side and was delighted to see a two-person glider at the far end. Carefully, she set her cup on the railing, curled herself up on the glider and wrapped herself in the blanket. She watched the steam from the tea drift up into the night sky before she took a sip.

"Oh Jase." She forced back a sob that threatened to escape. "You wouldn't believe this place. It's the town we always said we'd find one day." For a while she sat there, lulled by the distant sound of the waves that lapped at the shoreline, and missed the man she'd never get to marry.

Nell watched Maggie head out to the porch. The mother in her wanted to go out there and hug her until she cried out all that pain. But Maggie was a guest and Nell wanted to respect her privacy. It was one of those rare times in her life when she didn't know what to do. As she wavered between her options, she was startled by Paddy.

"Well now, isn't this something?" Nell looked over at her husband who was closing up the desk for the night. "Nell love," he called to her, "what's today's date?"

Before she could answer, Mick yelled over from the bar. "Tis the 26th. Me da's birthday." With that, he poured a shot of Jameson and raised it to the ceiling. As Mick toasted his father, Paddy told Nell that wasn't the only birthday.

When Nell asked what he meant, Paddy told her it was also Maggie's. As proof, he showed her the copy of Maggie's driver license. Nell closed her eyes in gratitude. Then she grabbed her husband and kissed him loudly.

"Every once in a while, Paddy O'Roarke," she said and put her hands on his shoulders, "you remind me why I married you." Then she told him he'd earned a second Guinness.

"Did ya' hear that Mick?" Before his bride could change her mind, he scampered over to the bar while Nell ran back to the kitchen.

Nell fixed Maggie a second cup of tea, filled a small plate with some desserts from the sweets table and brought them both out to the porch. "It's not birthday cake," Nell apologized, "but it's the best I could do on short notice."

Maggie was touched by the gesture and invited Nell to join her. The two women sat comfortably. Nell assured Maggie that the shops were indeed open on Sundays and she was happy to hear Maggie would stay with them for at least one more day. With a squeeze to Maggie's left hand, she sighed. "That is one of the most beautiful rings I've ever seen."

Maggie didn't respond at first. It took a couple of minutes, but she told Nell about the night that Jase proposed.

CHAPTER 15

They had lived together for almost two years and talked about marriage every so often. They were both in their late 30s and neither had been married before. Although Jase had once been engaged. Maggie had come home from work that night – on her birthday – and Charlie greeted her. Jase had placed a bowtie around his neck. She dumped her bag on the chair beside the door, knelt down and tugged at it.

"What's this?" She asked as she hugged him. Then she noticed that it wasn't Metallica or any other heavy metal band that usually assaulted her when she got home. It was Genesis. And not just any Genesis song. Follow You, Follow Me seemed to be on a loop.

"Jase?" She called out nervously as the vase full of sunflowers caught her eye. He came into the dining room with two glasses of wine. He handed one to her and told her dinner would be ready in about five minutes. He kissed her hello and held her hand for a minute.

Maggie pursed her lips and asked what was going on. "The table looks beautiful by the way," she said as she took a sip of wine. He looked at her with his soulful brown eyes. Without a word, he set his glass down and picked up a box from the table.

"What's in the box Jase?" She asked. Maggie knew the answer but was not yet sure she was ready for it. He hadn't let go of her hand when he told her that he knew marriage scared her.

"Terrifies me," she whispered.

"Given both our parents' marriages, I get it," he replied as he got down on one knee and started to sing along with the band. With that, he opened the box and inside was a ring – a round sapphire *encircled with diamonds.*

"Whadda ya say Mag, will you marry me?"

For a moment, Maggie just stared. At him. Then at the ring. Then back at him. Tears came. All she could do was nod.

He stood up, put the ring on her hand and kissed her. Maggie took a step back. She held out her hand with the ring on it and wiped her eyes with the other. The song began again.

"Genesis?"

Jase reminded her that she'd always said if she ever got married this would be her wedding song. "I just figured the lyrics said it all."

She kissed him again. They didn't tell anyone til the next night. She had wanted 24 hours for this to belong just to them. In that time, they painted a beautiful picture of the life they would build together.

"We never did get to dance to that song," she said to the sweet woman who sat quietly beside her. "Jase was in an accident about six months after he proposed. He didn't survive." Maggie went on to tell Nell that had been a year-and-a-half ago. And how for the past couple of weeks, she felt like she lived in slow motion. The walls had closed in around her and she wasn't strong enough to take it anymore.

"So last night I took Charlie to my sister's."

At Nell's silent question, Maggie said, "Charlie is our, my, yellow lab. And this morning, I threw a bag together, jumped in my Jeep and found my way here."

Nell patted Maggie's leg and told her how sorry she was and that she understood loss. Then she put an arm around her shoulder and hugged her.

Maggie pulled away from Nell and took her hand.

"Kathleen told me about Norah. I am so sorry. I never had children. I cannot even pretend to know how it feels to lose one."

They sat in silence for a couple of minutes, then Nell told Maggie that even though she'd had time to prepare, nothing prepares you. "Oh, and I was so angry." She patted Maggie's hand and told her she'd had a few choice words for the man upstairs.

"I imagine you would have," Maggie replied.

"But you know darlin' eventually the anger gave way to sadness. And the sadness is always here." Nell said and laid her hand on her heart. "But our Kathleen has made the suffering not as bad. Twas her needing me that got me through the darkest place I'd ever known." Then she told Maggie how one Saturday they were in the kitchen baking cookies. "It was a perfectly normal thing to be doin' with my granddaughter. And I heard someone laughing."

Nell seemed to be lost in the memory. Then with tears in her eyes, she said, "imagine my surprise when I realized *I* was the one laughing!" She told Maggie it was in that moment that she was able to forgive the good Lord for taking her Norah. "I know I will hug my daughter again one day. But for now," she said as she pulled herself off the glider, "I still have a job to do here." She gently cupped Maggie's chin and promised her that one day she would laugh again too. "And when you do, don't feel guilty about it." Nell wished her sweet dreams and went back inside.

For a while, Maggie sat there and stared at the ring. She loved the way it shone in the moonlight. She marveled again at how truly beautiful it was. It couldn't have been more perfect if she designed it herself. A one carat sapphire was surrounded by small diamonds in a scalloped setting. If you looked at it straight on, it had the appearance of a daisy-like flower. The band, in white gold, because Maggie did not like yellow gold, was designed to look like a vine. It was the most beautiful ring she'd ever seen.

"You know babe," she told the night air. "It hasn't been off my finger since you put it on." In an empty voice, she added, "now, it feels like a huge weight that I can't let go of."

CHAPTER 16

Maggie yawned, stretched and instinctively reached for Charlie who wasn't there. *He's at Lizzie's*, she thought, *and I'm in some place called Lantern Light Cove*. With another yawn, she sat up and breathed deeply. She reached for her phone. "No way," she said to the empty room.

She got out of bed and walked over to the doors that led to the balcony. When she opened one, the thin pink line ready to break on the horizon confirmed what she couldn't believe. It was 5:30.

"I'll be damned", she said with a smile. "For the first time since that horrible night, I slept past four-o'clock in the morning."

Maggie stepped out onto the balcony and shivered. She moved over to the railing and leaned on it. She found pure joy whenever she was able to watch the sun rise. Every so often, Jase would surprise her by waking her up in the middle of the night to drive to the shore. They would stop for coffee, take an oversized blanket, curl up in it and sit with their backs against the dunes. No words. Just peaceful silence while they watched streaks of pink and yellow and orange rise over the horizon. Brightly colored paintbrushes against a dark canvas.

On one of these mornings, about a month or so after Superstorm Sandy ravaged the East Coast, they walked close to the water's edge when something in the sand caught Maggie's eye. It was a seahorse. A seahorse – so perfect and intact – that at first, Maggie thought it was a plastic toy. But when she picked it up, the smell told her it was definitely not plastic. Even now, just the thought of that smell caused her to scrunch her nose in disgust. They took it home and placed it in a mason jar filled with sand and different colored sea glass.

The jar stands on their mantle; a reminder that it's possible to come through any storm whole and intact. It's what Jase always told her the seahorse would always represent for them. A seagull screeched, and shook Maggie out of the past. The pink ribbon on the horizon widened. It told her she had just enough time to run downstairs, grab a cup of coffee and get back up here to watch the sunrise.

With her hoodie thrown over her pajama top, she pulled on socks and crept down to the dining room and tried to be quiet. The breakfast buffet wasn't til 6:30, but she had her fingers crossed that she could find coffee.

As she turned into the dining room, she noticed a marked difference from supper the night before. The bar area was dark, and the stools were stacked behind it. The "family" table could now seat just four people. And while all the tables were set and draped with linens, the place settings were more casual than the beautiful pieces from the night before. Maggie stood in the empty room. She didn't *see* coffee, but she was certain she could smell it. She considered she'd peek into the kitchen, when the door swung open and Paddy bounced through it.

He stopped and grinned. "Top 'o the marnin to ya Maggie."

"And the rest of the day to you sir."

Her response prompted a hug from the inn keeper as he told her she was a credit to her ancestry. "Good enough to steal a cup of coffee," she asked.

With a wink, he tilted his head towards the swinging

door, and told her to help herself. She gave his cheek a loud kiss and told him *he* was a credit to his ancestry. Chuckling, Paddy continued to the front porch for the Sunday paper while Maggie continued to the kitchen.

Back up in her room, she grabbed a throw blanket and went out on the balcony. The railing was slatted in a way that she had a perfect view of the ocean when she was settled in one of the Adirondack chairs. With the mug clutched between her hands, Maggie watched the steam rise up and float off in the breeze. She took a sip, and thought, not for the first time, *the Beverly Hillbillies were wrong. Coffee, not oil, is black gold.*

Little by little, the night sky was erased and the golden sunrise promised a beautiful day. Although a chilly one. Maggie considered what clothes she'd thrown into her overnight bag and figured she'd be okay for today. But if she wanted to spend another night here, shopping was on the agenda. *Wow*, she thought. *I actually do wanna stay.* Maggie wasn't sure what to make of that, but she didn't dwell on it either.

"Well, shopping it is," she said to the seagull that landed on the far railing. "And unless you're on the hunt for coffee, I have no breakfast for you." Disappointed, the bird screeched and flew off. Maggie became aware of other sounds that had begun to interrupt the morning's silence.

A car horn beeped, then a door opened and closed. Traffic had started to pick up, Maggie assumed on Main Street. She was curious about the shops she'd find there. Somewhere in the distance a dog barked, and was greeted with several other barks in response. Maggie wondered if one of those dogs was Molly. Then she wondered how Charlie had managed without her.

I have to call Liz later this morning, she thought and took another sip of coffee. All was quiet again until Maggie heard the bells. The clear, unmistakable sound of church bells that called the faithful to come and pray. Maggie jumped up and almost dropped her mug. She rushed to the other end of the balcony and leaned over the railing. She craned her neck to locate the steeple. It was well hidden and Maggie wasn't even sure from which direction the bells rang. So, she stood there with her chin lifted to the sky. The sun warmed her face and the breeze played with her hair. She was at complete peace as she let the sound of church bells wash over her.

All of a sudden, she was a kid again where the church bells chimed every hour. It was how she knew it was time for dinner or time to go home. And every year on December first, those bells rang Christmas carols right up through January sixth. It was the one sound from her childhood that always made her feel safe. Maggie smiled. And for the first time, in a very long time, she *felt* the smile.

Not just on her lips, but in her heart. As if the emotional war that had raged deep inside her had thrown up the white flag and surrendered to the calm that was trying its best to settle around her. Maggie was unaware that she rubbed her thumb over her sapphire, but she was aware that it no longer felt heavy.

"Thanks babe," she said to Jase's memory. "I promise you. I will find my way." Maggie finished her coffee and went back inside to plan out all she wanted to do that day.

CHAPTER 17

Maggie showered, dressed, and out of habit, made the bed. She picked up a pen and the writing pad from the side table, grabbed her now empty mug and bounced down the stairs in search of food and more coffee. She made a small plate of fruit, a toasted bagel with cream cheese and a miniature apple danish. *Just one*, she told herself. With her second cup of coffee, she sat down at an empty table and began to make a list. She didn't get very far, as Mark and Chrissy stopped to say goodbye on their way to check out.

Maggie wished them good luck with all their plans and told them to be safe driving. She bit into her bagel, and wondered if the other guests had checked out. As soon as she thought it, the foursome came into the dining room to answer that question. She listened to them share a story from their anniversary dinner then started to organize her day.

"Obviously shopping", she wrote at the top of the list. Then felt a twinge of guilt. *Maybe Charlie should be my priority*, she thought. When Paddy stopped by her table to make sure she was okay, she told him she'd like to stay one more night. "Possibly two," she added.

With the flourish only a true Irishman possesses, he told her it was a fine and grand idea indeed. Maggie shook her head amused, then asked about Nell and Kathleen.

"My bride and granddaughter are at church." With a snort he added, "every Sunday and each holy day they go in an attempt to save my soul. But my soul don't need saving. And I'll not set another foot in *His* house until St. Patrick himself comes to me and explains why my Norah is up there with the Angels!"

Before Maggie could respond, someone from the kitchen popped their head out to tell Paddy he was needed. Maggie finished breakfast, went back upstairs to grab her keys and backpack then headed out to explore Lantern Light Cove.

CHAPTER 18

Once in the Jeep, Maggie wasn't sure which street to take. "But Main Street has to go the length of the peninsula. "Doesn't it?" She asked herself as she plugged in her phone and pulled up her country playlist. Certain she was right, Maggie turned left at the corner then called her sister.

Lizzie was distracted as she answered the phone. "Hey Mag, how's'. But she was interrupted with a yell of "Hi Aunt Maggie."

Maggie could see the happy chaos as if she were there. "Hey Bree," she said to her niece. Lizzie relayed the greeting.

"Love you," Bree yelled into the phone. Then Maggie heard Bree say goodbye.

"Our niece," Lizzie continued, "has decided to go to culinary school in Boston." When Maggie asked why Boston, Lizzie said that Bree wanted a change of scenery. Maggie was quiet at first, but said she understood.

"So," Lizzie asked, "what is life like in Lantern Light Cove? And have you bought me anything?"

Maggie ignored the question then told her sister all about the diner, supper at the B&B, and all the quaint little mom and pop stores she had yet to go into. "If you're okay with Charlie another night, I'd like to stay and explore. I can't describe it Liz, this town is. It's."

Lizzie finished the sentence for her. "It's the kind of town you always dreamed of."

Maggie just nodded, as if Lizzie could see her. Lizzie made Maggie promise to explore the town with an open heart. That maybe this was the fresh start she needed. Maggie tried to protest, but Lizzie stopped her.

"Whadda you always say Mag about moving on?"

Maggie answered slowly. "Don't just move on. Move forward."

Lizzie then suggested that Lantern Light Cove could be her chance to move forward. Before Maggie could say anything, Lizzie reminded her that Jase would want Maggie to be happy. "And I have to tell you Mag, today is the first day since Jase passed that you haven't sounded lost. Since you're such a big believer in signs, ask him for one. Maybe you'll find a cute little cottage where you can focus on your greeting cards and photos. Just make sure the house has room for me and Reggie to visit. With or without George."

Maggie again told Lizzie how much she would love Lantern Light Cove. As much as Lizzie wanted to hear all about it, she had to go. Danny and his friend Jimmy had come home for the weekend, but they had to head back to Northeastern. "Call me later. Love you."

Lizzie hung up before Maggie could say she loved her back. Maggie knew she'd driven the length of the peninsula when she saw the Tradewinds where the anniversary dinner had been. Just past the restaurant, she pulled up to a walled barrier. She jumped out and walked over to the wall.

The peninsula casually sloped down into a jetty at the bottom. The jetty curved, and formed a cove of sorts. Maggie released the breath she'd held as she leaned against the barrier and looked out at the ocean. She thought about what Lizzie said.

She was right. Jase would hate to see me so sad. Maybe it is time to let go of the past and move forward. With her eyes closed,

Maggie whispered a little prayer to ask Jase for that sign. Then she got back in the Jeep and drove back towards town. This time, however, she paid closer attention to her surroundings.

CHAPTER 19

To Maggie, it seemed that Lantern Light Cove was divided
into very distinct neighborhoods. The area near the tip of the
peninsula, she was certain, was for tourists. There were several
motels and cottages for rent. There was an arcade and the
restaurant. There was also an archway that led to docks where
people could take day cruises or fishing trips.

When she crossed over Mermaid Strand, Maggie noticed
people tending to small yards, and kids riding bikes. She also
noticed a dramatic difference in housing. The bay side of Main
Street had simple two-story cottages all very similar in size
and shape. The ocean side of Main also had cottages. But these
cottages were all very different in style, color and size. It was
as if two builders were given the tracts of land. One builder
had serious OCD issues, and the other didn't know how to color
inside the lines.

As she passed the cottages, she noticed average homes
near the school, city hall and post office. This area bordered the
shops which led into the historic part of town. The downtown
district was roughly eight blocks long. The diner and market
were at one end, with Murphy's Irish Pub and Wally's Hardware
at the other. Maggie found a parking spot somewhere in the
middle and got out to explore the Cove.

She stood on Main Street not sure which way to go, but
decided to get necessities out of the way. So, she looked up and
down. As she did, she tried to recall the stores she had driven
past earlier and Rosa's Boutique popped in her mind. But that
sounded dressier than what she wanted, so she decided to just

walk, certain she'd find something. A block and a half later, on the opposite side of the street, a store front caught her eye. The Clothes Horse. *Catchy name,* she thought, *and worth a look.*

Maggie was drawn to the burnt orange fisherman sweater on the mannequin in the window. She thanked the gods for credit cards. "This could be dangerous," she said as she opened the door and walked in. An hour later, Maggie walked out with two pairs of leggings, walking boots, socks, two women's thermals, a flannel shirt, and of course, the fisherman sweater. Back at the Jeep, she stashed her bags and thought how good it felt to shop! "Okay," she said, "time to explore.

As she meandered along Main Street, Maggie stopped to look in almost every store window. Some stores she went into and talked with the owners or sales clerks. She was impressed with the friendliness of everyone she met. She'd also noticed flyers in every window that promoted an art festival. At one store, she stopped to get a closer look.

The flyer informed her that this was the 19th annual festival and it showcased the work of local artists – painters, photographers, writers, musicians, sculptors and woodworkers. For a brief moment, Maggie wished she could be here for it. A flash of light pierced her eyes that forced her to look closer in the window.

What seemed to be a circus of glass animals of all different sizes hung on fishing line at various lengths. Some were colored, some were clear. When the sun hit the window, it was as if it created prisms that danced in the air. It took Maggie a second to focus, but when she did, she realized it was a pale green seahorse that captured her attention.

She couldn't help but wonder if this was "her sign", and

there was no way she would leave without it. Maggie yanked open the door with This & That painted in white antique letters and walked in.

CHAPTER 20

When she stepped inside, Maggie found herself in a very unique gift shop. There were greeting cards, all handmade. There were original paintings and photographs. Some framed, some not. Maggie whipped her head around to the display window. It occurred to her that they were probably all handblown glass. She was in awe. A customer was in the process of buying a vase, and the young woman behind the counter was illustrating the artist's process in creating his pieces.

Another woman came from a back room and approached Maggie. She was tall and slender with almond colored skin. Her crystal blue eyes danced above high cheekbones. Her thick hair was braided and hung below her right breast. Maggie couldn't call it gray because it shone like polished silver. She held out a hand to Maggie. "Welcome to This and That. My name is Unalii. Part owner. Part artist."

Maggie returned the smile. As she took the offered hand, she commented on the beauty of the store. Unalii thanked her and asked if there was anything she was interested in.

"Definitely the green seahorse," Maggie said as she pointed to the display window. When Maggie asked if all her stuff was done by local artists, the woman announced it was. There was no mistaken the pride in her voice, and she gave Maggie a tour of the shop. Once they made their way to the counter, she asked the sales clerk to get the seahorse out of the window.

Then she turned to Maggie. Unalii is the Cherokee word

for friend. Before Maggie could respond, she was quick to add that Maggie looked like she could use one. "Or maybe, like a lot of us transplants, you need a fresh start?"

Maggie bobbed her head with a maybe. She hesitated, then before she could stop herself, she asked Unalii if she ever took on new artists.

"I'm always looking to expand my base of artists. What is it that you have?"

Maggie paused again. But the sales clerk returned with the seahorse and Maggie acknowledged she was in this store for a reason. So, before she could back out, she explained that what she did was take pictures and add inspiring poems to them. "They're not inspirational like religious. They're inspiring, as in encouraging and uplifting. I also create my own greeting cards. Intrigued, Unalii asked Maggie if she had any samples. Maggie pulled out her phone and scrolled through photos, to find one of her favorites.

She'd been on the beach around dusk. It was a dreary day – it had matched her mood. As she walked, she came upon a bright yellow tennis ball that had been left behind. Because the sky was gray, the sand appeared dull, and the ball seemed that much brighter. The poem Maggie wrote read: *no matter where you go in life, one day you may turn around and find, the happiness you seek lies with the childhood dreams you left behind.*

Unalii didn't say anything at first, then asked Maggie if she had more of these. "Lots," she replied. Now it was the shop owner who nodded. She told Maggie she might be able to squeeze her into the festival. Maggie stopped her and suggested that maybe she could send the store a small sample of her work.

"Like a test run. Then next year I could do the festival."

Maggie was surprised at where her thoughts were going.

"Next year?" She asked. "For another visit, or have you decided to move here?" Maggie said she wasn't sure. But she was certain she was led to this place for a reason. The older woman said she understood.

"I was led here 45 years ago from Colorado. Fresh out of college and an abusive relationship, I knew I needed to get away. Six months and a hundred missteps later, I landed in the Cove. Married a good man. Raised four kids. Opened this." She said with arms spread wide. "And I love to discover new artists," she said as she nudged Maggie's shoulder.

As Maggie paid for the seahorse, Unalii gave her a business card. "When you get home, send me ten or twelve photos, matted. We'll figure out prices and consignment fees. I would like to have them for display for the festival." Maggie asked if there were a lot of artists who lived in the Cove. Unalii noticed that Maggie had dropped the word Lantern Light as only the locals did. Then she gave Maggie a brief history of her little town.

CHAPTER 21

Lantern Light Cove was founded in 1823. According to one legend, by pirates whose ship was pushed ashore during a hurricane. In reality, it was a group of fishermen looking for refuge during a nor'easter. Some rowboats were lowered into the water off the jetty, and men lit lanterns as a way to guide the ship into the cove. Just as it rounded the jetty, a strong wind knocked the back of the ship into the rocks causing some damage. After the storm, the men established a camp and set about making repairs.

As days passed, they found the shallow waters rich in oysters. Off shore, they would soon find the water swimming with blue fish, flounder, fluke, weakfish and striped bass. Additionally, the back bays were home to blue crabs and scallops. Never having had bay scallops before, the men discovered that these scallops, while smaller than sea scallops, were more tender and sweeter. Once repairs were made to the ship, several men decided they wanted to stay.

They sent word with the captain to have their families join them. The following Spring, the captain returned with families, supplies and several others who were looking to start over. Eventually, the encampment became a village; the village became a town; and the town became incorporated.

"For some reason the Cove seems to attract either those who want to start over, or those who don't seem to fit in anywhere else."

Maggie liked the thought of a place like that. "Sort of like the island of misfit toys," she added. Unalii chuckled. She never thought of it quite that way, but that did seem to sum it up.

Unalii shook off a memory she seemed to get lost in, then refocused on Maggie. "Artists are a different breed and don't tend to follow the "norms" of society. One or two painters found their way to the Cove. Then, a photographer here; a writer there. And before anyone knew what had happened, we had our own little artist colony."

Maggie mentioned the brightly colored cottages she had seen. Unalii confirmed that was indeed the Cove's center of creativity.

"And it's in stark contrast to the fishing village located directly across Main Street. That's the area where the families who make their living on the water live." She added that because of its rocky shoreline, Lantern Light Cove, never became a tourist destination. "Still, the summer months do attract day-trippers and over-nighters.

From Memorial Day through Labor Day, it's difficult to find parking or a seat at the diner. And usually, tourists pay no attention to traffic patterns. We locals just roll our eyes and try to convince ourselves that *they* are good for the economy."

Unalii finished by telling Maggie that almost twenty years ago some of the artists approached town council about an outdoor weekend art fair. Each year, it grew bigger. And now, every October, the town hosts a week-long Art Festival. "There's an outdoor craft fair in the park, easels with paintings line Main Street and a bandstand gets set up in the gazebo. And *that* week really is good for the economy."

The two women walked to the door. Maggie thanked Unalii and promised to send her pictures. Before she left, Maggie added that Unalii had given her a lot to think about.

CHAPTER 22

Back outside, Maggie's stomach reminded her it was past lunch. She considered the diner, but halfway down the next block, she came up on café tables in front of the Tea Shoppe. A waitress told her she could seat herself and would be back out with a menu. With her chicken salad on potato bread and raspberry iced tea, Maggie noticed the old-fashioned street lamps that seemed to run the length of Main Street. A jitney drove past, and Maggie fully appreciated the town's idea of public transportation.

Jase, this truly is the place we always wanted to find, she thought. Then she wondered if he somehow did lead her here. As Maggie paid the waitress, she felt something rub against her leg and heard a low meow. Under the table was a small calico cat with a collar and tag.

"Well, aren't you the cutest little thing," she said as she gave the cat her hand to smell. It rubbed her head against the offered hand, so Maggie felt comfortable enough to pick her up. The waitress noticed the cat and asked Tink why she had wandered up to Main Street.

"Tink?" Maggie asked. The waitress told Maggie that the cat belonged to Mrs. Donnelly who lived about a block and a half away.

Maggie looked at Tink's ID tag. "Of course you live on Seahorse Lane," she said to the cat who seemed quite content cradled in Maggie's arm. Maggie then asked for directions to Mrs. Donnelly's house and said she would take Tink home.

"Seahorse Lane is the next corner. Cross over Main. Mrs.

Donnelly lives at the end of the block on the right-hand side. We can call her and let her know you're coming." Then she asked Maggie's name and told her she didn't have to take Tink home. Maggie thanked her, but said she thought this is one of those things she's meant to do. The waitress accepted that response without question, then went into the café to call the cat's owner.

CHAPTER 23

Maggie ambled down Seahorse Lane, and once again noticed her ring no longer felt heavy on her hand. She was more and more convinced that Lantern Light Cove was exactly where she was meant to be. The lane was a narrow street a little more than one and a half blocks long. In total, there were seven houses on one side and six on the other. Maggie saw an elderly woman on the porch two houses in from the corner on the opposite side of the street.

If Maggie had to guess, she'd put Mrs. Donnelly in her early eighties. Her gray hair was pulled back off her face which had high cheekbones and friendly eyes behind granny glasses. Her hands appeared to be folded in prayer and the look focused on the little ball of fur that slept in Maggie's arms told Maggie that Tink was in trouble.

"I cannot thank you enough." The old woman introduced herself while she scolded the cat at the same time. "When I came back from church, I just assumed she was across the street." She pointed to a porch diagonal from her own.

Mrs. Donnelly didn't understand it. But ever since that family moved, Tink liked to lounge on the wide railing so she could soak up the afternoon sun. "I can't imagine why she would've gone all the way up to the tea shop."

Maggie followed the woman's gaze to the house across the street and noticed the "For Sale" sign out front. She had to stifle the giggle that had bubbled up in her throat. Maggie thought, *oh I'm sure I know why.* Just to confirm, she asked Mrs. Donnelly if she meant the house that's for sale.

As soon as Maggie started to talk, Tink stretched and squirmed out of her arms. Maggie watched her dart across the street, up the steps past the for-sale sign and jump up onto the railing. There she arched her back then curled up and went right back to sleep.

"See," Mrs. Donnelly exclaimed. Then she told Maggie that the house was quite lovely if she was looking to buy. Before Maggie could say anything, the old woman thanked her again, then waved to someone who drove by. From the corner of her eye, Maggie saw a black pick-up truck pass them. In a conspirator's whisper, Mrs. Donnelly informed her that was Luke. He's single. And she was determined to find him a good woman.

Maggie asked if Luke was aware of this. "Oh, he just humors me like I'm a dotty old woman and says he's fine on his own. Trust an old widow," Mrs. Donnelly said and squeezed Maggie's hand. "No one should be alone in life." The old woman looked across at Tink, told the cat to be home at supper time, thanked Maggie again, and went back inside.

Maggie walked over and stood in front of 28 Seahorse Lane. Somehow, she found herself in conversation with the cat. "So. Tink? Is it? Did Jase send you to find me?" At the sound of her name, the cat opened one eye then promptly closed it again. Up on the porch, Maggie turned to look up and down the street.

Seahorse Lane was one of those small streets squeezed in between two larger ones. She was certain there were several of them all around Lantern Light Cove. The houses were similar in size and style, but they were not cookie-cutter. Each had its own personality. All of them appeared to have porches, but a couple of them were screened in. And although it was currently quiet, the street showed signs of everyday life.

Two of the houses had kids' bikes parked out front. The corner house on this side of the street had a fenced in front yard with a puppy running around. A man was out front washing his car. Somewhere else on the street, music was coming through an open window. Otis Redding was letting people know that he was leaving Georgia and heading West. Maggie turned back around and walked over to look in one of the windows.

"Naturally, you have an open floor plan just like I've always wanted," she said to the house and backed up til she bumped on the railing where Tink was asleep. She began to scratch behind its ears. For a moment, she wondered if Tink got along with dogs. Then she dug for a pen and piece of paper to write down the realtor's phone number. Maggie thanked the cat that still basked in the sun, then raised her eyes to the afternoon sky and thanked Jase. "I think this is it babe," she said out loud. With a smile, she walked back to her Jeep. She knew she had a lot to work out.

CHAPTER 24

Maggie turned onto Oyster Road, surprised that she had to settle for a parking space about a block away from the B&B. As soon as she walked in the front door, she was greeted with Irish music and the reason there was no parking.

Besides the music, there was raucous laughter that spilled out from the dining room. Maggie peeked in. She saw the bar was open and about twenty people were crowded around one guy on a stool. Kathleen noticed her just as she turned back to take her bags upstairs.

"Maggie," she called out, "come meet my da." Before she could say no, Kathleen dragged her by the hand. "Da, this is Maggie. She's a guest here."

The man on the stool stood up. He was dressed in jeans, work boots and a white fisherman sweater. His hair was thick, wavy and jet black. It made his blue eyes somehow seem bluer. Her hand got lost in his paw when he shook it saying, "Liam Walsh. My daughter has mentioned you once or twice."

Maggie told him she was a remarkable young woman and he should be very proud of her.

"Oh, that I am," he said and draped an arm around Kathleen's shoulder. Liam offered Maggie a pint at the same time Paddy came out of the kitchen. When he noticed her, he asked if she could join them for dinner. Maggie apologized but said no to both. She'd been out all day and needed to go upstairs, get settled and make some phone calls.

Liam took note of Maggie's engagement ring, and was surprised that her fiancé wasn't with her. He was even more surprised when she turned around and bumped into Luke, and they spoke for a couple of minutes about Mrs. Donnelly's cat. As Luke watched Maggie head upstairs, Liam brought a pint over to his friend. He handed it to him. "I'm sure you've noticed that ring on the third finger of her left hand."

Luke cocked an eyebrow at Liam and raised his glass. "Slainte my friend." He added that he had indeed noticed the ring and that for him, she was off limits. "But a man can dream, can't he?" Laughing, Liam slapped Luke's back. "Yes he can." Both men watched Maggie walk up the stairs and out of sight.

CHAPTER 25

Once in her room, Maggie showered, then changed into a pair of tights and one of the thermals she'd bought earlier. She wanted tea, but she didn't want to face that crowd again. Not sure what to do, she was startled by the knock on her door. She opened it to find Nell with a tray.

"When I heard you declined dinner and a pint, I thought you might want some tea." Maggie told Nell she was a mind reader and invited her in. The inn keeper set the tray on the side table, then apologized for the commotion in the dining room.

"Liam surprised us with a visit. Word got out and then."

"And then a party broke out," Maggie finished for her. After she assured Nell that no apology was necessary, Maggie told her to go back to her guests and almost had to force Nell out the door. Once she did, Maggie walked over to the tray. The aroma released by the steam told Maggie it was lemon tea. There was also a small jar of honey, what appeared to be homemade banana bread and a small plate of fresh strawberries with a side of clotted cream. "Mind reader indeed," Maggie said as she poured a cup of tea and dipped a berry into the cream.

Maggie propped pillows against the head board, climbed onto the bed and curled her feet under her. Armed with phone, notepad and pen, she started to make calls and take notes. Her first call was to Lizzie. After she asked about Charlie, Maggie told her sister all about her day. From the seahorse in the window to the house on Seahorse Lane and all the "signs" in between. Then she told Lizzie that she planned to call a realtor in the morning. "Unless you think I'm crazy and this is all too fast."

Lizzie sighed in that way older sisters can when they have to deal with a younger sibling. "First, I am so happy to hear that you're getting back to your photos Mag. It's something you've always loved. Second, no. This is not too fast. It's almost two years in the making. And third, I think you are absolutely right about that house." Lizzie's tone softened, then she added. "I believe that Jase led you to where you need to be. It's okay to be happy Maggie."

They talked a little more about what photos she should send to Unalii, how they thought Charlie would handle the move and how they wished they could have a better relationship with their youngest sister. Before she hung up, Maggie said she'd head home after she spoke with a realtor and that she'd call Lizzie once she was on the road.

The next call was to Timmy, Jase's cousin. The house in Havertown had been Jase's grandmother's before he bought it. Tim had always loved the house, so Maggie wanted him to have the first chance at it. She had to leave a message and asked him to call her back the next night. Then she googled realtors in Lantern Light Cove. She wasn't the least bit surprised that there was just one real estate office in town. Their website said they opened at nine o'clock on Monday morning. Maggie jotted down the address. Then she made a list of photos she decided to send to Unalii. She considered what she had in her spare room and was certain she could mat and ship the photos no later than Thursday. After a couple more notes and reminders, Maggie stood up and stretched.

Armed with a second cup of tea, she walked out to the balcony. The moon was almost full and cast a beautiful beam of light across the waves. Maggie looked down at her ring and whispered, "no matter where I go babe, you'll always be with me." She stood there for a while to let the ocean breeze soothe her. Back inside, she slipped under the thick comforter and fell into a deep dreamless sleep.

CHAPTER 26

Maggie opened her eyes on Monday morning in total disbelief! The small alarm clock on the dresser said it was after eight, but Maggie called it a liar. "There is no way," she said as she reached for her phone. But that confirmed the clock's reading. With a yawn, she sat up and pushed the comforter aside. She made her way down to the dining room for coffee. When she saw Paddy, she asked what time check-out was.

"Can't I talk ya into another night love?" Maggie raised her eyebrows and told him she was certain he could talk people into doing just about anything. "But I do have to leave."

Disappointment crept into Paddy's face, but he told her checkout was at eleven and he would get her bill ready. As she turned, Maggie caught Liam coming out of the kitchen. When she asked him how long he'd be in town he told her he was here for a week.

"Then I'm gone again til Christmas." Maggie thought it must be tough.

Liam got a far-away look in his eye and agreed that it was. Then added, "but it's the only life I know." Maggie started to pour her coffee when Liam said, "Nell told me about your fiancé. I'm truly sorry."

Maggie thanked him and said she was sorry about Norah. There was an awkward silence between them, then Maggie said she needed to go pack.

"Please tell Kathleen I said goodbye." Liam said he would, wished her safe travels and headed back into the kitchen.

At 9:15, Maggie called the realtor and asked about 28

Seahorse Lane. The bubbly voice on the phone introduced herself as Kelly Benson and said she'd be happy to show her the house. They agreed to meet at ten. Maggie took one last look around then went to say goodbye to the O'Roarke's. She didn't want to share her plans just yet, but promised she would definitely be back.

Maggie stood outside the house on Seahorse Lane, and she felt calmer than she expected to. While she waited for the realtor, she decided to walk down the street to the bay. She leaned against a bulkhead and stared back up the lane.

Am I really going to do this? She wondered to herself. As she walked back up toward the house she was interested in, she had to admit that it felt right. She saw a young woman outside, approached her and asked if she was Miss Benson. She looked the way Maggie imagined she would. Cute, bubbly and full of confidence. She introduced herself as Kelly, then handed Maggie a business card and a listing sheet with pertinent information about the house. Up on the porch, Kelly took a key out of the lockbox and opened the door.

Maggie wandered from room to room and pictured herself there. As she did, she almost felt that her furniture was made for this house. She opened the back door to a small yard and swore she could hear Charlie bark at some random squirrel that had dared to trespass. Upstairs appeared to be in as good as shape as downstairs, with the exception of the hall bathroom. But even that had more to do with aesthetics than plumbing. Over all, Maggie knew there wouldn't be much that she would need to do

Back outside, Maggie thanked Kelly and said she was certain she'd make an offer; but wanted to look over a few things on the sheet she'd given her. Kelly told her to call anytime, then left to go back to her office. Maggie got in her Jeep, made a left onto Main since that would eventually turn into the road that led out of town.

She was also certain that in about two months, she would drive right back into Lantern Light Cove to begin her life without Jase. She passed the diner and thought of Joe and his story. Then she thought of Unalii and her story.

"The island of misfit toys indeed." She said out loud. "And I will fit in just fine."

CHAPTER 27

As much as Charlie loved belly rubs, he went crazy when he rode in a car with the windows down. Maggie took the long way home from her sister's house to make it up for leaving him. As she drove, she told him all about her plans and their new home.

"You're gonna love it boy," she said and rubbed his neck. "Although, I should warn you, there is a cat who likes to sleep on the railing."

At the word cat, Charlie's head whipped around as if there was one inside the Jeep. Maggie rubbed his neck and told him he would just have to get used to it. She pulled up to the house just as Timmy called. Maggie told him about her weekend getaway and that she'd decided to sell the house.

When he didn't reply immediately, Maggie started to wonder if she'd upset him. After what seemed several minutes, he said, "Mag, this couldn't come at a better time. Carly's pregnant and our lease is up next month." Then, he added, "you sound happy Mag. I think that Cove place will be good for you. And Mag," he hesitated, "you deserve to be happy. Jase would want that for you." She knew he was right. They talked a while, then he told her he'd call her in a day or two.

Over the next two weeks, everything fell into place. Maggie and Tim agreed on a price, and the sellers accepted her offer. As promised, Maggie sent a dozen matted photos to This & That, along with a proposal for consignment. Unalii called Maggie one morning. She couldn't contain her excitement as she gushed over the photos and promised to take a picture of the display to send her. She added that she signed the proposal and sent it back. Maggie told her about the move and asked if she needed part time help at the shop.

"Absolutely. My husband pesters me at least three times a week to cut back my hours. But are you sure part time would be enough?"

Maggie assured her part time was fine. "It'll give me the freedom to pursue photography." Before Maggie could change her mind, Unalii said, "you're hired."

Maggie then asked if she could recommend someone to do work inside the house.

"Luke Skala," she answered right away. "He's done work at both the shop and my house. My husband is useless at that stuff. I know I have his number somewhere."

Maggie told her it was no rush, when she found it to just let her know. Then she asked, "Luke? Is that Molly's dad Luke?"

Unalii thought for a second. "Molly's dad Lu, oh yes Molly the lab. Wait, you know Luke?"

Maggie shared the story of how Molly introduced herself on the beach, and that Luke showed up twice at the Oyster Bed while she was there.

Interesting, Unalii thought but didn't mention. She found the phone number, gave it to Maggie then said she had to run. "Need to rearrange things for the festival. Keep me posted on the move." Before she broke the connection she added, "welcome to the Cove."

CHAPTER 28

By the first week of November, Maggie had left her job. She purged, packed and scrubbed. The house in Havertown would close the Monday after Thanksgiving. All twelve photos sold at the festival, and Unalii had asked for more. Systematically, Maggie went room by room, and did her best not to get caught up in memories. Or trip over Charlie who followed her everywhere she went. While she stood in the middle of the spare room, and considered she might ship all the photos and mats straight to the shop, Charlie came in and plopped down beside her feet. He looked depressed.

"Oh my poor boy, it's gonna be okay." Maggie sat down beside him and hugged him close. As if he understood, she apologized and told him she knew how tough this was on him. She promised they'd get through the next couple of weeks, then things would settle down. He licked her face and thumped his tail on the floor. With a smile, she thought they could both use a break. She jumped up and told him it was time for a walk. The "w" word was another of his favorites and by the time Maggie got downstairs, he was in front of the side door with his paw stretched toward the knob.

At her kitchen table the next morning, Maggie opened up her calendar. She'd made a list of everything she needed to accomplish on a daily basis. Crossing each chore off was part of her OCD issues. "I don't care what they say Charlie, everyone has a little bit of OCD in them." Charlie barked in agreement, then wandered over to his bed and curled up in it. Call Luke was at the top of today's list.

A quick look at the clock and Maggie decided that seven thirty wasn't too early to call. "Construction guys are up by now. Right?" She asked herself and dialed his number.

A voice answered, "Skala Construction. This is Luke."

"Luke," she said. "I don't know if you remember me. My name is Maggie. I was in Lantern Light Cove back in September." Luke cut her off.

"Maggie. I hear you bought a house on Seahorse Lane."

Maggie was surprised until she reminded herself that small town news travels fast.

Luke said that it did, but told her he happened to run into her realtor one night at Murphy's Pub and she mentioned it.

"What can I do for you?" He asked.

She let him know that she wanted to do some work at the house both inside and out. Her settlement was December fifth, and if he could meet her there some time that week, she would appreciate it. Luke asked if the number she called from was the best way to reach her and promised to check his calendar when he got home and get back to her with a date.

Maggie thanked him, hung up, crossed off that task and spent the rest of the day methodically going through each item on her list. It dawned on her that every time she put a line through something, she inched closer to the next chapter in her life. Maggie was surprised to see how excited she was about where she was headed.

Luke looked at the phone and shook his head. Remember her? He didn't think he could forget her. Before he left, Liam told Luke about Maggie's fiancé. But it didn't change things. As long as she wore that ring, she was off limits. And now they would be neighbors. He didn't think she knew that and wondered if she'd care. He shook his head and put his phone back in his pocket. "Damn shame." He said out loud. Then walked back over to the architect on his current job.

Al said, "if that was the owner with another change. I'm outta here." Luke assured him it wasn't and they turned their attention back to the blue prints.

CHAPTER 29

Thanksgiving at Lizzie's was bittersweet. After their mom passed, Lizzie insisted it was the one holiday that the entire family came together. Her son, Maggie, Bree, and anyone else who had no place to go. Maggie thought about the way Jase cringed the first time she exposed him to the chaos. It didn't take long for it to become one of his favorite days of the year. It also had become an anchor of sorts for Bree with her mom's side of the family.

Right after Bree finished eighth grade, her mom got involved in missionary work; which was admirable. But a girl that age needed her mom, and Trish was always off somewhere else. Not to mention that Bree's dad had taken off when she was about seven and he spent his time in and out of jail for petty crime. Sometimes, Lizzie and Maggie wanted to kill their little sister. Bree grew up with her paternal grandmother in Delaware. And they were incredibly grateful for Nana T's patience and kindness when it came to their niece. It was Nana T that introduced Bree to her love of baking. This year, Bree insisted she make the desserts; and she impressed everyone with her caramel apple pie, pumpkin cheesecake and chocolate fudge cake.

After dinner, Maggie took Charlie and Reggie for a walk. Bree joined her. "So. Boston. Huh?" Maggie asked with a nudge to Bree's shoulder

Bree looked at her aunt. "So. Lantern Light Cove. Huh?"

Maggie laughed. "Touché."

The pavement was carpeted in leaves of orange, red and

gold that hadn't yet been raked. It was peaceful in the early evening light, and for a while they walked in silence. Until, Bree broke it.

"My mom wants to plan a trip home," she said. Then with a bitterness no teenage girl should know, she spat, "she wants to see her baby graduate."

Maggie put an arm around Bree's shoulder and sighed heavily. "I don't know why your mom took off the way she did, and I wish I could've spent more time with you."

Bree cut her off. "Aunt Mag, stop it. You and Aunt Liz have been awesome! You always made sure I knew that I had a family. And I love you both so much." Then Bree told Maggie that she'd taken extra classes and that she would be able complete her diploma in December, but still go back and walk in June.

"Things are getting bad in my neighborhood. And my nana is sick."

When Maggie questioned her, Bree revealed that Nana Tacarini had cancer, and not much time. Uncle Joe invited her to live with them. "But, that's a whole different school system. So, I thought I'd finish in December, maybe Aunt Lizzie would let me take Danny's room and I could get a job. Then graduate and head to Boston."

Maggie smiled at her niece. "Now Boston makes sense." Maggie was certain Lizzie would welcome Bree with open arms, and said so. "You know I will have a spare room in my house."

With a snicker Bree added, "So. Lantern Light Cove, huh?"

Maggie tapped the back of Bree's head and reminded her niece not to be a smart ass. Arm-in-arm, they made their way back to Lizzie's to figure out which options were best for Bree.

CHAPTER 30

The first Tuesday in December, Maggie packed up Charlie and some things she'd need before the movers arrived and set off for the Cove. When she spoke with Kelly the day before, Maggie was assured that it was okay to bring Charlie into the title company office. She hated when people left animals in cars. Settlement took less than an hour and before she knew it, she and Charlie were parked in front of their new home.

Just before she got out of the car, Tink came out of nowhere, ran up the steps and jumped on the railing. Maggie watched as the petite little cat arched her back, circled once, then curled up and went to sleep. Charlie noticed her too and was eager to get out and meet his new neighbor. Maggie tried to tell him that the cat might not like dogs.

"But don't take it personally boy. She's a cat. They rarely like anyone." Maggie got out and walked around to the passenger side. Before she let Charlie out, she hooked his leash and held it tight. Outside the Jeep, she told Charlie to sit. At the sound of the door closing, Tink stretched and sat up. She cocked her head to the left as if assessing the situation. Maggie was about to introduce them to each other when a man called out to her.

"Welcome to Lantern Light Cove." Maggie jumped and turned to see that Luke had pulled up in his truck.

"Oh my gosh, Luke, I thought we were supposed to meet on Thursday."

"That was the plan." He knelt beside Charlie. "And who's this?" He asked as he rubbed Charlie's neck with both hands.

"This is Charlie. And," she added when she noticed Molly inside the truck, "he loves to make new friends." Charlie barked. Molly answered. Luke mentioned that while they were supposed to meet on Thursday, he had to knock off work early.

"The owner of my current project has changed her mind. Again. My architect has threatened to quit. Again. And I need a break." He opened the door and Molly all but jumped over him to meet Charlie. They made a dash for the porch which caused Maggie to run after them to make sure nothing happened to Tink. The cat obviously had gotten bored with all of them and had already left. With notepad in hand, Luke told Maggie that if she had time now, he'd be happy to take a look at what she wanted done.

CHAPTER 31

Luke had built enough houses in his life to know how important that first moment was for the homeowner – the moment they unlocked the door and stepped over that threshold. So, he held the screen door with one hand and Molly's collar with the other, Maggie opened the front door and she and Charlie walked through.

She knelt beside him, rubbed his neck and whispered, "this is it boy. This is our fresh start." Almost as if he knew the significance of the occasion, Charlie sat still and looked from side to side. The lab waited until Maggie told him to go ahead. At her nudge, Charlie started to explore, his nails click-clacked across the hardwood floors. Maggie took a deep breath, and exhaled slowly. Then she stood up, turned around and invited Luke to come in.

Luke let go of Molly, and shook his head in appreciation. "Love the open floor plan."

Maggie agreed. "It was definitely one of the high points." The dogs had made their way to the back door, so Maggie figured they could start there.

Three steps led to a well-kept fenced-in yard. "I'm not sure if I want a small deck built onto the house, or if I want these steps to lead down to a patio." She told him that she counted on him to be honest about what would work and what wouldn't. "And of course, you will need to tell me why it would or wouldn't work."

Luke looked up from his note pad and raised an eyebrow. But Maggie went back inside, and Luke followed. She'd want to paint the first floor, but other than that, nothing else needed to be done. Next, they went upstairs. Luke stopped every so often to measure, tap on walls and make notes.

This level had two bedrooms and two bathrooms. They stopped at the first room, where Maggie wondered about the floors under the carpet and if they could be saved. Luke stomped on different areas, then pulled back a corner of the rug.

"If both rooms are the same, they'll just need to be sanded and polished." Luke said as he made some more notes. The main bathroom needed a complete remodel.

"The pink and tan tile needs to go." Maggie told him. Luke was relieved. He never understood that color combination either. She also wanted to redo the master bath. She'd like to replace the tub with a walk-in shower. "This will become the guest room and I think it's great if they have their own bathroom. The other room will be for my niece. She's gonna stay with me til she leaves for college."

Luke looked at her confused. "Wouldn't you take the master bedroom?"

Maggie hesitated. "As for me," she said with scrunched shoulders and clasped hands, "I hope. Pray, actually, that we can turn the attic into a master suite." With that, she opened the door at the end of the hallway and directed him up the attic stairs. "And by we, I mean you." She said as Luke followed her up to the attic.

Luke had expected his nose to be assaulted by the stale odor of a closed up attic, but all he encountered was dust. It floated in a shaft of light that streamed through the two windows at the front of the house. Hardwood flooring had been laid at one point and on initial inspection looked to be in decent condition.

Maggie hoped to be able to have windows installed in the back wall with a window seat. She wanted a bathroom up here with a walk-in shower, simple pedestal sink and toilet. At the front of the house, she wanted an office space with maybe a half wall to separate it from the bedroom. "I know it's a lot of work, but on the plus side I am not in any real rush."

Luke stood in the middle of the attic and tried to take in the dimensions mentally. He looked at the notes he'd made, then said he needed to run out to his truck for a tape measure. Maggie followed him outside and got a box out of her jeep. Back inside, she told Luke she wanted to start on the kitchen and to just holler if he needed her.

With the dogs back in, she set up Charlie's bed in a corner of the living room and was amazed that both labs managed to curl up in it. "It looks like you made your first friend," she whispered to Charlie.

In the kitchen, Maggie plugged in her iPod player and turned it to her cleaning playlist. She sang along with Smoky Robinson's Going To A Go-Go and got to work. After she scrubbed the refrigerator, she went out to bring in the cooler she had packed and transferred its items. With the kitchen window open, the room was chilly, but the fresh air felt good.

She took out the oven racks, then set the oven to self-clean. When Boogie Shoes came on, Maggie added dance steps to her cleaning. Then she remembered she wasn't alone in the house as she heard Luke come down from the attic. She felt the flush of embarrassment and was glad she hadn't gotten caught. With the kitchen done, she tackled the half bath, then took her cleaning supplies upstairs.

In the attic, Luke could faintly hear the music that drifted up through the vents. Her taste ran from classic rock to Motown to country, and a lot of stuff in between. He liked the variety. When he finished his list for the attic, he made his way down to the master bedroom. He knew this floor would be the easiest to complete. He stepped into the main bathroom to take some measurements. He liked her plans for the house. He liked her music. He liked that she had a dog. He liked that he felt comfortable around her. Before he could think of anything else he liked about her, the sapphire ring she wore popped into his head.

"Don't go there Luke," he said out loud as he walked out of the bathroom and right into Maggie. In unison they both apologized and then took a step backward laughing.

Maggie asked Luke where he wasn't going. At his confused look, she reminded him what he said as they ran into each other. Luke just shook his head.

Maggie didn't press him. Instead, she offered him lunch. "I have some stuff in for sandwiches and a six-pack of Smithwick's if you're interested." He said sure, and that he just needed to go out back to make notes for what she wanted there.

While Luke was outside, Maggie went into the kitchen. She set out paper plates and napkins, then took out lunchmeat, bread and two beers. When she realized she didn't have silverware, she was glad she had gotten squeeze bottles of mustard and mayo. Luke came back in at about the same time the dogs realized there was food. Suddenly, the two labs sat on one side of the island and sniffed the air. Before she gave Charlie a slice of cheese, Maggie asked if she could give one to Molly.

"Sure," Luke said and opened the beers. "Just beware that

if you give her cheese, she'll find her way up here every day."

Maggie turned back from the dogs. "*Up* here?" She asked. Before he could answer, her phone rang and she walked out to the front porch.

Luke watched her walk away and told the dogs that he was an idiot. They barked in agreement. When they sensed there'd be no more snacks, they walked over to the door and Luke let them out to play in the yard.

CHAPTER 32

Maggie came back inside. The look on her face told Luke that the phone call had upset her. "You okay?"

"That was my niece," she answered. Her grandmother had been admitted to the hospital. "Nana T raised Bree. She has cancer. That's why Bree is coming to stay with me." Maggie lost herself in a long-forgotten memory, and stayed there for a moment. With a sad smile, she continued.

"She's going to Boston next September, culinary and hospitality program. I'm hoping she'll be able to get some experience at Joe's or Tradewinds."

Luke suggested the bakery as well. "Tony Bagliotti's a good guy. And a trained pastry chef. I bet he'd be happy to teach her some basics. And I'd be happy to ask."

Maggie loved that idea and thanked him. She pointed to his note pad. "So," she asked, "what's the damage?"

After he gulped down the rest of his beer, he asked her if she wanted another.

"That bad huh?" She asked and pulled out two more bottles.

"First, it can all be done. Everything you want is possible." When he hesitated, Maggie said, "I feel like there's a but coming."

"But," Luke replied.

Then it dawned on Maggie. *He's not sure if I can afford it.* "Luke, I know this won't be cheap. But I promise, I can handle this."

Then she explained that when she sold her house in

Pennsylvania, she basically paid cash for this house. "I don't have a mortgage. I also don't have a car payment." Maggie took a bite of her sandwich, and added that she lived very simply. "I've been good with my savings and I have a part time job at Unalii's shop that starts in February."

Luke took a long swallow and nodded in appreciation. He noticed the time and asked Maggie if he could help her bring anything else in before he went home.

"And home would be where exactly?" Maggie asked as she cleaned up from lunch.

Sheepishly, Luke jerked his thumb to the left. "One block down. And I don't know why I never said anything before."

"Mm mm," was her response. Maggie told him she'd be fine, that she only had one or two more boxes to bring in, but she wanted to introduce Charlie to the neighborhood while it was still light. They walked with both dogs out the front door. Luke told Maggie he'd have an estimate and timeframe by the end of the week. Before he left, she told him that if he ever needed to leave Molly with her it was no problem.

Luke climbed into his truck and watched her walk up the street through the rearview mirror. "Yep," he said, "don't even go there."

Back from their walk, Maggie brought the rest of her things in from the Jeep. She locked up downstairs and made her way up to the main bathroom. After that was scrubbed, she hung a shower curtain and towels. She set up the air mattress in what would be Bree's room. Before she finished for the night, she brought Charlie's bed up too, and decided she wanted a hot shower.

"To be honest boy," she said and rubbed his head, "I really

need a hot shower. A long, hot shower."

By seven o'clock, Maggie laid on her temporary bed and tried to get comfortable. She stood the one lamp she brought with her on a box she had turned upside down. With that on, she took out her calendar to look at the next day's list of things to do, but was too tired to see it. Charlie was already curled up in his bed. Maggie turned the light off and whispered good night to him. As she fell asleep, Jase was not the man she had on her mind.

CHAPTER 33

The next couple of days were a blur. Furniture was delivered and boxes were piled in every room. Cable was hooked up and Maggie had Saturday plans for whatever was on Hallmark. She met with Unalii, who welcomed her as if they had been lifelong friends. From there, Maggie made her way to Grrranimals, the local pet store. Which, conveniently was right down the street from Dorsey's Market and Deli. In each shop she went into, Maggie either introduced herself, or was welcomed as the new kid in town. She wandered along Main Street unable to hide her happiness at simply being there. She was in love with all the mom-and-pop stores and friendly people she'd met.

Mrs. Donnelly came over Thursday afternoon with an actual Bundt cake, and Maggie invited her to stay for an early supper of soup and salad. The two women talked easily and Mrs. Donnelly didn't hesitate to share small town news. When she got around to Luke, Mrs. Donnelly winked and said she noticed his truck parked outside Maggie's house for quite a while on Tuesday.

Maggie assured the sweet old lady that their relationship was purely professional.

With a sip of her after dinner whiskey, which she insisted was the secret to a long life, Mrs. Donnelly looked hard at Maggie. "My dear girl, if that's true, then you are a damn fool." Shocked, Maggie almost choked on her wine. Mrs. Donnelly continued. "I recognize heartbreak. I've lived through it. And you Maggie," she said cupping Maggie's chin, "have faced heartache. That heart of yours needs healing. And trust me,

Luke is quite interested in you."

At the look on Maggie's face, Mrs. Donnelly continued. She and Luke had a dinner date every Sunday. "You first met Luke when you were here in September. He's mentioned you several times in the past couple of months. And in the years I've known him, he's never mentioned any woman." Mrs. Donnelly stood up because she had to be home in time for Wheel of Fortune. "I have a wee bit of a crush on that Pat Sajak."

Maggie walked her across the street and thanked her for the cake. Before she went inside, the old lady grabbed Maggie's hand. "Even if you're not ready to let someone in right now, one day, you will. And when that day comes, if you've already shut Luke out, you will regret it." With a hug, she whispered, "he's one of the good ones."

Back at her own house, Maggie poured a second glass of wine, grabbed a throw and went out on the porch. She curled up on the swing the former owners left behind, took a long sip and looked up and down her street. Most of the houses on this block and the next were decorated for the holidays. Maggie's nose hinted that there might be snow in the not-too-distant future. As the lights on her street started to twinkle in the dark, Maggie thought about how she would decorate her house. She made a mental note of what she'd need to buy.

A little while later, Luke called. He let Maggie know that he had estimates for her as well as a timeline.

"Estimates?" She asked. "As in plural?"

"Don't panic," he replied. "I've broken down each job separately. This way, you can plan around your budget and prioritize the work." Then he told Maggie he had to drive down to Tuckerton the next day and asked if he could take her up on her offer to drop Molly off. "I hate to leave her alone for an entire day. And if you'd like, I could grab a pizza on the way home. Then, we could sit down and go over everything."

Maggie hesitated, as she thought about what Mrs. Donnelly had said. *Get a grip Maggie*, she thought, *he didn't ask you out on a date*. She told Luke she'd be happy to take Molly and that pizza sounded good. After they hung up, she told Charlie he had a play date in the morning. "C'mon boy," she said with a smile. "Tonight, we get to sleep in our bed."

CHAPTER 34

Maggie woke up Friday morning to light snowflakes that drifted down from a steel gray sky. With her morning coffee, she found her shopping list and added a shovel to it. She texted Luke to let him know she was up and he promptly texted back the thumbs up emoji. She opened the back door for Charlie, then walked to the front. As she stepped out on the porch, Luke pulled up. With Molly on a leash, he walked her to the back yard, opened the gate and let her go. He handed the leash to Maggie and thanked her again.

"It's no problem," she said. "Would you like some coffee?" He waved her off and told her he had a thermos full. He climbed into the driver's seat, called out that he should be back by four-thirty and took off up the street.

Maggie watched him leave. Before she could wonder why he was so short with her, shivers sent her back inside for more coffee so she could start her day. Since she had yet to drop in on Joe and Angie, Maggie decided to treat herself to breakfast.

When the bell over the diner door announced a customer, Joe looked up from the counter he had just wiped clean. He greeted Maggie with a booming laugh. "Well look who's come back for that fresh start." Joe came around the counter to hug her. "Welcome to the Cove Philly." He called out to his wife in the kitchen. "Angie. Come see who's here."

Angie wiped her hands on her apron and came out to greet Maggie. She told her how happy they were when they heard she'd bought the house on Seahorse Lane. "I know we didn't meet when you first came, but Joe told me about you. He thought you might be back." She said all this to Maggie as she led her to a counter stool as if they'd been friends forever.

Angie asked if Maggie had met any of her neighbors. Before Maggie could respond, Angie filled her in on most of them, while she took her breakfast order. "We own the only diner in town," Angie said when Maggie asked her how she knew everyone. "Sooner or later, they all come through that door."

As Maggie waited for her breakfast, she talked to Joe about the possibility of her niece being able to get some kitchen experience. He told her he'd be glad to help Bree and promised to work something out with Angie. With one more thing crossed off her list, Maggie ate breakfast and took the time to enjoy the atmosphere of a small-town diner. A place where someone could sit by themselves and feel perfectly comfortable. Before she left, Maggie thanked them both and promised to become a regular.

Outside, the wet snow had left a slippery layer of sleet on the sidewalks then it turned and took off up the coast. The air had turned colder, and Maggie thought that things could ice up. She added rock salt to her list. Certain the hardware store would have everything she needed; Maggie drove the couple of blocks to Wally's.

As she drove, she noticed large red bows on each of the street lamps and the strands of garland that connected one to the other. From Black Friday through New Year's Eve, the town piped carols through outdoor speakers. Outside the Jeep, Maggie stood on the sidewalk and looked back down Main Street. She imagined at night, with the lights and storefronts, the street would look like a postcard. She looked at it from different angles like she would if she saw it through the lens of her camera and was excited at the possibilities. Maggie was surprised at excited she was to be getting back into photography. Briefly, she let herself think about Jase and how happy this would make him. Then she turned toward Wally's.

CHAPTER 35

Wally's Hardware was a two-story brick building on a corner lot. It stood at the opposite end of the avenue from Joe's Diner. A red Radio Flyer wagon was on display in the window that faced Main Street. Maggie would come to learn that the wagon remained there all year long, but was decorated to match the seasons.

At this time of year, the wagon was filled with brightly wrapped boxes that spilled over into fake snow. A vintage wooden sled was propped up in one corner, while in the other corner, there was a shovel and snow blower, each with a big red bow. Two child-sized mannequins were building a snowman out of Styrofoam balls to complete the scene.

Maggie entered the store and was greeted with the aroma of fresh popcorn that lured her to the old-fashioned popcorn stand in the corner by the display window. "May I help you?" A man asked.

Maggie pulled herself away. "Yes. Please."

He noticed the extensive list in her hand. "You must be the newest member of our little community," he said. Dressed in tan khakis and a blue chambray shirt with Wally's Hardware embroidered on the pocket, Maggie considered he might be the owner.

"Oh no," he said as he pulled out cheaters. He told Maggie he just worked here. "My grandfather," he added with a jerk of his thumb to the back of the store, "is Wally. Until he retires, I'm just an employee." He adjusted his glasses and said, "now let's look at this list."

They walked around the first floor, picked up items and made small talk. Maggie told him that she did just move here and that she needed to have some work done on the house. She learned his name was Robert and that like a lot of others, this was a family run store. He rung up the shovel, rock salt, batteries and flashlight. "I can put these in your car while you go upstairs," he said with a nod to the steps on the opposite wall.

Maggie looked over her shoulder and saw the sign that informed her Santa's headquarters was upstairs. She pointed to her Jeep, told Robert it was unlocked and headed up to Wally's version of the North Pole.

The upstairs at Wally's was indeed Santa's headquarters, and Maggie felt as giddy as a school girl as she wandered around. The perimeter of the floor was entirely lined with artificial trees – tall, thin, short, fat. If an artificial tree was your thing, you could be certain to find it here. Some were decorated with handmade ornaments you could buy. Others were bare and just twinkled with lights. There was an entire aisle dedicated to candy canes and peppermint sticks. Another aisle was home to ribbon in every possible color, width and material you could imagine. There was a large bin filled with packs of silver tinsel; but if you preferred garland, they had that too. There were holiday-themed table linens, kitchen and bathroom towels and tree skirts.

At the far end of the floor, a large table was set up for children to be able to paint wooden ornaments while their parents shopped. Maggie watched a little boy who appeared very serious as he dipped his brush in red paint for the train he was intently focused on. When a clerk asked Maggie if she needed help. Maggie thanked her but said no. She waved the paper in her hand. "I have my list and I'm checking it twice."

Maggie finished her shopping and went back downstairs with her bags. Robert was with another customer and she didn't want to interrupt him. So, she caught his eye and mouthed thank you. Her final stop was to pick up beer because she wasn't sure if Luke drank wine. It was already after two by the time Maggie got home.

CHAPTER 36

When Maggie opened the front door, Charlie and Molly streaked to the back one. After she begged their forgiveness because they were left alone all day, she got them treats and let them out. While they played, Maggie went to get her bags from the car. For the next hour, she organized the unpacked boxes still in the living room.

Anything marked "Holiday Decorations" she moved to one corner and added the stuff she purchased at Wally's. A couple of other boxes belonged upstairs, the other two were books she wasn't sure she wanted to keep. After a shower she threw on jeans, a long-sleeve tee shirt and warm wool socks. Downstairs, she poured herself a glass of wine and thought about the conversation she had with Mrs. Donnelly.

Maggie didn't think Luke was interested in her, given the way he acted that morning. Even if he was, it didn't matter. She didn't want to get involved with anyone. "And I certainly don't want to get involved with someone who works for me," she said to the dogs that she had just let back in. "What do you two think?" She asked. They barked twice in unison. Unsure of what two barks meant, Maggie decided they just wanted something to eat. When Luke called to say he'd be there in half an hour, Maggie decided to occupy her thoughts with how she planned to decorate while she made a salad and set the table.

Luke hung up and thought about that morning. He knew he'd been short with Maggie, but he didn't know if she'd noticed. He thought about the way she looked when he pulled up to drop Molly off.

Flannel pajama pants, hoodie and Uggs. She had that just rolled out of bed air around her that can be so sexy. It took everything he had not to run up those steps, grab her and kiss out all his frustration. He considered that he would just leave the estimate with her, so she could review it and tell him she'd get another bid. Then he'd have no reason to be around her. But damn it, he genuinely liked her. Not just physically. She was intelligent, witty, and yes, beautiful. Luke also knew that no one in the Cove, or the surrounding area would be as honest with her as he would. And if she hired him, then that would be one more reason she was off limits.

Armed with the knowledge he'd never get involved with someone he worked for; Luke parked his truck. He got out with the pizza and the estimate, convinced that as long as they worked together, they could be just friends. That resolve melted as soon as Maggie opened the door and smiled at him.

CHAPTER 37

Luke stood in the doorway frozen. The wind stirred and he picked up her scent. Vanilla and coconut. Her gray long sleeved tee changed her eyes from blue to slate. On her feet were bright pink wool socks. Charlie and Molly barked and thumped their tails against the hardwood floors.

When she noticed his reaction to her choice of footwear, Maggie took the pizza out of his hands. "You can find anything on the internet," she said and turned toward the kitchen.

Briefly, Luke felt like he was a man who had come home from work to his woman and their kids. He closed the door, knelt and first rubbed Molly's neck, then Charlie's. He took two biscuits out of his pocket and gave one to each; after he made them promise not to tell Maggie. When he stood back up, Luke took in the furniture that wasn't there before.

The living room wasn't fully unpacked, but he could already see how she planned to decorate. In front of the windows, she had a full-sized soft leather couch in a light cocoa shade. It had a recliner that matched. There were throw pillows in burnt orange, golden yellow and sage green. What looked like a handmade patchwork quilt lay across the back of the sofa, and a throw blanket in softer colors was tossed across the recliner. There was a beautiful curio cabinet in one corner. Luke took the time to admire the craftsmanship while he ran his hand along the frame made of pine. Its glass shelves were still empty, but Luke imagined Maggie would fill it with framed photos and treasured knick-knacks.

He turned toward the kitchen, then stopped short. A

weathered barn table, not unlike his own stood in the center of the dining area. It was surrounded by oversized chairs and he was in love. It was easy to imagine dinner at that table every night. Maggie had set the table with real plates, silverware and cloth napkins. *For pizza and salad,* he thought when he noticed the large bowl and bottles of dressing.

Like the throw pillows, Maggie's plates were a mix of bright colors. He knew if he turned one over, the "fiestaware" stamp would be on the bottom. His mom had collected it for years. "Tread carefully Luke," he whispered to himself.

"Any chance you left French fries in the truck?" Maggie asked as she put the pizza box in the oven to keep warm.

Startled, Luke asked, "French fries?"

She added to her glass of wine and told him that pizza and fries were her favorite Friday night dinner. Luke said he'd remember that for next time. Then surprised her by taking wine over beer and asked if she wanted to eat first. With an eyebrow raised over the rim of her glass she asked if the estimate would ruin her appetite. Luke just shook his head and sat.

While she served salad and pizza, Maggie asked him about the jobs he currently had and where exactly was Tuckerton. They found it easy to talk about everything but the work she wanted done. Before either of them knew it, four hours passed and she hadn't even opened the estimate. As Maggie cleaned up, she promised Luke she would look over everything and call him in the morning. "I have a ballpark figure of what the work should cost." She told him and picked up the envelope. "So, unless this estimate is outrageous. You're hired."

Luke thanked her again for taking Molly and they walked

to the front door. Luke mentioned Wally's when he saw the bags in the corner. "Ooh, that reminds me. Would you be able to hang my outside Christmas lights for me?"

Luke stepped out onto the porch. "Yes. As a carpenter. And as a man. I am pretty sure that I am *able* to hang Christmas lights."

Maggie apologized. She hadn't intended to insult his manhood. "I should've asked if you *would* hang the lights for me."

Luke told her he could do it tomorrow, said good night and left. Back inside, Maggie checked the doors, turned out the lights and made her way upstairs. Charlie climbed up into bed and nuzzled her neck with a whimper.

"I know boy. The only other man I've ever been that comfortable with was your dad." She kissed the top of his head and whispered, "I just don't know if I'm ready." Charlie let out a heavy sigh then curled up at the foot of the bed. Maggie drifted off into a dreamless sleep.

CHAPTER 38

Maggie snuggled deeper into her comforter and begged Charlie for ten more minutes. "I know you want to go out boy. But it's so nice under the blankets." As soon as she pulled the covers over her head, she regretted it. Charlie took it as a sign that Maggie wanted to play and used his teeth to pull the blanket off. She had no choice but to surrender and get out of bed.

A blast of cold air slapped Maggie awake when she opened the back door to let Charlie out. She rubbed her arms and wondered if she had what she needed to bake cookies. Charlie hated the cold and barked to get back in before Maggie was able to fill his bowls with water and food.

"You're so goofy," she said and dropped a k-cup into her Keurig. "You hate the cold, but I have to drag you in from the snow." Maggie jumped at the knock on the door. It was only eight o'clock. "Luke, I didn't expect you," she said as she opened the door. Then screamed. "Oh my god." Lizzie and Bree stood there with overnight bags. Maggie hugged them tight. Reggie ran past her when Charlie barked.

"What are you two doing here?" She stepped back to let them in, but before she could ask again, Lizzie cut her off.

"More importantly. Who is Luke? And when did you expect him?"

Maggie ignored the implication and explained that Luke was her contractor. He would be there sometime today to hang her lights.

"Is he cute?" Lizzie persisted. In a way that only sisters understand, Maggie dismissed her and turned to Bree. "Would you like to see your room?" After they both said hi to Charlie, Maggie gave them a tour and told them her plans for the renovation.

In the kitchen, Maggie got a second cup of coffee and offered her sister and niece their preferred diet Pepsi. "I assume you plan to spend the night," Maggie said. "I would love to show you around town." Maggie then mentioned to Bree that she might be able to get some kitchen experience at the diner. She didn't mention Luke's friend at the bakery. *Lizzie would be all over that*, she thought to herself. Maggie suggested they take their bags upstairs while she got changed. Then they would go explore the Cove.

On her way back downstairs, Maggie heard a third dog and cringed. She was certain that Lizzie was grilling Luke. Oh my god she mouthed when she heard her ask Luke what he thought of Maggie.

"Lizzie!" Maggie yelled. "Stop." She offered Luke coffee, then told him to ignore her sister. "She means no harm." She shot Lizzie a "knock it off" look, and added, "sometimes she just can't help herself."

With a huff, Lizzie pretended to be insulted and sat down. Luke accepted the coffee, asked where the lights were and went out on the porch to get started. As soon as the door closed behind him, Lizzie started to say something but Maggie cut her off.

"Don't." She said and pointed her finger at Lizzie. "Yes, he seems like a good guy; and yes, he is handsome. But I have yet to take this ring off my finger." She waved her left hand at Lizzie. "And that tells me that I am not ready to get involved with anyone."

Before Lizzie could respond, Bree broke the tension. "Aunt Mag, when you do take it off, can I have it?" There was a moment of silence, then all three burst into laughter. Maggie hugged Bree.

"Yes." She promised. "When I finally take it off, the ring is yours." As they left the house, Maggie told Luke that if he needed to, he could leave Molly with the other two dogs. Then she almost pushed Lizzie down the steps before she could say anything else to him.

CHAPTER 39

Luke watched them walk up the street arm-in-arm. They seemed like they were really close. He promised himself he'd call his sister in Arizona later that afternoon, then got back to the lights. It brought back memories of holidays when his daughters were young. The early years when he thought him and Colleen were happy.

Like today, he'd be out on the porch stringing lights. His daughters would be at the windows giving him direction. Kaitlyn, always the perfectionist, would tell him things weren't straight or even. Emily, the daredevil, would tell him they needed more lights so Santa could see their house from the North Pole. Luke wouldn't see either of them for the holidays this year. Kaitlyn and her husband would be in Italy to visit his grandparents. Emily would be in Disney with her college roommates. They had all come here for Thanksgiving, and Luke never pressured them about Christmas. His ex-wife did enough of that for both of them.

When one of the dogs barked, Luke shook off the memories and started to laugh. All three had their noses pressed up against the window. "What do you guys think?" He asked the trio. "Personally, I don't think she needs Santa to see the house, but I don't think it has to be straight as a ruler either." All three barked in agreement.

It took him almost two hours. When he finished, he plugged them in then walked out to the street to see how it looked. He didn't notice Mrs. Donnelly until she spoke. She carried a blue gift bag and exclaimed that the lights looked beautiful. "I'm so glad you two are decorating for the holidays, Luke."

Luke looked with kindness at the old woman who treated him like a son. But he knew how her mind worked, and he didn't want her to get the wrong idea. "Maeve, we've talked about this. I'm just doing work for Maggie at the house and she asked me if I would hang the lights for her. She and I are not together the way you want to believe we are."

Mrs. Donnelly looked up at him and adjusted her glasses. "Why not foolish boy?" She asked. Before he could respond she reminded him that time was short and he better get a move on.

"What's in the bag?" He asked to change the subject. She told him that she finally finished the blanket she'd knitted for the Jenkins baby. They had brought little Phillip home last week and she wanted to drop it off to them. Luke watched her walk up to the house two doors down from Maggie's. He thought the lights were fine. He went back in to get Molly and take her home. Church bells rang in the distance. It was noon. Luke figured he had enough time to shower and make it to Murphy's for kickoff. The Ohio State / Michigan game would start soon. And no self-respecting Buckeye fan from western Pennsylvania would dare miss that one.

Luke's phone rang as he walked in his door. Since his mom was the only one who called the landline, he couldn't ignore it. "Hey mom," he said. "Ready for the big game?" His mom told him that his dad had the condo decked out in red and white. "As if anyone in this development cares about the rivalry. He had me drive all over Scottsdale for bratwurst!" When she brought up the holidays, Luke cut her off.

"Mom, I'll be okay here on my own for Christmas. It's not

like when you were still in Stony Creek and I could drive with Molly. What would I do with her?" Although Luke was sure he could leave her with Maggie, he didn't dare mention that name to Evelyn Skala. She'd have their wedding planned before they even had a first date. "Mom, don't mean to cut you off, but I need to get a move on if I'm gonna make kick-off. Give dad a hug and I'll call you next week." He told her he loved her too, then hung up grateful for the excuse of the game. For a minute, Luke stared at the yellow wall phone with the rotary dial.

When he bought the house, he couldn't bring himself to get rid of it. His daughters thought he was crazy and didn't have a clue how to use it. But for Luke, it was a throwback to his childhood and an easier way of life. He grabbed a bottle of Bud out of the icebox, walked into the living room and turned on ESPN Gameday.

The drone of the commentators was background noise as Luke took a good look around the house. He didn't like to admit that he didn't want to be alone. He never imagined he'd ever get divorced. But it had been seven years since his marriage ended. There had been some dates, but nothing serious. He moved East, stumbled into the Cove and poured everything into his work.

In the five years he lived here, he never decorated for the holidays. He was single and lived with a dog. What did he have to decorate for? "Maggie's single and lives with a dog. And she's decorating." He said to the empty room. Restless, he started to pace. He knew he had to do something. Or he'd end up doing something stupid. If he went to Murphy's he'd tie one on, Luke went up to the attic instead. He brought down the one carton marked "Christmas decorations". It didn't hold much.

His stocking from when he was a kid, some handmade ornaments his girls had made for him, and a box with his old Lionel train set for around the tree. He figured it was a start, but it wasn't enough. The bags from Wally's popped into his head. Santa's workshop on the second floor should have everything he'd need. Since he had to stop there anyway to check on some work orders, he could kill two birds with one stone. As he passed Mrs. Donnelly's, he thought, *I'll be damned. I guess I am decorating this year.*

CHAPTER 40

It was late afternoon by the time Maggie, Lizzie and Bree had gotten home. Luke had somehow managed to outline the frame in the white lights, which he plugged in so she could see it. "Oh Maggie," Lizzie sighed. "It looks like a gingerbread house."

Maggie didn't say anything. The silent knowledge sisters share passed between them and Lizzie squeezed Maggie's hand. "I'm good Liz," she said and squeezed back. "C'mon, let's go inside."

Charlie and Reggie greeted them, Molly and Luke were gone. Maggie sent Luke a text to thank him and ask him to stop by on Sunday to go over the estimate. While Bree decided to take care of dinner, Lizzie and Maggie began to go through the decorations and made a list of what she still needed.

Maggie always decorated for the season, not just a single holiday. She found her winter throws and linens, and tossed them into the washer. While Lizzie concentrated on the garland of holly and lights to wrap around the banister, Maggie cleared out a corner for the tree. Any box with ornaments ended up there, along with lights, tree stand and blanket. It wasn't long before snowmen and angels had taken up residence in the living room, dining room and kitchen. By the time they were ready to eat, Maggie had managed to get through everything without too many tears.

"Something smells good Bree," Maggie said and took out plates.

"It's basic stromboli Aunt Mag. One vegetable, one with

sausage and cheese. You could make these."

Maggie was certain she couldn't. After everything was cleaned up, the sisters and their niece talked til almost midnight. Bree went to bed and reminded Lizzie they would need to leave before noon the next day. Lizzie and Maggie sat up a little longer.

"Has she heard from Trish?" Maggie asked Lizzie.

Lizzie shook her head. "If she has, I don't know. This is her last week at school, then she'll come to stay with me. Nana T is on hospice and won't make it to Christmas."

Maggie brushed away a tear as she pictured Bree's nana and how tough it must've been on both of them. Lizzie then said that her son Danny and his friend Jimmy would be home on the twenty-third, but they had to leave the day after Christmas for California. They did offer to help pack up Bree's stuff when they got down. "I don't suppose I can talk you into coming home for Christmas."

"I am home Liz." She softly reminded her sister. "And I think it's important for me to be here this Christmas." They sat in silence for a little while, then Lizzie told Maggie how much she liked Lantern Light Cove.

"It truly is the small town you've always wanted. Quaint and quirky people. Fun little shops." Then added, "And I think Luke would be good for you." Before Maggie responded, Lizzie said that she wouldn't bring it up again.

"Sure you will." Maggie said. "But at least you'll wait a couple of days before you do." Maggie told Lizzie to take her room and she would sleep on the couch.

After Lizzie went up, Maggie curled up on the sofa. For a while, she stared out the window and watched the night. It was less than three months ago that she found her way here. And now she was in a house she'd bought and would decorate for the holidays. Her house. In Lantern Light Cove. She thought about Jase, then she thought about Luke.

Lizzie is right, she thought. *He probably would be good for me. And Jase would actually like him.* She fingered the bottom of her engagement ring and thought again of Jase. "I'm just not ready babe," she whispered and drifted off to sleep.

CHAPTER 41

Maggie woke to the smell of bacon and coffee. She stretched, yawned and sat up. Since Charlie hadn't woken her up, she got to sleep later than usual. In the kitchen, Maggie told Bree she didn't have to cook every meal.

"It's what I love to do Aunt Mag. Kinda like you and your camera." When Maggie didn't respond, Bree turned around from the stove. "Do you think you'll get back into it? Or just sell what you have and let it go?"

Maggie stared at her niece and wondered, not for the first time, how she survived such screwed-up parents. She didn't answer and instead walked over to steal a piece of bacon. The clear knob on the percolator showed the coffee had reached the perfect color. A deep inhale reminded Maggie that nothing smelled like home more than stove top percolating coffee. "When did you learn how to use a percolator?" Maggie asked and poured herself a cup.

Bree shrugged. "Nana T." Then wiped away a tear. Maggie hugged her niece before Bree turned back to the stove and began to work on omelets.

"I'm glad I decided to finish early. At least she'll know I graduated. And she saw the acceptance letter from Boston U so she knows I'll be doing what I love. She always said how important that was."

Maggie started to set the table. "I'm glad you'll be in Boston. Danny'll be there for your first two years. At least. And it's always good to know someone when you move to a new place."

Bree decided not to remind her aunt that she didn't know anyone when she picked up and moved to her new house. Instead, she popped bread into the toaster and asked Maggie to wake up Aunt Lizzie.

"Don't bother, I'm awake." She mumbled from the stairs. "Sort of." She added as she came into the kitchen. She poured orange juice and asked what was wrong with them. "It's seven o'clock in the morning. On a Sunday. Day of rest." Maggie ignored the whining.

"You sure you want me to stay with you Aunt Liz? Even if it's just a couple of weeks. I'm an early riser." Bree said and slid an omelet onto her aunt's plate.

"Why can't you be a normal teenager and sleep til noon on the weekend?" Liz asked while she slathered butter on her toast and sliced into her breakfast.

Maggie listened with a smile. Liz had said those exact same words to her when they were teenagers. Liz interrupted Maggie's thoughts. "She gets this from you. And why are you laughing?"

Between forkfuls of her own omelet, Maggie said, "it all feels like home."

By ten o'clock, Lizzie, Bree and Reggie were packed and ready to leave. Bree promised to take a good look at her bedroom furniture and let Maggie know what she would and wouldn't need. When Lizzie hugged Maggie, she reminded her that she didn't have to be alone for Christmas.

"How can you say I'm alone?" She asked. "I have Charlie." Charlie barked on cue, as Maggie tried to make Lizzie understand that she needed this first holiday in her new home. Lizzie claimed to understand, but Maggie didn't think she did.

Lizzie hated to be alone. Since Danny would only be there for a couple of days, and George had to go out of town for work, Maggie was glad Bree would be with Liz through the New Year.

Maggie watched them drive away then told Charlie that she gave Lizzie about a year and a half before she convinces George they have to move up here. "What do you think?" Charlie barked twice. Maggie assumed he thought so too. When she grabbed his leash off the hook, he immediately sat down at the front door and waited for Maggie to take him for a walk.

CHAPTER 42

Luke got up Sunday morning, made coffee and let Molly out. He started to go through the stuff he'd bought at Wally's. With Molly back in he said, "I wanna decorate, but I don't wanna overdo it. Right girl?" She didn't respond. Instead, she sat in front of her food bowl and looked at him impatiently. He filled her bowl and started to unravel the outside lights. Out on the porch, the cold damp seeped through his sweatshirt. A small coastal storm was headed their way but he didn't expect it til late afternoon. Molly pushed the screen door open, sniffed the air and turned right around to go curl up on the couch.

"Is this your idea of help?" Luke asked as he walked out to his truck for the ladder. He started to screw hooks into the porch roof to hang the lights on, and got lost in the conversation he'd had with his sister the night before.

Calista Skala, Callie, had gone to nursing school in Pittsburgh. Once she passed her boards, she took a travel position and ended up in Scottsdale. There, she fell in love with the weather, the city, and the man she married. About two years ago, their parents had decided they'd had enough winters in Western Pennsylvania to last them the rest of their lives and relocated. Callie idolized her big brother and they tried to speak at least once a week. She called after the Ohio State game, but the conversation soon turned more personal. Luke knew he could talk to her about Maggie without his sister automatically hearing wedding bells. This morning, Luke felt easier, less edgy. His sister had been right. *I can't compete with a ghost*, he'd told himself.

"And as long as she wears that ring Mol," he said to the dog that had come back outside, "she's not ready to give up the ghost." Molly looked at him as if he were crazy. "Yeah, I'm not sure if I used that phrase the right way either, but you get my drift." With all the hooks in place to hold the wires, Luke started to string the lights.

His hands began to sting from the cold, so Luke brought Molly inside and decided to light a fire. As much as he liked Maggie's open floor plan, she didn't have a fireplace. Luke didn't think he could live in a house without one. He saw he missed a call from Maeve. Her granddaughter had surprised her this morning so she had to cancel Sunday supper. Luke was certain the surprise visit was related to the impending storm. And although he'd miss Maeve, he hoped that one day soon she would accept her granddaughter's offer to move in with her.

"Well girl," he said to the lab, "it's just you and me today." It was one of the rare Sundays he didn't have dinner with the widow Donnelly. He checked the icebox to make sure he had food in and was certain they wouldn't starve. But he made a mental note to go grocery shopping. With a beer in hand, he sat at the dining room table and pulled out invoices. He snorted to himself when he thought about the perfectly good office set up in a spare room. *But my desk isn't this close to the beer*, he thought to himself. As Luke started to go through the paperwork he'd put off, he thought about that day almost five years ago when he first stumbled into the Cove.

CHAPTER 43

In March 2010, a nor'easter crawled up the eastern seaboard. The storm formed off the coast of North Carolina and hit New Jersey particularly hard. Wind gusts of 50-60 mph were reported state wide, and some areas reported wind gusts up to 70 mph. Powerlines came down, trees toppled over and debris was strewn everywhere. Some parts of the state reported close to five inches of rain. The governor declared a state of emergency, and at the height of the storm, almost 500,000 customers were without power. Wind and rain closed parts of the NJ Turnpike and almost shut down the NJ Transit system completely. Major damage occurred to thousands of businesses and residences in flood prone areas.

Two weeks after the storm, a friend of Luke's called to see if he wanted to come East for a couple of months. There was plenty of construction work available. Luke knew carpenters would be in high demand. And he needed a change. So, Luke left his apartment, loaded Molly into his truck and drove straight through to Philly. He spent two days with his oldest daughter who was a sophomore at the University of Pennsylvania.

Luke's friend had offered to put them up for however long Luke needed. Those first weeks, they put in 10-hour days, six days a week. One Sunday, in mid-April, Luke decided to take Molly to the beach for the first time. He took the wrong exit off the Garden State Parkway and drove straight into Lantern Light Cove.

When Luke looked up from his paper work, he was surprised to see it was late afternoon. The sky was ominous and wind lifted piles of leaves that waited to be picked up and tossed them all over Seahorse Lane. A light rain had started to fall, and Luke knew he had to take Molly out before it got any worse. "C'mon girl," he said and put her leash on. "We still have about fifteen minutes before it gets bad." They made it back right before a wind gust snapped off a dead branch and tossed it in the middle of the street. Lights flickered, and the December sky opened up. Cold, relentless rain pummeled Lantern Light Cove.

Luke grabbed a couple of logs from under a tarp on the porch and added them to the fire. He took some blankets and made a pile for Molly to burrow under on the couch. As he was about to start on hamburgers, his phone rang.

"Maggie. Is everything okay?" Maggie assured him she was.

"I'm calling for two reasons. One is the estimate. But first, I wanted to make sure that Mrs. Donnelly was gonna be okay with the storm." Before Luke could answer, Maggie told him she didn't know her that well but she didn't want the elderly woman to ride out the storm by herself.

Luke told Maggie she had nothing to worry about. Maeve's granddaughter was with her, and he was certain they'd be fine. Relieved, Maggie then told Luke that she was good with his numbers. "I'm not sure when you can get started, but Bree's room is a priority."

Luke understood and said he thought he could have all the work on the second floor done by the first week in March. "It could be sooner, but that will depend on the other jobs I've got going right now." Luke told Maggie that she needed to start to look at tile, faucets and paint chips. He said that Wally's had a decent selection, and if she wanted, she could set up an account there and Luke could charge the supplies to her account.

"This way, you'll know exactly what you pay for." Maggie liked that idea and said she would take care of it this week. Before they hung up, Luke told her he had a fireplace if she lost power. And that she and Charlie were welcome to come down if they got too cold.

"Thanks," she said, "but we should be okay. Although after the lights flickered, I added a generator to my shopping list." Luke agreed that was a good idea and told her the invitation still stood. She thanked him again.

Then added, "I've got lots of blankets. And wool socks in all different colors!" She ended the call before he could say anything. With a shake of his head, he thought about those brightly colored wool socks and what she'd look like out of them and the rest of her clothes.

Before those thoughts went any further, Luke went back to the ground beef, grabbed another beer and pulled out a package of American cheese. "How long do you think this has been in there?" He asked Molly who had come into the kitchen to investigate the meat that was on the counter.

Luke smelled the cheese and decided it was okay to eat. The two buns he pulled from the freezer were coated in white crystals. *The toaster oven will take care of that*, he thought. He found an opened bag of potato chips in the cabinet. One bite told him they were stale, but edible. "It's time to go grocery shopping Mol. We'll have to make a list."

He had to settle for fried burgers because the grill plate in the fireplace needed a good cleaning. While he waited, he replayed his conversation with Maggie. Luke was certain that if Maeve was alone, Maggie would have dragged her and the cat over to Maggie's to ride out the storm. And she barely knew the woman. He thought of how she offered to take Molly whenever he needed her to, yet she hardly knew him. He recalled that Saturday at the Oyster Bed. Most people would've blown off a teenager they didn't know. But Maggie talked with Kathleen as if she were the most important person in her life. Luke thought Maggie O'Neill might just be the most genuine person he'd ever met. And damn he wanted to get to know her better.

But Callie's words rang in his ears. Luke bit into his burger and remembered how Callie had try to warn him about his ex-wife. He broke off a piece of meat and tossed it to Molly. "And that," he said, "was one warning I definitely should've listened to."

CHAPTER 44

Luke and Colleen got married before they were twenty-two years old. They'd been together for about six months when she got pregnant. Callie sat in his apartment one night and tried to talk him out of it. But Luke lived by a code and this was the right thing to do. He knew he wasn't in love with her. He liked her. They got along fine. He was, however, in love with the baby she carried; and had been from the second she told him she was "late". Sure, they were young, and he was trying to get his construction business off the ground, but he was certain it would all work out. He bought a small house with a yard not too far from his parents. And by the time Kaitlyn was born, they had settled into a comfortable routine.

After a while, Colleen got bored. She resented her life as a housewife and the hours Luke worked. Although she never seemed to mind the money he made when he worked those hours. By the time Emily had come along, Colleen had gotten a job at a bank and had started to take night classes. Luke hated the idea of daycare; his mom had always stayed home with him and Callie. But he couldn't fault Colleen for wanting a life outside the house. He may be old fashioned, but times had changed. If he was honest back then, he would've admitted that he and Colleen were simply going through the motions of being a family. Other people saw it. It was Callie who had the guts to say it. His daughters, however, were a completely different story.

Kaitlyn and Emily were five years apart and as different as two people could be. But, to Luke's delight, were as close as any two sisters could ever hope to be. Kaitlyn loved princesses, was a straight A student and by the time she was eight, she knew she wanted to be in medicine. Emily was a tomboy and an athlete and had no idea what she wanted to be when she grew up. Luke never missed a recital or soccer game, a debate or school play. Whatever the girls were doing, he made sure he was a part of it.

While Colleen started to make a name for herself in the corporate world, Luke and his daughters were living like the family he'd always hoped to have. That ended the day after Kaitlyn graduated high school. Colleen told Luke she thought they should separate. He didn't fight for custody. Girls needed their mom. So, Luke moved out; but saw them twice a week for dinner, and whenever they had time for him. That December, Colleen asked for a divorce. She'd been offered a position at her bank's headquarters in Delaware. She accepted the offer and would move as soon as Emily finished middle school. Colleen's current husband Mark, was a VP in that office. And, Luke learned, Colleen had started seeing said current husband about six months before she and Luke separated. Luke could've fought the move across state lines, but he didn't. Instead, he let them go. With nothing to keep him grounded, Luke spiraled out of control.

Every night after work he was at the bar. If he wasn't there, he would drink alone in his apartment. There were a couple of one-night stands, but the last thing he wanted was to get involved with anyone. Instead, he kept to himself. And drank. His mom begged him to get help. His dad got after him at least once a day. Each time he thought he hit rock bottom, he sunk a little deeper. His business and friendships started to suffer, but this caused Luke to drink more. That first Christmas without his girls, Luke thought about ending it all. Then Callie showed up at his apartment.

Luke opened the door to see his sister with a small black ball in her hands. It was moving. She thrust it at Luke. "This is Molly. She was abandoned down on Maguire Avenue. Hence the name. You need something to focus on other than your self-pity. She needs someone to take care of her." She pushed pass him and set a box down with food, bowls, toys and a leash. Coming back to the door, she kissed Luke on the cheek. "I think it was meant to be. Merry Christmas." She closed the door behind her and was gone.

CHAPTER 45

Luke stood there for a minute. Hungover. And angry. What the hell am I supposed to do with a puppy, he thought. He was about to go after his sister when Molly started to squirm. She barked once then licked his face. Before he knew it, the dog nuzzled Luke under his chin. "I don't know girl," he whispered. "I'm probably the last thing you need."

Together they stumbled over to the couch. Luke held Molly tight as he plopped down on a cushion. He didn't realize he'd been crying til the puppy started to lick his tears. It was in that instant he knew he needed to turn things around.

Luke hoisted himself off the couch and decided to take Molly for a walk. "Let's see if your house-trained girl," he said. When he pulled the leash out of the box, Molly sat up and wagged her tail. As soon as she was on the sidewalk, she stopped to pee, so Luke figured she was trained in that area. Judging by her size, Luke thought she was about three months. 'What kind of person abandons a puppy?' He wondered as they made their way around the block. Once she finished her business, they went back home. He put Molly down to explore and took a good look at his apartment. That was when he saw exactly how low he'd sunk.

As Molly wandered, Luke cleaned. "Awful lot of beer cans," he said and filled a large trash bag. Next was the expired food that had started to smell inside the icebox. He took those bags to the dumpster behind his building. When he came back, he found Molly by the door. She barked when she saw him and rubbed his leg. Luke picked her up and felt her trembling. It dawned on him that she thought he deserted her.

"Oh girl no," he said softly and hugged her close. "I'm so sorry." He held her out to look at her. He promised he'd never leave her. Molly licked his face as if she understood every word he said. Luke sat her down again and began to pick up clothes that had fallen to the floor wherever he took them off. He tossed them in the washer. He stripped his bed and was assaulted with the smell of stale beer and sweat. His nose wrinkled in disgust as he added the sheets to the laundry. He opened the windows to let fresh air in, and was hit with a blast of arctic air. But the cold felt good. He took the blanket off the back of the sofa and wrapped it around the puppy.

Molly snuggled deeper into it. Luke watched her and thought she looked content. And he smiled. For the first time in a long time, he genuinely smiled. He called Callie. When she answered, he simply said, "thank you."

"You're welcome. I leave for Arizona the day after New Year's. Mom wants to have a family dinner and I certainly hope you'll be there." Luke promised he would. That call was followed by one to his parents. He apologized to his mom for the way he worried her and told his dad that he really was okay.

"Not just words this time. I promise." Luke declined the supper invitation because he was cleaning. His mom heard the sincerity in his tone. She fought the tears of gratitude that she knew would upset him. Luke offered to treat to Mario's for Callie's going away dinner. After he loaded the dishwasher, dusted, swept and swiffered, he decided he needed a long, hot shower.

Under the steady stream of hot water, Luke felt all the tension that had bottled up inside him wash away. He knew he'd screwed up, but refused to see how bad things had gotten. Luke stepped out of the tub and wiped the steam away from the bathroom mirror. I look like hell, he thought. As he shaved off the three-day growth of stubble, he decided he needed a haircut.

Once the steam cleared completely, Luke took a long hard honest look at himself. And he didn't like what he saw. He had left the bathroom door open so Molly would know where he was, and noticed her curled up in the doorway fast asleep. "I think it's time for a change Molly girl," he said as he stepped over her.

At the sound of his voice the pup stood up and padded over to him. Luke scooped her up and walked into the kitchen. He popped a frozen dinner in the microwave, then filled Molly's food and water bowls. After they ate, Luke made his bed and put away his clothes. Darkness hung outside the open window and Luke was surprised to see that it was almost nine o'clock. "Alright girl," he said. "One more bathroom break then lights out."

Later, as he lay in bed with the puppy curled up beside him, Luke took a pen and pad of paper from his nightstand. He began to make notes on the three different jobs he was working. He figured if the weather cooperated, he could wrap up all three jobs by mid-February. Since he was serious that he needed to make a change, he decided he wouldn't take on any new work. Briefly, he thought about Arizona. Callie had taken a travel nurse assignment there and he was sure she'd stay.

"She hates winter." He said to Molly as he scratched behind her ear. But Luke knew he would never be happy out West while his two daughters were on the East Coast. When a yawn escaped his throat, he put the pen and paper down and turned out the light. He told Molly not to worry. "I promise. I will figure out a way for you and me to start over together." The puppy yawned in response, stretched, then nosed her way up under his arm. Luke fell asleep with the feel of her hot breath on his cheek.

A loud crack brought Luke back to the present as he jumped from his chair and knocked his plate to the floor. In two strides he had the front door thrown open. The wind had uprooted an old oak and dropped it across Seahorse Lane. Miraculously, it hadn't pulled down any wires. Luke closed the door. "That's gonna be a real mess Mol." He stopped mid-sentence as he noticed that the dog had gulped down the rest of his dinner.

"Stale chips and all, huh?" He asked and bent over to pick up the plate and papers that had also fallen. The wind rapped loud against the windows and pelted sleet against them in a relentless assault. Luke opted to sleep on the couch with Molly stretched out on one end. He turned on Turner Movie Classics and hoped to find Hitchcock or John Wayne. Instead, he stumbled onto a Bogart marathon, so he settled for Key Largo. As his eyes fluttered closed, the first time he saw Maggie on the beach popped into his mind. "I should be more like Bogie," he mumbled through his sigh. "He always gets the girl."

CHAPTER 46

The day after the storm, Maggie was woken up by the loud buzz of a chainsaw. Before she investigated outside, she inspected inside. She started in the attic, went floor by floor, room by room and was relieved to see not a hint of damage anywhere. Outside was a different story.

Mother Nature had laid a carpet of leaves and twigs across the front porch. She noticed a work crew breaking down a tree that had fallen, and several large branches had blocked the steps of the house directly across the street. Closer to the bay, there was some minor flooding. Maggie wondered when high tide was, but thought, *all in all, Seahorse Lane fared quite well.*

Happy to see neighbors come out to help each other, Maggie figured her porch could wait and made her way over to see if she could help with the branches. Luke came out of Maeve's after he checked on the leak in her mud room. He told her he could patch it, but reminded her the roof was twenty years old and needed to be replaced.

"But Luke," she started to complain. Luke put up his hand to stop her.

"Maeve, that roof has been through Sandy, a couple of blizzards and I don't know how many nor'easters. It can't last forever." When tears filled her eyes, his heart broke. He loved this woman like a mom and remembered the day she showed up at his house with a cake.

He'd been unpacking boxes, trying to get Molly situated and wondering how long it would take for the pizza to get there when he heard the knock on the door. Thinking it was his dinner, he was stunned to see a little old lady on his porch. Even more stunned to see she had a cake in her hands. Luke was speechless. Through the screen she'd told him her name was Maeve Donnelly and that she lived up on the next block.

"I wanted to welcome you to Lantern Light Cove," she said and offered him the cake. Luke had to bite the inside of his cheek not to laugh. She was so sincere.

Finally, he stuttered, "I, I'm Luke." He opened the door and thanked her for the cake. "I would invite you in, but it's a mess." She told him that was fine then asked if he was married. Not sure where she was going with that, he didn't respond. Instead, he introduced her to Molly who had smelled food and came to see if it was for her.

Maeve stood in the doorway and looked at what he'd unpacked so far. "A dog, a couch, a TV and beer," she said with a nod to the empty Budweiser carton on the counter. "Definitely not married." She accused him.

"Divorced," he said simply. And in case she wanted to play matchmaker, he added that he was happy that way and didn't want to get involved with anyone.

"Maybe not today," she told him and left. Luke shook his head as he watched her make her way up the street. Back inside, he thought the cake was something his mom would've done. He broke off a piece of the cake and knew moving here was the right decision.

Three days later, Maeve invited him to her house for a home-cooked meal. It was then he learned she was a widow, her son lived in Florida and her closest grandchild was a lawyer in New York. And, he noted, her house needed some work. That was how their weekly dinner date began. Over the years, Luke had met Maeve's family, and he did what he could to help her. Luke knew that she wanted to stay in the house; but now, he needed her to understand that another storm like last night would be disastrous.

He didn't want to scare Maeve, so he explained all this to her granddaughter, who thankfully agreed. Luke left the two women to talk, so he could go check on the two job sites he had at the other end of the Cove.

Glad to see the limbs had been moved from the house next door, Luke noticed Maggie sweeping her porch and for a minute he stood there and watched. Her hair had been thrown up in a ponytail, but one tendril had slipped out and moved in time with each pass of the broom. Her sleeves were rolled up to reveal a small tattoo on the inside of her right wrist. Luke squinted to see if he could make out the details when a car beeped. The honk caused Luke to jump and Maggie to look up. From the street he called out to see if she needed any help.

"No. I'm good." She assured him the leaves on the porch was the worst of it for her. When she asked about Maeve, he shook his head. He told her about the leak in the mud room and how the roof needs to be replaced.

"Siobhan will try to talk her into selling. Again." He said, "but she's a stubborn Irish woman who doesn't want to leave."

Maggie told him that to say an Irish woman is stubborn is like saying water is wet. "Being stubborn is in our DNA."

"Thanks for the warning." Luke replied. "I'll keep that in mind when I'm at your house."

She then told him she'd go to Wally's later to set up the account and pick out tiles and paint. He asked if he could come back that afternoon.

"I'd like to see what you picked and check my measurements. I'll be able to get Bree's bedroom done before Christmas. But I thought I'd wait til after the holidays to tackle the rest of the upstairs." Maggie thought that was a good idea and told him that since he'd be here later, he could leave Molly with her and Charlie.

Something in the air sizzled with a sexual tension they both felt. Luke suggested dinner and saw the fear creep into Maggie's eyes. In frustration, he blew out a loud breath. "Relax Maggie. I don't date clients. We're two people having dinner because they need to eat."

Embarrassed, Maggie looked away. "Luke. I'm. It's not that I don't." It was her turn to sigh in frustration. "We should probably talk."

When he saw how distressed she'd become, Luke felt like a real jerk. He tried to apologize, but Maggie cut him off.

"Do you like soup?" She asked to lighten the mood. "I make a mean tomato bisque."

"I like anything someone else cooks." When he offered to pick up a loaf of Italian bread, she told him she made that too. *Of course you do*, he thought, and walked back home.

CHAPTER 47

The next two weeks flew by. Luke and Maggie cleared the air between them and true to his word, Luke had Bree's room finished the week before Christmas. It had turned out better than she imagined. The original floors were beautiful once sanded, stained and polished. For Bree's Christmas present, Maggie had ordered brand new bedding and an area rug. The walls were painted a soft dove gray and the rug was cream with darker gray swirled through.

Bree insisted she didn't need anything new, and Maggie made arrangements to have her furniture delivered the day after Christmas. She decided she could make the furniture look new with some chalk paint. She hoped Bree would like the comforter she'd ordered. It was coral and cream swirled with small specks of silver. She had Luke install soft gray mini blinds and she'd gotten floor-length cream-colored sheers to hang over them.

Nana T passed away the day after Bree finished her finals and Maggie made the trip to Delaware for the service. It was the same day Luke showed up with Sam, one of his workers, to start on Bree's room.

Luke's jaw dropped when she opened the door in a little black dress and heels. She told him about the funeral and handed Luke a key to the house. Once he regained his ability to speak, Luke made some comment about late night visits. Maggie looked him in the eye and considered her response. She didn't take the bait. Secretly, his reaction to the way she looked woke up desires she thought she buried with Jase. Maggie told him she didn't think she'd be home til later that night and asked him to feed Charlie dinner. The two-hour drive gave her time to think about the day after the storm and their conversation.

With the soup on simmer in the slow cooker, Maggie rolled out the bread to rise. She set the table and tried hard to not make it look like "date night". After she baked the bread, she took one of the loaves and some soup over to Maeve. She introduced herself to Siobhan, and they exchanged numbers. Maggie told her she could call any time.

From there she drove to Wally's set up her account and brought home some sample tiles to see how they would work.

She managed to shower and change about five minutes before Luke was at her door. Like the table, she tried hard to dress down for dinner in black tights, a cream thermal and black, gray and green checked flannel. "And naturally, green wool socks," she said as she checked the side mirror to switch lanes.

Dinner turned out to be more comfortable than she imagined. After some small talk, and over Luke's second bowl of soup, Maggie told him all about Jase. How they had met when she decided to take courses at community college. Her class was in one of the out buildings. She'd gotten there and noticed a red pickup truck parked in front. She thought it might belong to the instructor, but when she walked in, there was a guy at one of the desks. She knew he was a student. And she was hooked. Luke raised his eyebrows in a question.

"It seems I have a thing for men who drive red pickup trucks."

At first, Luke could only stare at her. Then laughed so hard he almost choked. "I'm sorry," he said after a long gulp of water. "Guys who drive red pickups?" That was one he'd never heard before.

Maggie knew how silly it sounded and shook her head. "I

don't know why it is. It just is." Then she gave Luke the cliff notes version of her life with Jase. Their first date. How she moved in with him. The night he proposed. Maggie grew quiet, took a sip of wine and stared at the back door as if she expected someone to walk through. Luke knew what she hadn't told him yet, but didn't push her. Finally, she looked at Luke and let a tear spill down her cheek. "Six months after he proposed, he was killed in a hit-and-run accident."

She poured more wine and took several sips before she told him that it will be two years in March that he passed. "I have been so angry and bitter. Angry at Jase because he went out that night. Angry at Tommy for because he left the scene." She added that as for Kevin, one of her best friends, she had been so pissed that he tried to cover it up. "I can't tell you how many people have told me that I need to move on."

Maggie held her left hand in her right and took a long look at the sapphire-diamond ring she wore; then looked up at Luke. "But we all grieve in our own way. At our own pace. I don't think anyone has the right to tell someone how long they're allowed to grieve for someone they loved and had planned a life with."

She looked so vulnerable. 'Like a scared and lost little girl,' he thought. And he wanted nothing more than to hug all that hurt out of her. Instead, he said, "you're right. You need to work through it in your time." Maggie looked up almost as if she'd forgotten he was there. Then she smiled at him.

"I know that one day I'll be ready to take this ring off. And maybe on that day, I'll be able to let someone else in." She reached out to put her hand on his arm. "But Luke," she said, "today is not that day."

Luke nodded. "No Maggie, today is not that day. Today,

you're my client and I don't get involved with clients." He stood up and started to clear the table. He added that one day, she'd no longer be his client. "And when that day comes, maybe I'll trade my black truck in for a red one." With a wink, he called for Molly.

Maggie walked him out. He advised her not to let Joe taste the soup, or he'd have it on the menu at the diner and claim it as his own. Maggie leaned against the closed door. She finally felt like she could let go of the burden she'd clung to for the past two years.

The loud honk of a truck's horn blasted Maggie back to the present moment. It saved her from missing her exit. After she replayed that conversation in her head, she started to see Luke in a different light. Before those thoughts went any further, she pulled into the church parking lot.

CHAPTER 48

Maggie made it to the church a minute before the service began. She saw her sister and brother-in-law and slid into the pew beside them. Maggie reached around George, and asked Lizzie if anyone had heard from Trish. She was answered with an eye roll and head shake. Maggie clenched a fist and exhaled. She calmed herself with memories of the woman she had come to pay respect to.

Nana T had been very involved with her church, and it seemed that the entire congregation had turned out to honor her. *It says an awful lot about that woman for all these people to show up on a cold wet December morning*, Maggie thought. With a silent prayer, she thanked the kind and gentle old woman who raised Bree into the young woman she'd become. The one request Nana T had made for her service was that the recording of Mahalia Jackson's Amazing Grace be played as her recessional. It was one of two church songs that always brought tears to Maggie's eyes. With the first notes, Lizzie handed Maggie a tissue. Maggie leaned over and whispered, "it could be worse. They could've started with Ave Maria."

After the service, Bree found her aunts outside church. She hugged them and thanked them for coming. "I'm gonna ride in the limo with Uncle Joe and his family, but." Her words trailed off.

Maggie brushed back a strand of Bree's hair. "You don't have to go in the limo Bree. You can ride with me. Your Uncle Joe would understand."

As if on cue, Bree's uncle approached. He said hello to

Lizzie and George, then turned to Maggie. "What would I understand?" He asked.

Bree told him she'd rather not ride in the limo. "It kinda creeps me out," she added.

Joe whispered, "me too." He told Bree that he offered her the limo out of respect. "But I understand if you would rather ride with your aunt." He did tell Maggie that he would like Bree to stand with them at the grave site.

From the cemetery, everyone was invited back to Nana T's. Maggie and Lizzie watched as most of nana's friends approached Bree. They hugged her and offered their condolences. Maggie thrilled to hear one woman tell Bree she expected to see her on the Food Network one day. Bree tried to humor the older woman.

"Mrs. Robbins, I'll be happy to be able to get a job after I graduate.

The woman had stopped to put on her coat. She cupped Bree's chin. "You listen to me young lady. Your nana believed you could do anything. And you provided desserts to enough church socials for me to know she was right." Bree tried to interrupt, but Mrs. Robbins continued. "Do not settle for a job after you graduate. If ever a young woman deserved her dreams to come true, it's you. Don't you ever sell yourself short. You have a gift." She hugged Bree, then whispered, "we will miss you beautiful one. But you go show those Bostonians what a simple girl from Delaware can do."

Bree hugged the woman back and promised she would try to make her nana proud.

"Oh child," she responded. "You already have."

By about six o'clock, it was only family left at the house.

Maggie changed out of her dress and heels and asked Bree where the boxes were to be loaded in the Jeep. While Joe helped Maggie with that, Bree sat with each of Joe's kids to say goodbye. Once the boxes were loaded, Joe told Bree he had something for her. He disappeared into the kitchen and came out with a small leather binder held together with a rubber band. As Joe handed it to Bree, her eyes filled up.

"Uncle Joe, I can't," she stammered as she shook her head no.

"Bree, she wouldn't want anyone else to have it."

Bree laughed and cried at the same time. She held the binder up to her aunts and told them it was Nana T's recipe book.

"Oh how wonderful," the sisters exclaimed together. Then Maggie added, "once you move in, I expect you to make a recipe at least once a week."

Bree said they wouldn't taste as good, but she'd try. Then it was time to leave. After another half hour of hugs and goodbyes, Maggie got on the road. She texted Luke to let him know she'd be home around nine or nine thirty, and thanked him again for watching Charlie. A country station started to play Rascal Flatts' I'm Movin' On. "No," Maggie told the radio. "Not moving on. Moving forward."

CHAPTER 49

Maggie woke up Christmas Eve to the hum of a motor. She brushed her ear and burrowed deeper into her comforter. She felt a tap, tap, tap on her right shoulder, she guessed Tink wanted breakfast. Maggie had offered to watch her so Maeve could go to Florida for Christmas without worrying.

Maggie opened her eyes startled to find the little calico staring at her. Maggie squinted her eyes and stared back. She never had a cat and wasn't sure if Tink wanted breakfast, or the bed. After a minute or two, she turned away. "No human in history has ever won a staring contest with a cat." She said as she pulled herself out of bed.

A quick look out the window caused Maggie to squeal with delight. A coating of snow lay peacefully on the grass as well as the sidewalks. "Looks like a white Christmas after all," she said but stopped when she saw Tink curled up asleep in the middle of the comforter.

"So, you just wanted me out of the bed?" She asked and walked over to scratch Tink behind the ears. Tink's response was to stretch her front legs, then curl right back up to sleep. Maggie kissed the top of her head. "Whatever happens little one, you will always have a home here," she whispered. Since she wouldn't be able to make the bed that morning, Maggie grabbed the hoodie off the back of her door and went downstairs.

In the living room, she found Charlie curled up in his bed. "What happened boy?" She asked and reached down to scratch under his chin. "Did the itty-bitty cat chase the big bad dog out of mommy's bed?" She reminded him that the cat was there for at least two weeks. "You two might want to work out a schedule."

Maggie went around the room and plugged in the Christmas lights. She found the TV channel with the yule log; then put on her I-pod holiday play list. Out in the kitchen, Maggie turned those window lights on too. When Charlie heard the back door open, he got up. Maggie let him out to play in the snow and watched him. She couldn't help but laugh as he ran around the yard and tried to catch snowflakes. Once he was back in and dried off, she fed him and filled Tink's bowl. Charlie looked at the chocolate chip she had taken from one of the tins on the counter. She swore he licked his lips. Maggie took out another. "You can have one," she said and tossed it his way. "And only because it's Christmas."

Maggie took her coffee, curled up on the couch and planned out her holiday. She'd had several offers for dinner. Everyone she dropped homemade cookies off to had invited her. And each time her response was the same. She truly did appreciate it, but Maggie believed she needed to have this Christmas, this way.

Nell was the one person who seemed to understand when they talked about it at Saturday supper three nights earlier. It had been the first time Maggie had been to the Oyster Bed since she'd moved there. She'd been glad to be able to catch up with the O'Roarkes and Kathleen. Maggie hoped Liam had made it home last night, to give his daughter the only present she wanted.

As for her own Christmas dinner, Maggie had decided on seafood. Not the seven fishes meal celebrated by Italians on Christmas Eve. She would have shrimp and scallops with linguini in a garlic white sauce. But that was for tomorrow. Today was all about photos.

CHAPTER 50

Ever since that first day outside Wally's, when Maggie took in Main Street all decorated, she wanted to photograph it. Unalii had shown Maggie that her "art" would sell. Maggie had always wanted to create greeting cards, and she was mildly successful at craft fairs. But the opportunity to sell them in a store like This & That sparked something inside her. Being able to create a holiday collection could take her cards to the next level. And she was certain this town would provide the perfect settings for Christmas cards.

Maggie learned that all the merchants on Main Street turned their lights on at noon on Christmas Eve, and kept them on for forty-five hours. It was one hour for each of the fishermen who sought shelter in the cove from that long ago storm. Maggie thought it was a beautiful tradition. Even more, she knew that once the stores closed, Main Street would be deserted, but beautifully lit.

The snow continued to gently drift down from the pale gray sky, which in her opinion, would only enhance the pictures. She also planned on the midnight service at church. Not to attend it, but after she saw it in daylight, she could fully visualize how it would photograph at night. First though, she wanted to take some wreaths down to the beach and "carelessly" toss them on the dunes for some nature Christmas scenes. With just a couple of hours of daylight left, Maggie got off the couch to start her day.

Later that afternoon, as she examined the photos from the beach, she was glad she decided to bring Charlie with her.

She managed to get him to sit still in front of the jetty and hold a wreath in his mouth. A few flurries floated around him. At the precise moment she took the picture, a lone seagull landed on one of the rocks behind him. It was perfect.

The result inspired her to consider photos with other animals. She was certain she could borrow Molly for some and use Tink in others. Around six o'clock Luke called to see if she wanted to go to Murphy's Tavern.

"On Christmas Eve?" She asked incredulously.

Luke explained that Murph stays open til ten on Christmas Eve. "Ya know. For those of us who don't have anywhere to be."

Maggie thought about that. "Well, that's nice. I guess." She declined and told him her plans for the night, and asked if she could borrow Molly for some pictures. Luke had no problem with that then asked Maggie if she had plans for Christmas Day.

"Yes." She replied, "but you might think it's weird."

"Weirder than your attraction to men who drive red pickups?"

"Ha ha." Then she told him how she stayed in her pajamas and has an all-day movie marathon. She makes breakfast, which includes mimosas, and opens whatever presents are under the tree. Her first movie is always the original *Miracle on 34th Street*. After that, she talks with family and friends, pulls together munchies and watches *A Christmas Carol*; the one with George C. Scott.

"Well of course," Luke interrupted.

"Finally," she said, "I make dinner. This year it's seafood and linguini. After dinner, I clean up everything, make popcorn and watch *It's A Wonderful Life*. The black and white version."

Maggie remembered Luke would not see his daughters this year. She quickly added, "you are more than welcome to join me for any or all of those festivities."

Luke said he might take her up on that offer. He told her to be careful while out taking pictures, wished her Merry Christmas and hung up. "She likes the old black and whites," he said to the empty room. "Imagine that."

CHAPTER 51

Around nine o'clock, Maggie dressed in layers and stopped by the door to pull on gloves. Charlie looked up at her expectantly. "Sorry Charlie. But I cannot focus on my work and keep an eye on you at the same time." She used a cookie to lead him back to his bed and escaped out the front door. She was startled to see Luke leaning against her Jeep with Molly by his side.

"What are you doing here?" Maggie asked as she shifted her camera bag onto her shoulder.

Luke held up his hand and told Maggie she couldn't get mad at him. When he didn't say anything else, Maggie did.

"And what is it I am not allowed to get mad at you for?"

Luke turned his head, then looked back at her. "I'm old school." He waved his arm toward Main Street. "And this is a great town. A safe town. But." Again, he stopped.

"Buuuuut?" Maggie asked.

"I'm old school." He said again.

"Yes Luke. We've established your old school." Then it dawned on her. "You don't want me out and about at night by myself."

As Luke stuttered his reasons for why he was there, Maggie listened and struggled not to tap her foot to an impatient beat, by they were wasting time. It wasn't that he didn't think she could take care of herself. But sometimes bad things happen in nice towns. And he knows that they're friends. Nothing more. He wasn't trying to overstep boundaries. "It's just that."

"You're old school." Maggie finished for him.

Luke stuffed his hands into the pockets of his jeans. He shrugged. "Yeah. Something like that."

Maggie stared back at him and bit on her lower lip to keep from laughing. She was actually touched by his concern for her safety. "Well, it's nice to see that chivalry is alive and well in Lantern Light Cove. C'mon Mol," she said and opened the door to let her in. She told the dogs to behave and not to bother Tink then went down to the Jeep.

"Tink?" Luke asked. Before she could respond, he answered his own question. "Oh that's right. Maeve's cat is crashing at your place while she's away."

Maggie walked around to the driver's side. With a look back at the house, she said, "crashing. Taking over. Not sure." Luke snorted, climbed into the passenger side and said he was definitely not a cat person.

CHAPTER 52

Maggie drove down Main Street and tried not to see it. She wanted her first impression of it all lit up to come once she stood on the side walk and looked back down along the avenue. Grateful that the street was deserted, she parked around the corner from Wally's.

Maggie opened the back of the Jeep, took out a tripod and handed it to Luke. Even though she knew she had everything she needed, she checked her camera bag one more time. Maggie slung her camera around her neck, zipped the bag, locked the Jeep and told Luke she was ready to go. As they turned the corner, Maggie stopped so suddenly that Luke almost walked right into her.

"Is everything?" He started to ask.

"Shh" she hushed, and cut him off.

They stood still in utter silence. There was pure wonder on Maggie's face, and he wished he could see this the way she saw it. Maggie took in every angle, every shadow, every single inch of the ideal Christmas card scene.

Each storefront was trimmed in white lights that created a gingerbread house effect. Every one of the old-fashioned lampposts were adorned with large red bows whose tails swayed in the night air. Thick boughs of holly were strung from post to post across Main Street like holiday arches to pass under. There was a thin layer of untouched snow on the sidewalks. The night was clear and several dozen stars punched holes in the black sky. When a light wind stirred the snow, starlight reflected on it like diamonds had dusted the pavement.

As Luke started to walk, Maggie pulled on his arm. "We need to walk in the street." When he asked why, Maggie pointed at the sidewalk. "It looks like snow fell after the shops had closed and everyone had gone home. There's not a single footprint."

She moved out into the street then told him that it was clear people have been out in their cars, but not walking. "Do you know how rare it is to have a chance like this? That sidewalk snow is pristine. No one has stepped on it."

Before Luke could respond, she added, "and you won't either. At least until I get my photos." With that, she took the tripod and set it up in the middle of the intersection.

It took a couple of minutes, but Maggie got the camera set up with the lens she wanted. The fact that she was able to adjust the angle of the tripod made it easier to take street length photos. She didn't need to physically move it quite as often. After she was satisfied with those, she took the camera and changed the lens. Then she moved in a zigzag pattern up and down the block. At one point, she stood directly under one of the holly arches, looked straight up, and clicked away.

Luke watched it all in complete amazement. Never in his life had he considered how greeting cards were made. But he had a new found respect for the people who created them. When Maggie came back and picked up the tripod, Luke wondered if they were done.

"With this block. Yes." With an almost wicked smile, she told him they had four more blocks to cover. Then she took off for the next intersection. All Luke could do was follow.

Two hours after they parked, Maggie and Luke were back in the Jeep. She cranked up the heat and silently thanked whoever invented heated seats. While they shared coffee from the thermos she had filled, Maggie told Luke she was headed to the church next. She offered to drive him home first, but Luke wanted to go with her. He could only imagine how she would take those photos. The DJ on the radio announced that Santa's sleigh had been sighted over the Empire State Building. Maggie figured they had just enough time to get to the church before people showed up for midnight services.

CHAPTER 53

Maggie was able to park on the street in a spot that offered a clear view of one side of the church. They sat in silence. Luke watched her take this in the same way she had when they stood on the sidewalk outside Wally's. When she opened her door, Luke asked if she wanted the tripod. "Thanks. But no. It wouldn't provide the same effect." Luke pretended to understand.

The bells in the steeple began to ring Silent Night. Within the first few notes, the air became hushed with reverence. At the church steps, Maggie noted thick boughs of holly draped across the front of the church. She appreciated the consistency with the decorations from Main Street, and started to see a holiday card "collection" with holly as a common denominator.

The side of the church she had approached from had six large stained-glass windows that ran the length of the building. Each window was framed with a large wreath. The impression was a halo effect around the solitary figure etched into the glass. Maggie was transported back to catechism classes from her childhood. She pointed at the window closest to the alter. "Peter. James. Thomas." She leaned into Luke, and whispered. "I bet there are six windows like this on the other side, but with different figures portrayed in the glass."

Luke was impressed with her knowledge of the Apostles. Maggie shuddered, but not from the cold. The memory of the nuns from grade school could still cause anxiety to perch in her chest. When they crossed the wide steps in front of the church, Maggie stopped short on the other side and gasped. "Oh Luke, look at that stable. It's beautiful."

If she'd been facing him, she might have noticed the brief flash of pride in his eyes. But her focus was on the stable he had built and donated to the church the Christmas before.

Its beauty laid in its simplicity. The sides and front were open, with a pillar on either end to hold up the roof. The floor was covered in hay. Life-sized statues of Mary and Joseph knelt on either side of an empty manger. The statue of the baby Jesus would be placed there at the end of the service. Two shepherds stood outside the stable, while several realistic lambs lay inside. A donkey and a cow stood off to the left, and Maggie expected that any moment they would start to bray and moo at her intrusion.

Luke then told her that on January 6th, statutes of the three wise men bearing gifts would be added to the scene. "Little Christmas," Maggie murmured. Nodding, Luke said it would stay up for about a week after that. An angel was attached to one side of the roof. A spot light was positioned with a strategically drilled hole that created the illusion of the Christmas Star. It was one of the most beautiful settings of the birth of Christ that Maggie had ever seen.

Maggie heard someone open the front doors and saw that people had started to file in. She led Luke back to the Jeep and waited. A couple of people at the threshold to the church stopped to turn and look up at flurries that seemed to be heaven sent. It was the moment Maggie had waited for – her camera started to click.

By the time they got back to Maggie's, the snow had ended. In the distance, the steeple bells began to clang and welcome Christmas Day. Maggie stood on the top step, closed her eyes and let the night air embrace her.

"Merry Christmas Luke." She whispered when she opened her eyes.

Before either of them knew what was happening, he pulled her close and kissed her. Not rough. Not passionate. But soft. Sweet. For a split second, Maggie leaned into that kiss. Then Luke, who could feel the ring on her left hand, broke away.

"I'm sorry," he said but leaned his head down to touch hers.

Maggie stepped back too. "It's okay." She lightly touched her fingers to his lips. "We'll chalk it up to holiday magic." She said simply.

Before he could respond, the dogs started to beg for attention. Maggie opened the door. Charlie and Molly raced down the steps and tossed snow around then try to eat it. Maggie carried her camera bag in, and came back out with a box wrapped in silver and gold, and a small silver bag with a large gold bow. She called Charlie up to the porch and handed the presents to Luke.

"What's this?" He asked.

"Everyone should have something to open on Christmas morning," she replied. "The box is yours; the bag is Molly's."

Luke was speechless. On tiptoe, Maggie reached up and kissed his cheek. "Merry Christmas Luke." Then she turned with Charlie and went inside.

As Luke and Molly walked home, he took in the lights and the smoke that drifted up and out of chimneys into the brisk night air. *God how he loved that smell.* The lights from his own house welcomed him home. In wonder, Luke thought this might've been the best Christmas Eve he'd ever had.

CHAPTER 54

Maggie jumped out of bed on Christmas morning like a child who'd been good all year to get on Santa's nice list. Tink, who had slept at the foot of her bed, did not appreciate the disturbance. She stood, arched, stretched and promptly turned her back to ignore Maggie. Maggie rolled her eyes, apologized and leaned over to kiss the top of the cat's head. "Merry Christmas Tink."

Charlie greeted Maggie at the bottom of the stairs with a bark and a raised paw. When she sat on the bottom step, he sat and thumped his tail. Maggie hugged him close. "Merry Christmas my handsome boy," she whispered. "Remember last year?" She asked and hugged him closer. "You were my only reason for getting out of bed."

He followed her into the kitchen so he could go out and come right back in to escape the cold. *We really have come a long way since then,* she thought as she fed Charlie and made coffee. In a repeat of yesterday, she turned on the lights and relit the yule log on the television. She made room for Charlie to curl up on the couch with her, and thought about the night before.

Absentmindedly she patted Charlie's flank, as she considered that she had a good number of photos for a full holiday card collection. "Tomorrow, I need to talk to Unalii about a local printer," she told Charlie.

Aside from the greeting cards, she had some genuinely authentic small town Christmas photographs. She knew she'd have to work with some of them, but definitely good stock photos. It surprised her how much she enjoyed having Luke with her while she worked. Normally, she flew solo when on a shoot. She didn't like the distraction. If she were honest, once she had a vision in her head of what she wanted, she forgot other people existed. Unless, of course, they were part of the photograph.

Luke was different, she thought. He was easy to be around and he seemed to respect her need to focus. He didn't constantly interrupt with questions.

"Or worse," she said and leaned into Charlie, "suggestions." She touched her fingers to her lips as if she could still feel his kiss. "Not going there today, boy." She told Charlie and stood up. She had one hour to get their walk in, make French toast, bacon and a pitcher of mimosas before her Christmas movie marathon began.

She pulled on boots and grabbed her coat off the hook by the door. Charlie jumped off the couch and followed her. They stopped on the porch to plug in the outdoor lights. She was just about to head down the steps when Luke drove by. He beeped and waved, but kept on going. Maggie watched him disappear up the street. She thought it was strange he didn't stop. Charlie's bark reminded Maggie they were on a schedule.

"You're right boy. Let's go." They skipped down the steps and turned toward the bay. Determined to enjoy every single second of the holiday, Maggie put Luke, and the kiss, out of her mind.

Luke reached the stop sign at the top of the street. For a minute, he thought he should turn around and thank her for the presents. She was right, everyone should have something to open on Christmas morning. The framed picture of Molly had instantly become one of his favorite gifts.

It was obvious she'd taken her to the beach one day, he thought. "Did she take you there without Charlie?" He asked and rubbed Molly's back. Molly turned her head from the window to look at him adoringly. Then she licked his face and turned her head back out in the cold December air. Luke thought more about the picture.

Luke assumed she'd had both dogs with her, but he didn't see how she could've separated them. The picture was all Molly. If he had to guess, Molly had chased a gull and had run into the waves. She captured the blue sky, bright yellow sun and white mist that sprayed around the black dog. It looked like Molly had jumped at a gray and white seagull that floated above the brown stone jetty in the near distance. The colors were distinct and vibrant and Luke was in awe of Maggie's talent.

"Of course," Luke told Molly, "if I had stopped when I passed her this morning, I could've asked about the photo op."

Again, Molly turned and licked Luke in the face. "Knock it off." He laughed and pushed her back. They were at the beach, and for a couple of minutes, Luke stood there mesmerized at the flow of the waves that rolled in and out. He threw Molly's ball in no particular direction and she chased after it. Luke started to think about last night on Maggie's porch, but Molly interrupted his thoughts when she dropped the ball at his feet. He crouched down, hugged her and rubbed the sides of her neck.

"Today is all about you and me girl." He threw the ball again. "We'll save those other thoughts for tomorrow." Before he followed the dog down the beach, he took out his phone and texted Maggie. *Thanks for the picture. It's perfect. Molly thanks you too. Merry Christmas.*

CHAPTER 55

After their walk, Maggie made her breakfast and took it into the living room. *A Miracle on 34th Street* was starting. Each time she watched this movie, she wondered what it would be like to sit at the window of a high-rise apartment and watch Macy's Thanksgiving Day parade from that vantage point. Just as quickly, she remembered that she never wanted to live in a big city. And, as she always did, Maggie teared up at the end of the movie when Natalie Wood jumped out of the car and ran up to the house. It reminded Maggie how lost she used to feel. How all she ever wanted was to find her home. That place where she belonged. With the credits rolling, Maggie stood up and stretched.

She started to clean up and thought *well, we found that place. Didn't we?* "Although," she said to the house, "you don't have a fireplace." Thoughts of a fireplace, reminded her of Luke's house. Thoughts of Luke's house, reminded her of Luke. Thoughts of Luke, reminded her of the kiss. Charlie barked at Maggie's plate in the hope of some leftover bacon.

"And we aren't gonna think about that today. Are we boy?" She said and grabbed her phone to call Lizzie. Maggie noticed she missed Luke's text. She read it. Then she read it again and thought it sounded off somehow. She told Charlie that Molly would not be coming to see him today. And for a moment, she wondered if Luke was upset with her for some reason.

"Maybe he didn't like his gift?" She wondered out loud. Before she could wonder anymore, her phone rang. She was greeted with Lizzie and Bree singing "We Wish You A Merry Christmas."

"You two oughta take that show on the road," she said into the speaker phone when they finished. Maggie talked with Bree first, then Lizzie. The two sisters talked for almost an hour. Maggie was thrilled to hear that after 25 years, George was finally able to surprise Lizzie on Christmas.

"So, a trip to St. Thomas over Valentine's Day. Very romantic."

Lizzie thought it would be. "Maybe you and Luke could join us." She said hopefully.

"I'm sorry." Maggie replied. "Me and Luke? We are not a couple." Before Lizzie could say anything, Maggie added, "I'm not sure he's even speaking to me." She then told Lizzie about the drive-by this morning, followed by the very short text. "I think he's upset because he kissed me, but." Maggie stopped short when Lizzie screamed into the phone.

"Kissed you? What? And you waited this long to mention that?" Maggie started to tell Lizzie about the photo shoot on Christmas Eve, but George interrupted and reminded Lizzie that George's family would be there soon. "I have to go Mag, but you better believe I want to hear all about this kiss." They hung up with a promise to talk in a day or two.

She'd no sooner hung up with Lizzie, when the phone rang again. "Merry Christmas Maeve," she said.

"I don't mean to bother you Maggie, but I wanted to check on Tink and make sure she isn't too much trouble."

Maggie assured Maeve that her cat was no trouble at all, that she was fine. "Really Maeve, all she does is eat, drink, use her litter box and sleep. Once in a while she lets me play with her for about five minutes." Maeve told her that sounded about right and said she'd let her know when her return flight would be.

Before Maeve could hang up, her son Brendan got on. "Merry Christmas Maggie. Do you have a couple of minutes?" He asked in a tone that said something was wrong. Brendan told Maggie everything was fine, but Maeve had fallen. He added that he wanted her to stay longer than she had planned. "Weather in the Cove can be bad in the winter, and my mom," he trailed off.

"Is a stubborn old Irish woman." Maggie finished for him. Brendan snorted, but agreed.

"Honestly, I wish she would make the decision to move down here. She has her own suite. A golf cart to get around. And other people her age."

Maggie told him it sounded wonderful, and wished him luck with that talk. "And if she's concerned about Tink, the cat can stay as long as Maeve needs her to." Brendan thanked her and said he'd be in touch.

As if she knew they'd been talking about her, Tink appeared in the kitchen. Maggie reached down to pick her up and the cat rested her head on Maggie's shoulder. Then turned her face into the curve of Maggie's neck and began to purr.

"Do you miss her girl?" Maggie asked as she stroked the cat's back. Maggie had no idea how soothing a cat's purr could be. In the living room, Maggie dropped Tink onto the couch and watched as she pawed at a blanket until she got it the way she wanted. Then she circled once, and burrowed deep into it. Maggie wondered if the pretty little calico was now a permanent part of the family.

She sliced cheese and fruit, and grabbed crackers to add to the plate. Maggie bit into a strawberry as her mind wandered back to the night before. She had to admit she wasn't upset about the kiss. Charlie barked a reminder her she wasn't thinking about that today. "You're right," she said and tossed him a piece of cheese. She was on the couch with two minutes to spare before Ebenezer and Jacob Marley had their reunion.

CHAPTER 56

Back home after the beach, Luke straightened up and showered. He wondered how Maggie's marathon was going, then turned on the TV and started his own movie marathon. "Okay, so it's just one movie Mol, but who doesn't like *A Christmas Story* for 24 hours?" He asked her as he made something to eat.

"Seriously. A BB gun. A leg lamp. And Flick's tongue frozen on a flagpole. If that doesn't scream Christmas, I don't know what does."

Before he could lay down on the couch, his phone rang. "Merry Christmas mom." He said as he answered it. "No. I'm not alone. In fact, I'm lying here with a beautiful girl by my side."

His mom replied that while Molly was indeed beautiful, it isn't the same as not being alone. Luke assured his mom he was fine. There was plenty of things to keep him occupied. He was glad to hear that both his daughters had called their grandmother; although with the time difference in Italy, like Luke, she spoke with Kaitlyn on Christmas Eve.

"Well," his mom conceded, "you sound okay."

Luke was dumbfounded. "If I didn't know any better mom, I'd swear you were upset that I'm okay." They talked a little more, then she put his dad on.

After they hung up, he called Callie. He told her about Christmas Eve. How he pulled Maggie in for a kiss and the gifts she had for him and Molly. Then he admitted that the avoided her this morning.

"Luke!" She admonished him. "Have you spoken to her at all today?"

"Sort of," he responded.

"Texted? Are you serious?" Luke interrupted his sister to ask if she could hold off on her disappointment until after Christmas. Callie decided not to push it. Instead, she suggested that if Maggie wasn't upset about the kiss, then maybe she's more ready to move on than she thinks. After she hung up, Luke thought about what Callie had said. "Maybe Callie is right. After all, Maggie didn't end the kiss. I did."

With a beer in hand, he thought about how easy it was to be around her. She made him laugh and after last night, he started to think about getting back to what he loved to do. He decided that maybe it was time to take a chance again. When Molly rubbed up against his leg, Luke apologized. "You're right girl, today is for you and me." But he promised himself he'd call Maggie in the morning and see if she'd like to go on an actual date Friday night.

CHAPTER 57

The day after Christmas, Maggie finally got out of her Christmas pajamas and took a shower. While she had enjoyed yesterday, if she were honest, she wished Luke had decided to join her. The thought jolted her. It forced her to admit that she was thinking about a man other than Jase and she had no idea what to do about it.

As she stepped out of the shower, she watched Tink bat the shower curtain with her paw. Then she jumped up on the side of the tub and proceeded to lick the water off the liner. "You really are a weird cat. Or maybe you're normal and all cats are weird."

Back in her room, Maggie noticed a missed call on her phone. The movers would be there between one and five. That gave her plenty of time to clean, straighten up and get to Wally's to pick up the chalk paint for Bree's furniture. By noon, Maggie had everything done she needed to do. Her stomach rumbled to remind her she hadn't eaten.

"Cheeseburger, onion rings and home brewed iced tea is just what the doctor ordered." She told Charlie to be good and ran up to the diner.

Maggie was about to walk into Joe's when she heard a man call her name. She assumed it was Luke, and was surprised to see Liam approach her. Maggie stepped away from the door. "Merry Christmas," she said when he was close enough, she didn't have to yell.

"Nollaig Shona," he replied in his best Irish brogue as he hugged her and kissed her on the cheek. They made small talk for a while. He wanted to know if she was settled and if she was happy with her choice. There was a twinkle in his eye when he asked how Christmas Eve was with Luke.

"Small town grape vines never cease to amaze me," she said with her hand on his arm. Then she asked about the O'Roarkes and Kathleen. She hoped they had a wonderful holiday.

Liam assured her they had, but added that he hated the thought of going out on the boat again. "Between you and me, I might give my land legs another try." Then Liam grew serious. "Actually Maggie," he began. "I had hoped to talk to you about Kathleen."

He took her hand and became serious. "I'd like to ask you a favor." He went on to tell Maggie that Kathleen seemed like she had a lot on her mind. "Things she doesn't want to talk to her da about." He leaned in closer as people passed by them. "Nell is great, but her and Paddy are from a different generation."

Maggie thought she knew what he wanted to say, but she let Liam finish. "The thing is, I don't want to tell Kathleen she should call you. And I thought maybe you could come up with a reason to call her."

Maggie put her hand back on Liam's arm. "Oh my god," she cried. "This is perfect. She can help me with my arts and crafts project." She told Liam that her niece, who is about the same age as Kathleen, would be moving in with her. Bree's bedroom set would be delivered today, and Maggie had plans to chalk paint it before Bree arrived. "I could tell Kathleen that I need her expert teenage opinion."

Liam hugged Maggie. His brogue returned when he told her he thought that was a fine idea. He kissed her again and wished her a Happy New Year in case he didn't see her before he sailed. Maggie wished him the same then went in to get her lunch. Neither of them had noticed Luke parked across the street.

That same day, Luke had driven out to the lumber yard and then the plumbing supply store. He wouldn't start on Maggie's bathroom til the day after tomorrow, but wanted to make sure his order was in. As he drove back into the Cove, he found himself singing along with the radio and he had to laugh. He hadn't felt this happy in a long, long time; and he knew it had to do with Maggie. He wished he'd gone to dinner at her house the night before, "but nothing I can do about that now. Maybe, if I do it right, she'll say yes to a dinner date on Friday night."

Luke was surprised at how much he wanted this. He thought about it a lot the night before. He didn't want to be alone. He knew that. He also knew that all this time he had waited for the right woman to show him what it was he did want. And that realization hit him like a ton of bricks. He saw Maggie about to go into the diner. On a whim, he pulled over and parked. He had one foot out of the truck when Liam approach her.

It was like a knife to his stomach as he watched them laugh, hug and casually touch. "You're right Callie. Maggie is ready to move on. But not with me." Luke didn't follow Maggie into the diner. Instead, he steered his pick-up down to Murphy's Pub and proceeded to drink his lunch.

CHAPTER 58

Lunch became dinner. Dinner became dessert. All liquid. Murphy had a private car and driver he used for his patrons who had one too many. It was an expense he gladly paid to keep people safe. His own brother had been killed by a drunk driver when he was barely sixteen and Murph had never forgotten it. From the moment Luke climbed onto a barstool, Murph had heard all about Maggie and Liam and moving on together. He knew that Liam had no interest in Maggie, but Luke didn't want to hear it. Like every other drunk, Luke had all the answers and repeated his story to anyone who would listen. By ten o'clock Murph had heard enough. Luke had started to slur his words and made no sense at all.

"Oh you will be one hurtin' boy tomorrow friend." He said as he poured Luke into that private car and wished him luck.

Marty cracked the window to give Luke fresh cold air. "Don't be puking in me back seat Luke."

Luke burped and said "'K".

Marty was shocked when Murph said Luke needed a ride home. In all the time Luke had lived at the Cove, Marty had never seen him get drunk. As he listened to him mutter, Marty figured it was a woman. "Then again," he said, "it usually was." When they got to Luke's house, Marty offered to walk him up the steps.

"Mar." Hiccup. "Mar." Hiccup. "Marty." Luke said with a pat on his shoulder. "What was the question?" Before Marty could answer, Luke said, "I amember."

Outside the car, Luke said, "You're a good man Marty.

But I'm a grown man and can." He waved his hand towards his house, "ya' know. Walk up a flight of steps."

The porch and house were dark. As Luke fumbled with his key, Molly started to bark. Luke held a finger to his lips and told the dog to hush. Somehow, he fit the key in the lock. Molly charged out, ran down the steps and peed on the sidewalk. Luke turned the porch light on and grabbed Molly's leash. At the sound of that, she ran back up and sat in front of him. Luke looked at his dog and patted his chest with both hands. Molly stood on her hind legs as if hugging him.

Luke said, "I know you would never play games with me would you Mols?" She barked and sat back down. Luke managed to hook her leash onto her collar. Luke closed the door, but left his keys in the lock. Then he set out up the street to tell Maggie exactly what he thought of women who did play games.

CHAPTER 59

Maggie was startled awake. She couldn't imagine who was at her door this late. When she heard Molly's bark, she yanked it open. "Oh my god Luke, is everything al?"

She stopped and stepped back when she noticed he was weaving. "Are you drunk?" She asked surprised.

"I've been thinking," he said. Then burped. "Scuse me." He stopped as if he'd forgotten something. "Oh yeah," he continued. "Women lie, cheat and pretend until something better comes along." He burped again. "Maybe you should find a different contactor." He slapped his chest, and repeated, "Con. Trac. Tor." Then he pulled Molly's leash, "c'mon girl."

Maggie, grabbed his arm. "You're not taking her anywhere. She may need a walk, but she doesn't need a stagger."

She pulled Molly inside then told Luke he could either leave or crash on her couch. When he didn't reply, she added. "You have exactly ten seconds to turn around and try to find your way home or come inside. I'd like to go to bed."

Luke stumbled onto the couch. As Maggie went to get a pillow and blanket, he muttered something about her being the same person as his ex. His snores echoed through the living room before she got back downstairs. She covered him with a comforter and stared at him.

"Not sure what this is all about Luke," she whispered, "but you better believe you have a lot of explaining to do tomorrow."

The next morning, Maggie thought she heard something, but just as quickly thought she imagined it. Then images from the night before flashed through her mind. She bolted up and shook her head. "Oh no, no, no," she said as she jumped out of bed and ran down stairs.

"If you're gonna do the walk of the shame," she snapped, "you're gonna know why you're doing it." Luke froze. There was a jackhammer pounding inside his head and someone had stuffed his mouth with cotton. He wasn't sure what was coming, but was certain he deserved it. In slow motion, he turned to face Maggie.

Luke started to apologize, but Maggie cut him off.

"No. You don't get to talk. You said an awful lot last night. Now it's my turn." She started with his ex-wife. "I'm not Colleen. I don't lie, cheat, or pretend." She held up her hands and told him what you see is what you get. "Don't you ever compare me to her again."

Luke started to open his mouth. "I'm still talking," Maggie spat.

"Also, not sure what you thought you saw outside the diner, but contrary to what you believe, I am not the new girl in town who goes around and samples the merchandise until she finds what she wants."

Luke winced. He felt the sting as if she'd slapped him. And she should have.

"Finally, if you want me to find a new contractor, I will. Because last night I saw I side of you that I don't like. And I certainly don't respect." Out of steam, Maggie sat on the bottom step and forced herself not to cry.

Luke wanted to sit beside her and hug her. But instinct told him not to. When he looked down at Molly, he realized for the first time that he put her at risk.

"Maggie, I am so sorry. I don't want you to get another

contractor. I know I hurt you." Luke rubbed his hand across his mouth. "Worse, I could've gotten Molly hurt."

He knelt beside Molly and whispered how sorry he was. He kissed the top of her head to ask her forgiveness. Maggie couldn't help but smile when Molly stared at Luke with adoration and licked his face. Luke looked up at Maggie. "If you'll let me, I'd like to make you dinner tonight and have that talk."

Maggie knew he was sincere but it didn't matter. She had to bite her upper lip because she didn't trust herself to speak. She blew out the breath she'd held and suggested that the next night might be better.

"Mag, I am." But she stopped him and told him he should just go.

"I need some time Luke." After he left, Maggie sat on the step numb.

Once she pulled herself together, Maggie was able to go about her day. She reached out to Kathleen who seemed happy to come to Maggie's and help her with the furniture the next day. She spent an hour on the phone with Lizzie to let know her everything that had happened.

"Don't be too hard on him Mag, if you ask me, he sounds scared." Maggie snorted and told her that made two of them.

Lizzie was patient. "I know you are. But he must care an awful lot if he got that upset and that drunk because he saw you talking to someone."

Before Maggie could interrupt her, Lizzie went on to say that she didn't think Luke was a jealous man but that he had probably been really hurt by his ex. Maggie had thought the same thing but did not admit this to her sister.

"Listen Mag, you're very good at reading people. Let it settle for today. Did he screw up? Big time." Lizzie insisted. "Is he paying for it? I bet more than you know."

Maggie sighed. This time it was Lizzie who snorted. "You know I'm right. I still think he's worth a chance. But only you can decide that Mag."

They switched topics and Maggie told Lizzie about Kathleen and Bree's furniture. Lizzie was happy to hear that Bree would be able to meet someone her age. After they hung up, Maggie had nothing to occupy her mind. She decided she needed the ocean and spent the rest of the afternoon with Charlie. It didn't take long for the water to soothe her frayed nerves

CHAPTER 60

An ice-cold shower, several Advils and a three-hour nap reduced the pounding in Luke's head to a dull ache. It took a gallon of water, but the cotton in his mouth finally washed away. He called one of his workers to drive him to Murph's to pick up his truck. Luke considered he should stop in to thank Murphy, but he wasn't in the mood to be harassed. Instead, he ran into Joe's ordered a greasy lunch to go and went home. He certainly didn't want to get yelled at, but he needed some advice. He texted Callie. Less than ten seconds after he hit send, his phone rang.

"You did what?" She yelled in his ear.

Calmly, Luke responded. "Cal, I know I screwed up. Right now, I physically hurt. I'm embarrassed and ashamed of the things I said. On the upside."

Callie interjected. "Oh good. You think there's an upside."

Luke noted the sarcasm that dripped in her voice. He was silent for a minute before he told her that all of this has made him see how much he wants to try with Maggie.

Callie hated that her brother was alone. She knew what a good guy and father he was. If this woman has made him want to try, she said a silent prayer that Maggie would forgive Luke and take a gamble on him. She decided Luke had suffered enough so she was kinder when she spoke again. She told him not to push Maggie. "But when, *if*, you get to talk, be honest Luke. About how you feel and all your fears."

Luke knew she was right, but admitted how hard that would be.

"Yes. It will be hard. But if you can't be honest about all of that, especially with yourself, you don't stand a chance with anyone. Certainly not a woman like Maggie from what you told me." Callie told him she loved him and wished him luck before she hung up and left him to think about everything she said.

Luke did think about it and knew his sister was right. Since he felt a little more human again, he decided to make the rest of the day about Molly. "I owe you big time girl," he said. He then asked her how she felt about the beach, a bath and a good steak dinner. She barked in eager excitement. Luke thought that people should love as unconditionally as pets do. He drove to the end of the peninsula. There was not as much beach there, but he was certain there'd be no Maggie there either.

The next day, Luke got up and checked his phone. Maggie hadn't cancelled, so he started to scrub his house from top to bottom. The windows were thrown open to let fresh air in. Still not sure what to make for dinner, he decided on seafood because she seemed to like it. "And you can't get any fresher than the fish market." He told Molly.

He carefully lifted the fireplace grill off the hooks he'd installed. At the sink, he scrubbed it to remove any steak residue from last night's dinner. Once that was done, he checked his spice cabinet and made a list of what he needed. He knew white wine went better with fish, so he added that. But since Maggie preferred red, he picked up a bottle of that too. And if she was in a beer mood, he'd thrown in a six pack of Smithick's as well.

Out on the porch, Luke found a package. Confused, he picked it up. As soon as he felt the thick envelope, he knew what it was. He'd forgotten about the order he placed on Christmas, but the timing was perfect. Just before he climbed into his truck, Luke texted Maggie to see if six o'clock worked.

Maggie was certain her text alert was from Luke, but didn't answer right away. She still wasn't sure what she wanted to do. Kathleen had come over, they'd mixed the chalk paint and were just about to get started. Maggie had pushed up her sleeves and Kathleen noticed the tattoo on Maggie's right arm. It was an old-fashioned skeleton key with a heart at one end and the word forgiveness as the stem of the key. When she asked about it, Maggie explained that what she has learned in life is that *forgiveness is the key.*

"I designed the tattoo because every so often, I need to be reminded of that." With a shake of her head, she added, "like right now." Maggie picked up her phone and texted Luke that six o'clock was fine. Then she turned her attention to Kathleen and the task at hand.

Maggie had laid a tarp on Bree's floor. The bed was put together, but the box spring and mattress were in the hallway to give them room to work. With the ceiling fan on and windows opened for ventilation, they tackled the dresser first. As they worked, Maggie tried to sound casual when she asked about Kathleen's life. How her senior year was going? Did she have a boyfriend? Had she decided on college?

Kathleen was silent for a minute. "I guess I'm learning a lesson about forgiveness myself." Someone Kathleen had thought was a good friend started a rumor about her. All because a boy that girl liked had been interested in Kathleen. But out of friendship, Kathleen turned him down.

Maggie took her time before she responded. "First of all," Maggie began, "that girl isn't a true friend if she started a rumor about you for something you have no control over. Second," she continued, "if you genuinely like this boy, then you're cheating yourself by not giving him a chance."

As she listened to herself, Maggie picked up on the fact that this advice could be about her and Luke. She brushed that thought away and went on to tell Kathleen that if she didn't like this boy then be honest about that too. "As long as you stay true to who you are, I promise it will all work out."

With the first coat of paint on the dresser and drawers, they stood and stretched. It was already three o'clock and Maggie decided they needed to stop here. They cleaned up and Maggie closed the door behind them.

"Don't you want to leave that open for ventilation?" Kathleen asked as they went downstairs.

Maggie thought if she kept the fan on and windows crack it would be good enough. "Besides, if I leave the door open, I'm pretty sure the cat will wander in there and come out streaked bluish gray."

Kathleen thought that made sense. As she thanked Maggie for inviting her up, she stopped and turned around. "Why did you ask me to come up?" Before Maggie could answer, Kathleen continued. "Oh my god. Did my da ask you?" Maggie held up her hand to stop her.

"He was concerned and thought you could use a female to talk to. And you can." She assured Kathleen and hugged her. "Any time. I think once Bree moves up in another week, you and she will get along great. You're a lot alike."

Kathleen offered to come back after Mass the next day to do the second coat. "That would be great. And don't be too hard on your dad when you talk to him. He only spoke to me because he was worried about you." Kathleen said she'd think about that and left. With nothing to distract her, Maggie got ready for dinner.

CHAPTER 61

Maggie opened her closet and stared. She didn't want to dress too casual, but she didn't want to dress too flirty either. For an hour, she pulled things out and put them back. In the end, she opted for dark grey leggings and a cream-colored chunky turtleneck sweater. She chose black ankle-high boots. A light touch of mascara and lip gloss and she was good to go.

On the way down to Luke's she talked to Charlie. "Listen boy, tonight you're my wing man. If it looks like mommy is uncomfortable, bark twice and we're outta there. Got it?"

Charlie barked once and Maggie said, "Yes. Just like that. But twice."

She emphasized that by holding up two fingers. Charlie barked once. Maggie told him again that he truly was a dopey dog. Before she knocked, Maggie tried to settle the butterflies that had erupted in her stomach. She looked down at Charlie, and whispered, "wing man," as Luke opened the door.

Maggie wasn't sure what to expect when she stepped inside, and was pleasantly surprised at how comfortable it was. He had an oversized dark blue sofa, with an oversized chair in stripes of blue, cream and green. What looked to be homemade afghans were draped over the backs of each.

"I know they're bold. Almost obnoxious. And they don't go with the furniture. But my Gram knitted them." Luke told her. "Can't seem to get rid of them."

"You shouldn't." Maggie replied and jumped when something in the fire popped. Maggie walked over but stopped short. "Are. Are you cooking in the fireplace?" She asked not sure she was seeing right.

"Yeah. Hope you like sea bass." He then showed Maggie the hooks he drilled into the sides so that he could hang a grill over the fire. "This way, I can barbecue inside no matter what the weather is outside." He started for the kitchen then called back. "Red, white or beer?"

When she didn't answer, Luke came back to the living room. He caught her mesmerized by the fireplace. *He has fillets on cedar planks on an open fire.* She thought. *Now that's a first.* Maggie looked back and asked what he'd said.

"Red, white or beer." She looked confused. Then it clicked. "I know I'm supposed to say white because it's fish. But I prefer red."

As he got her a glass of wine, Maggie continued to explore. She was glad he had gotten a tree, and she noticed the photo of Molly displayed on the mantle. The radio was tuned to a country station and Maggie softly sang along with the Dixie Chicks *Landslide*.

She turned into the dining room and once again stopped short. Luke didn't have an open floor plan like she did, but he had managed to combine the kitchen and dining room into one space. Like her, he had a large barn table. But his was more weathered. As she ran a finger along it, she felt an etching. There were letters scratched into it: k-a-i.

He handed her a glass, tapped it with his beer and said cheers. With a nod to the letters, he said that he'd come home one day to find seven-year-old Kaitlyn in a time out. Colleen had caught her trying to carve her name on the table. "I was concerned that somehow she'd gotten hold of a penknife; but Colleen seemed to be focused more on how the table looked."

Luke thought that memory defined Colleen better than he ever could. But he shook it off and went over to the oven to check on the potatoes.

"Well, the table looks lovely." Maggie noted the vase of fresh flowers he placed as a centerpiece. *He really is trying*, she thought. "So, what's on the menu?" She asked as she leaned against the kitchen island.

Luke told her sea bass fillets, twice-baked potatoes and green beans. "I also stopped at Bagliotti's for cannoli." As he walked out to take the fish off the grill, Maggie made herself comfortable at the table. After he prepared the plates, he poured more wine for her and grabbed another beer for himself.

Maggie was impressed; and told him so.

"Don't be." Luke replied. "When you think about it, the grill does all the work. But thank you."

With a large swallow of liquid courage, Luke began *the talk* with an apology. "First, I am so sorry about the other night. I was rude and I was cruel. I could say that I don't know what came over me, but that would be a lie. And Callie told me I needed to be honest about my feelings and my fears. So, here goes."

Luke then told Maggie about Colleen. How she had pretended to be someone she wasn't for most of their time together. That *she* had cheated and *she* had lied. He told her that she had destroyed his trust in relationships and since the divorce he swore he would never get serious with anyone again. He told her that he was okay on his own. He worked, he had friends, and he always came home to Molly.

At the sound of her name, both dogs wandered over to the table. After a minute of being ignored, they went back to the living room and laid down in front of the fire. Their interruption gave Luke some time to regather his thoughts.

Luke stared hard into Maggie's eyes. "That all changed the first day I saw you on the beach. Those couple of minutes we talked, you woke something up in me. But then the sun flashed off the sapphire." He nodded to her hand. "At the time, I didn't know your story. But any woman who wears a ring on that particular finger is off limits. I don't cheat." He emphasized.

"When you decided to move here, you turned my world upside down. And the more time I spent with you, the more time I wanted to spend with you. Christmas Eve was one of the best nights I've had in a long, long time. And not because we shared a kiss." He stopped himself before he got lost in that kiss. He stayed focused on the present.

"The day after Christmas, I had planned to ask you out to dinner. On a date." He took a mouthful of potatoes and washed it down with another gulp of beer. "When I saw you with Liam, all those Colleen-generated fears slapped me in the face. So instead of following you into Joe's, I decided on Murph's. And well, you know the rest."

CHAPTER 62

Maggie didn't respond at first. Instead, she asked for a little more wine. When Luke sat back down, she covered his hand with hers. "First of all, as far as Liam goes, they were holiday hugs and kisses. Nothing more. He had stopped to ask me if I could help Kathleen. There are some things she's going through that she needs a woman to talk to. That's all."

Luke could feel the flush rise in his cheeks and felt like a complete idiot.

"And I am truly sorry for the hurt Colleen caused you. I have never understood why people cheat. But I can understand why that would make you not trust. And why you would be afraid. I have my own fears."

Before Luke could ask, she stopped him. Maggie looked away for a second, then turned back to face him. "Feelings and fears, huh?" Luke didn't push her, but Maggie continued.

She told him how her whole life her own insecurities made her think she would never find someone to love her. So, she created a persona of a strong independent woman who didn't need anyone.

"In reality, I was a scared little girl who desperately wanted her happily-ever-after. I'm forty-two years old and I've never been married. Never had kids. My fears are very real."

Luke was stunned. How could *she* think no one could love her?

She then told Luke that Jase had been kind and so sure of us and strong enough to carry her through her fears. She was in her late thirties when they met. It was the very first time that she felt worthy. They had planned a life together. "Then, just like that," she said with a snap of her fingers, "that life was gone."

They sat in silence. Each of them lost in a life that could've been. When the dogs barked, Maggie started to clear the table. Luke got up to help.

"When I came here, it wasn't to find someone. It was for me to find a way to move forward. Yet, there you were. Every time I turned around. There you were."

Luke smirked but agreed that it did seem that way.

"And yes, Christmas Eve was beautiful. The kiss surprised me, but it was nice. It was sweet." They stood at the sink close enough to touch. Maggie covered his hand with hers and told Luke she wanted to spend time with him too.

"But you have to understand Luke, that we have to go slow. And, you have to trust me." She reached up and pulled him in for a kiss. "Because I promise. If I'm kissing you, you're the only man I'm kissing."

She turned towards the table, but Luke pulled her back. This time the kiss was anything but soft. His tongue probed and he tasted the wine she'd been drinking. Luke lost all thought and wanted to drink more of her. He wanted to get drunk on her.

Maggie placed her hands on his chest and pulled away. "Slow," she said and smiled up at him. "I believe the word I used was sloooooooow."

He gave her another quick kiss, then snorted. "Slow. Got it." He said and held up his hands.

Molly came into the kitchen and sat by the back door. Charlie followed. "I'll let them out," Maggie said. As she opened the door, she noticed the photo he had hung beside it. The picture was of a yellow tennis ball left on the beach with a poem about childhood dreams. It was one of the ones she sent Unalli. Maggie stifled her giggle.

When Luke asked what was so funny, Maggie touched the ball in the glass. "Isn't that great?" He asked. "I found it at the art festival last Fall and I fell in love with it."

Maggie turned to face him. "It was always one of my favorites." At Luke's puzzled look, Maggie told him it was one of hers.

"One of?" "Yours?"

"Yes," she said. "One of mine. This," she said and laid her hand on the glass "is one of the things I do with my photographs."

Luke asked her if she was serious. Maggie assured him she was.

"I thought the photos were for greeting cards." Maggie told him that some are, and some are for other uses. She opened the back door and called for the dogs. "C'mon Charlie, it's time to go."

Luke started to complain that it was still early, but then he looked at the clock. "When did it get to be tomorrow?" He asked when he saw that it was after midnight. "Let me grab my coat. Mols and I will walk you home." Before they left, he grabbed the package from under the tree.

Maggie was curious, but didn't ask. At her door, she thanked him again for dinner and kissed him on the cheek. She tried to sneak inside before it led to more, but Luke stopped her.

He pushed the package into her hands and kissed her forehead. "Merry Christmas," he snickered and left her puzzled.

Inside, Maggie looked in the bag and squealed in delight. She turned it upside down over the couch and watched as a half-dozen pairs of brightly colored wool socks fell out.

CHAPTER 63

By Tuesday, Bree's room was finished. With the bed made and curtains hung, Kathleen promised Maggie that Bree would love it. As Kathleen was leaving, Maggie wished her a Happy New Year and told her to have fun on her date. Then she thought of her own plans for that night.

Luke was taking her to Murphy's Pub for an early supper around five, and Maggie liked the idea that their first official date would be on New Year's Eve. She wasn't ready to jump into bed with Luke, but unlike the other night, she planned to dress flirty tonight.

She decided on a swing dress with a low scoop neck and flared sleeves. Her dark blue sodalite pendulum necklace hung so the point rested just above her cleavage. The crystal matched the blue in the black, blue and cream swirled pattern of the dress. Silver hoop earrings, black tights and knee-high boots completed the outfit. As she twirled around in front of the mirror, Maggie watched the dress float out around her. She felt pretty. From Luke's reaction when she opened the door, she knew she nailed it.

"Wow." Was all Luke could think to say. "You look amazing." From behind his back, he pulled a single long-stemmed white rose.

"It's beautiful." Maggie said as he handed her the flower and told her it's meant to represent new beginnings. Maggie loved the symbolism and leaned up to kiss him. Before it went too far, Luke reluctantly pulled back.

"Slow." He said but held her a moment longer.

"Slow." Maggie echoed. "You two," Maggie said, then stopped. Tink had made herself comfortable in a corner of the couch. "You *three* behave." Charlie and Molly barked. Maggie was certain the cat looked up and rolled her eyes at them.

Murphy's was everything an Irish pub is supposed to be. Maggie thought it was a larger version of the bar at the Oyster Bed. Rich dark wood with a brass rail footrest. The bar itself was oval and tonight there were three bartenders. High top tables ran along one wall. At the far end, a band was setting up on the small stage in front of a make shift dance floor. Boisterous is the word that came to mind; and there was a distinct feel of camaraderie as people greeted each other with hugs and "get my friend a pint." Maggie thought she heard "Come Out Ye Black and Tans" coming from the jukebox.

"Well, Luke me boyo," a man shouted in their ear from behind. A large mitt clasped Luke's shoulder, as he leaned in closer. "Would this be the lovely lass who had you worked into a drunken dither the other night?"

Luke hugged the older man and wished him a happy new year. Maggie held out her hand and told him she believed she was that woman. Murph let out a roar and hugged Maggie so tight he lifted her off her feet.

Once he set her back down, the old man said "allow me to introduce myself. I'm Murph, and this," he said with arms spread wide, "is my kingdom." As he escorted them to two empty stools, Murph called to one of the guys behind the bar. "Brian, their first round is on me." He then moved through the crowd very much like a king in his kingdom.

They both ordered pints. Luke opted for traditional fish and chips while Maggie went with Guinness Pie. Their food came as the band took the stage. They opened their set with A Soldier's Song. The air had changed from camaraderie to reverence. Maggie noticed several older men, some with visible scars, stood and sang with tears in their eyes. With his red hair, long red beard and burly build, Murph resembled the quintessential ancient Irishman. Maggie watched him as he sang along with his fist on his heart.

After several more fight songs, the band slowed things down and Maggie recognized the first notes of Grace. As if transformed into another world, Luke watched Maggie fall into a trance-like state. Mesmerized, she sang about the love between Joseph Plunkett and Grace Gifford. Maggie swayed to the lyrics, and a tear escaped down her cheek. When it ended, Maggie turned to Luke and asked if he could ever imagine a love that strong. He didn't trust himself to speak and was grateful when Murph intervened.

With a kiss to Maggie's cheek, he said, "it does an old man good to see Joe and Grace's love live on." Maggie told him the song always makes her cry.

"Darlin, it should bring a tear to every eye." Brian brought Murph over a shot of Jameson. He toasted Luke and Maggie. "In the name of old Erin, here's wishing you good cheer, good luck and good fortune for many a year." He slammed back the whiskey, wished them happy new year and made his way through the crowd to mingle with his patrons.

CHAPTER 64

An hour before midnight, the pub was three deep all around the bar. Pinned in by claustrophobia, Maggie asked if they could leave. They snuck out before Murph looped back around. By the time they got back to her house and let the dogs out, they had about five minutes til midnight.

Maggie pulled Luke outside as fireworks went off somewhere in the Cove. They couldn't see them. But their bursts broke up the night sky with a warm glow in pale shades of pink, yellow, green and blue. Maggie told Luke to make a wish. "This is the purest moment in time. The mistakes of last year are behind us, and a fresh start lays before us."

"New beginnings?" He asked.

Maggie smiled. "Exactly. New beginnings."

They held hands until the warm glow of colors faded back into the dark night. One star broke through the blackness, as if the Universe had blessed them. They welcomed the New Year with a kiss.

The next morning, Maggie tiptoed down the stairs. Luke had crashed on her couch and she didn't want to wake him. As quiet as she could, she let the dogs out and back in. She left a note where Luke could see it and crept out of the house.

Every January first, Maggie made it a point to be on the beach at sunrise. This was the first time she didn't have to be up two hours before dawn to do it. This ritual was spiritual for Maggie, although this year it was more. As the horizon lightened with pink and orange, Maggie took note of the sun, almost white against the dark water, ready to peek over the waves.

With her hands clasped together, Maggie thought of Jase. His dark hair, the eyes that could read her soul, and his smile that could charm everyone he met. She almost felt his strong arms wrap around her. "Babe, it's time to say goodbye." A lone seagull cried out once as it flew overhead.

With a nod to the bird, Maggie told Jase that Luke is a good man. "You and he would've been friends in a different life. But," she added, "if I'm going to give him, us, a real chance, I have to let go. You will always have a place in my heart. I cannot even tell you what." Maggie stopped to brush away a tear. "Thank you, for all you gave me. Most of all, for the courage to take a chance on love."

Maggie stood at the water's edge and blew a kiss into the wind. She let the new day wash over her. When she got back home, Luke was still asleep, but he stirred when she closed the door. Maggie ran upstairs and placed the sapphire ring in her jewelry box. Then she went back downstairs to make breakfast for her and the man she knew she had started to fall in love with.

CHAPTER 65

Bree's first week in Lantern Light Cove was hectic, but good. Maggie had taken her up to the diner where she and Angie worked out a schedule. Then she'd gone to the bakery to meet Mr. Bagliotti. While she appreciated the opportunity at Joes, as Angie would help show her how to run a kitchen properly; Mr. Bagliotti would teach her the art of cake decorating and he also encouraged her to experiment with new recipes. If Bree were honest, she loved to bake more than she liked to cook. That first Saturday, Maggie and Luke brought Bree to supper at The Oyster Bed. And her aunt had been right, she and Kathleen hit it off immediately. It surprised Bree since she'd always been sort of a loner, but she was glad to have someone her own age to hang out with. Especially since she noticed that Luke and her aunt spent a lot of time together.

As for her bedroom, Bree was certain that her aunt had bought her new furniture. Until she opened the top drawer and saw her name in purple crayon scrawled inside it. Bree shuddered as she traced her finger over it. Nana T was so mad at her. Yet she was so proud that she spelled Sabrina correctly. She picked up the framed photo of her nana and stared at it.

"You punished me by making me sit in the kitchen with you while you baked. And now here I am. About to start down the path to my own pastry shop."

Bree was startled when she heard Maggie's voice. "Is that what you want to do Bree? Open your own pastry shop?"

Bree told Maggie how she and her nana had gone into Philadelphia one weekend and stayed overnight. As they wandered around Center City, they stopped inside a small shop. Bree fell in love with the aromas, the display cases that showed off beautifully decorated cupcakes and cookies, and the people who sat there with their coffees, baked goods and books or laptops. She looked up at her nana and told her that someday she would own one just like it.

"She squeezed my hand and said she didn't doubt it."

CHAPTER 66

January turned into February and Maggie and Bree settled into a routine. Each of them worked three days a week. Bree at the diner and bakery, Maggie at the gift shop. On Maggie's off days, she spent time on her greeting cards and photos. Bree spent her free time on recipes and cake decorating. Maggie insisted that Bree take one day each week and do something fun. Those days, Bree spent with Charlie and Tink. It worried Maggie that Bree spent so much time alone. But she knew there was nothing she could do since kids her age were in school during the day; and there wasn't a lot of night life for teenagers in the Cove. So, she was delighted when Bree mentioned the Valentine's dance at the high school.

"We get to go dress shopping?" Maggie clapped her hands, while Bree held hers in prayer. "Aunt Mag, please don't get crazy. Kathleen asked me to go because Scott is a drummer and his band is playing. She doesn't want to go by herself since he'll be on stage." Then she mumbled something about some girl who had started a rumor about her.

Maggie recalled the conversation she'd had with Kathleen the day they'd painted Bree's furniture. Then she asked Bree if there was anyone she might be interested in. Bree couldn't hide the dejected look that washed over her.

"No. Aunt Mag. There's no one I'm interested in. And what would be the point?"

Maggie reached over for Bree's hand. "I don't understand what you mean."

Bree started to talk about her parents. How they picked

up and left her like she meant nothing. So maybe she was nothing. And if they could walk away so easily, why would anyone want to stay with her.

"And what if I'm like them? What if I do meet someone and he falls in love with me and I decide to up and leave? That would be cruel. But maybe that's just in my DNA." Bree broke down as sobs hitched in her throat.

Maggie was shocked. The shock was replaced by anger. Not for the first time, she wanted to strangle her little sister. She tugged on Bree's hand and coaxed her away from the table to the couch. Maggie sat with her arms around Bree until the young girl's tears subsided.

"I'm sorry Aunt Maggie, I don't know what came over me."

Maggie handed her a tissue and told her there was no need to apologize. "I am so sorry for what they put you through. But Bree, you are not them."

Before Bree could interrupt Maggie stopped her. "I am absolutely certain you are nothing like them. You worry whether or not you *are* like them which tells me you aren't. You're you. Intelligent. Kind. Beautiful. Driven. Talented."

Bree didn't believe Maggie. She told her that since she was her aunt Maggie had to say that.

"Maybe," Maggie considered. But I also believe it."

Bree didn't agree. "I don't know Aunt Mag, the thought of getting involved with someone scares me."

Maggie told her she understood. She reminded Bree that it wasn't until she was in her late 30s that she found someone.

"Yeah. And then he was taken from you."

Maggie tread carefully around Bree's bitterness. "Yes. He was. And I was so angry about that. But I've learned that people come into our lives for a reason, and sometimes they leave us for a reason."

She brushed a tear away from Bree's cheek. When she continued, Maggie told her she believed that she was brought to Jase so she could learn to trust in love. "And then he led me here. To Luke. And one day, you will find someone to love. It may take years, but he's out there. In the meantime, focus on you and your dream."

Maggie stood up. "But now, *we* get to find you the perfect outfit for that dance."

Reluctantly, Bree got off the couch and allowed her aunt to take her shopping.

CHAPTER 67

By the end of April, Luke had completed the second floor. He had to finish a couple of other jobs, but promised Maggie he could start on the attic by the end of summer. Bree didn't remember much about Uncle Jase, but she knew that her aunt had been heartbroken. She was happy to see Maggie with Luke, because she saw how happy Maggie was when he was around. Even though Bree hadn't met any guys she liked, she had made some new friends at the dance. There was one kid named Connor Donovan who she thought was cute. But when he approached Bree, Kathleen steered her away.

Maggie noticed that Bree seemed more relaxed. When she mentioned it, Bree brushed it off. She still got sad, and there were times that she struggled with how much she missed Nana T, but Maggie had been right. Whenever she made one of her nana's recipes, she did feel close to her. Each time she tried something new in the kitchen, or learned a new decorating trick, Bree's confidence grew. By the end of June, Mr. Bagliotti allowed Bree to decorate the special-order cakes.

One night as she sat at the table and toyed with a new recipe, she thought about her first six months in Lantern Light. Bree recognized that "the Cove" had become her home. Even though she'd never met Mrs. Donnelly, she was upset when her son called to say that his mom had suffered a stroke. Maeve was okay, but they all decided she'd be safer with them in Florida. Maeve's granddaughter would be down to oversee the sale the house, but he could not bring Tink to Florida as both he and his wife were allergic. Maggie was happy to make the cat a permanent member of the family.

July fourth promised to be the hottest day of the summer. But Bree didn't care. Her Aunt Lizzie and Uncle George had come up to spend the week. She hadn't thought about how much she'd missed them. She hoped her cousin Danny would be able to come, but he and a couple of his friends were driving cross-country to see how many roller coasters they could ride over their summer break. She asked him if he lost a bet or something. He told her to talk to him again after her first year of college. That thought brought her back to reality.

She would leave for Boston in less than six weeks. She was terrified and excited, confident and unsure. When she talked to her aunts the night before, they reassured her that it was all normal.

"How do I look Tink," she asked the cat that had taken to sleeping on her bed. Bree applied some lip gloss and spun around in her new sundress. It was cornflower blue with little yellow daisies embroidered across the neckline. She paired it with yellow flip-flops and had a gotten a pedicure with hot pink polish.

"You look adorable," her aunts exclaimed when she walked into the kitchen.

Bree looked at them in horror. "Adorable is not what an 18-year-old girl wants to be," she huffed.

"How 'bout hot?" Luke chimed in as he looked up from the steak he was marinating for the grill. "Although I probably shouldn't think of you as hot. Scratch that." He said as Maggie through a towel at him. Her Uncle George came in from the yard and whistled. Bree shook her head and sighed in that dismissive way teenage girls have when they're around adults.

Luke asked about the concert and Bree explained that it was the same band from high school. "They're actually pretty good. Besides," she added, "Kathleen is still crushing on the drummer." Lizzie asked Bree if she had a crush on anyone.

"No," she answered, in a tone that abruptly ended the conversation. She was grateful when Kathleen breezed in and said they had about six minutes to get to Main Street for the next jitney that would take them to the bandstand.

CHAPTER 68

After they left, Maggie told Lizzie about the conversation she'd had with Bree about relationships. Lizzie wanted to cry. George grabbed two beers, and motioned for Luke to join him outside. While they waited for the grill to get hot, Luke asked George about Bree's parents. He'd never pressed Maggie about it, but he didn't understand what happened. George had been with Lizzie since high school, he knew the story well.

Trish had been a wild child, and there were times that Lizzie and Maggie were convinced their parents had brought the wrong baby home from the hospital. After their parents' divorce, Trish spiraled. At seventeen, she met Johnny Tacarini. At eighteen she was pregnant and they moved in with his mom in Delaware. By the time Bree was five, Johnny had been running on Trish for three years. He left two years later, and Trish did a complete three-sixty.

"She found God." George said between swallows of beer. "Which is all fine and good. But it came at the expense of her daughter."

George finished off his beer and opened another. Luke could see the anger in George's eyes, but he kept it in check. Trish began to do missionary work. "It's admirable. But she left Bree with her nana so she could stay in school. These trips became longer and longer. This last one took her to somewhere in Africa three years ago."

"Three years?" Luke yelled. "How do you leave your kid for three years?"

George tilted his bottle in Luke's direction. "Exactly. It's a wonder, and a credit to her nana, that Bree is not completely screwed up."

When Lizzie and Maggie came out with the steak and potatoes, both men decided to change the subject. The rest of the night they talked about anything but Bree. The attic renovation. Danny's trip across country. And of course, George's beloved Phillies.

The rest of the summer flew by and the day before Bree was to leave for Boston her mom called. Maggie was half-way up the stairs when she heard Bree on the phone.

"Are you serious? No. No. Don't. You know what, don't ever call me again." Bree threw open her door and almost knocked Maggie over.

"Bree, what happened?"

She waved her phone in the air and started to rant. "Her. She happened. Like she always does right before something's supposed to be about me."

Maggie didn't need to know anything else. It was obvious Bree had heard from her mom. She put her hand out and told Bree to give her the phone. Bree handed it over, but said she'd already hung up.

"Good." Then she scrolled through the phone, pushed some buttons and handed it back. "Now she's blocked."

Bree was dumbfounded. "Block? Can I? Am I allowed?"

Maggie pushed a strand of hair behind Bree's ear. "Sweetie, you're eighteen. You're no longer a minor that she has any control over."

Bree slid down the wall and sat on the floor. "I'm eighteen. She can't." Bree looked up at her aunt. She couldn't control the laughter that bubbled up and out of her.

Maggie sat down and put an arm around her shoulder. Bree quieted, then the hysterics started again. Once she got herself under control, Maggie would lose it. And then Bree would start all over again. Luke found them like that an hour later when he got home with pizza and fries to celebrate Bree's last night.

CHAPTER 69

College was a whole different world for Bree, and it took her a couple of weeks to get adjusted. She'd been out of school for almost nine months and she struggled a little to get back into classroom mode. Her roommate, Melissa, was from Connecticut. She was a petite blond and very fashion forward. Unlike Bree, who just about lived in sweats. Mel's parents owned a boutique hotel in Greenwich and an upscale restaurant in Manhattan. They had been high school sweethearts and married for twenty-three years. She and Bree were from two completely different backgrounds. But they got along great.

Like Bree, Mel wasn't a big party person and was focused on school. Melissa's major was hospitality. She'd planned to take over the hotel one day. It took them about a month to be able to find their way around campus without getting lost. One Saturday in October, Bree suggested they play tourist and explore Boston.

As a little girl, Nana T would often take Bree to Philadelphia for day trips. She thought it was important for Bree to learn about the history of America. Since they lived an hour's drive away it was easy for them. It took a lot of coaxing from her nana to get Bree to walk past the imposing statue of Benjamin Franklin, but his institute eventually became one of Bree's favorite places to visit. And of course, there was the Liberty Bell, Betsy Ross' house, the Constitution Center and Elfreth's Alley – where the houses and cobblestones still look like they did in the Revolutionary Era.

Boston's Freedom Trail brought all those memories back

to Bree. In front of the Old North Church, she remembered how her nana tried to get her to memorize The Midnight Ride of Paul Revere. "I managed to learn the first verse," she told Melissa. "Then I gave up."

Melissa told Bree that she looked completely at home in Boston. "I am. I guess it reminds me a lot of Philadelphia in certain ways." That was the first time Bree considered she could make Boston her home.

Over Christmas break that year, Melissa invited Bree to her parents' house for a couple of days. One night, they went into New York and had dinner at her parents' restaurant. The tour of the kitchen fueled Bree's ambitions further. But she declined the offer to help the pastry chef. Bree wasn't sure she was ready to handle a blow torch. While they dined, Bree recognized some of the patrons as people she'd seen on the Food Network. Unable to believe her luck, she thought, *Nana T must be looking down and jumping for joy.*

Classes were more difficult in her second semester, and sometimes Bree wondered what she was doing. She was grateful that Danny was in the area. He would come by and have dinner with her once a week, sometimes his friend Jimmy came with him. For the most part, Bree spent her time in the library.

At the end of that semester, one of their instructors told the students about the possibility of enrolling in classes at Le Cordon Bleu. There was a six-week Summer intensive program in London that could earn Bree the basic certificate in pastry. She had no idea what all of that would cost. And she wasn't sure how she'd afford it, but she promised herself she'd find a way. *Can't worry about that now,* she thought as she loaded up her car.

Freshman year was behind her, and Bree was excited to be

going home. She wanted to catch up with Kathleen, and spend time with Charlie, Molly and Tink. She thought maybe she could pick up time at Tradewinds in addition to the bakery and the diner to fund the England trip. After she got out of the city, Bree jumped onto I95 and found a classic rock station. With the radio up and the windows down, she blasted Bon Jovi's "Livin' On A Prayer." As she drove, she bobbed her head in time with the music. "You and me both Jon. You and me both."

CHAPTER 70

Maggie was on the porch swing when Bree pulled up. As she watched her niece get out of the car, Maggie was surprised to see how mature she seemed. *Bree has always been older than her years*, Maggie thought, *but this is different.*

Maggie bounced down the steps and hugged Bree. Then it hit her. She held Bree at arm's length. "Confident." She stated.

Bree looked at her aunt with a raised eyebrow. "Huh?"

Maggie led Bree up the steps. "I couldn't figure out what was different. You've gained confidence in yourself. And it shows here." She said and waved her hand around Bree's face.

Bree took the compliment gracefully. "I've learned a lot this year Aunt Mag. And there's something I want to talk to you and Luke about. Is he home?"

Maggie stopped before they walked inside. She asked why Bree thought this was Luke's home.

"Oh please." Then she pushed past Maggie and fell on the floor to hug the dogs who'd ran over to her. "Where's Tink," she asked them. "Did you finally vote her off the island?"

As if on cue, there was meow from the stairs. Bree butt-crawled over to scoop up the cat who nuzzled her under the neck. "If I didn't know any better, I'd swear you missed me," she said. Somehow, she managed to stand up, grab her backpack and head up to her room with Tink still settled in her arms.

Maggie followed Bree upstairs. She was excited to see her reaction.

Bree stopped at her door. Confused.

"Wait. Where's my room?" She turned around. Maggie

didn't answer but Bree could see the excitement that wanted to burst out of her.

"You now have the master bed and bath. And this," she said as she closed the door, "has become the guest room."

Bree wasn't sure what to say. "Why? You didn't have to do that."

Maggie walked ahead of Bree with one of the boxes from her car. "It was Luke's idea. He figured after living in a dorm, the extra space and private bathroom is something you've earned." Maggie added that she hated when he was right.

"Does this mean the attic is finished?" Bree asked as Tink jumped out of her arms and curled up on one of the bed pillows.

"It would appear she comes with the bed," Maggie gestured toward the cat. "She hasn't gone back in the other room since we moved your furniture."

Bree scratched Tink behind her ears. "That's okay. I even missed this little furball."

"And yes, the attic is finished. I can't wait for you to come up and see it." After two more trips, Bree's car was unpacked. Then Maggie dragged her upstairs for the grand tour.

At the top of the steps, Bree stopped and gasped. "Oh. Aunt Mag, this is way more than I imagined."

Maggie could only nod in agreement. "He finished it a little over a month ago and I'm still in awe of it."

Luke had installed a window with a window seat. On either side were floor-to-ceiling recessed shelves. At the far left, a door opened onto a bathroom complete with toilet, vanity and shower stall. Bree noticed two half walls that seemed to create a separate room. This is where Maggie had her bed set up. On either side of the bed were tall night stands that Maggie used as dressers. On the wall opposite the bed, an antiqued coffee table stood. Maggie had hung a flat screen TV above it. Past the far half wall, Bree found Maggie's office space. She had a desk, more recessed shelving and her computer set up. In the corner farthest from the top of the stairs, Luke had built a closet. True to Maggie's style, there were colors everywhere.

The office area walls were soft yellow. Maggie had framed several of her favorite photographs and hung them. She chalk-painted her desk a dusky blue. Her desk accessories were all painted hot pink. The dusky blue from the desk carried over to the walls of the bedroom area. There, the rug under the bed was cream colored with splashes of forest green, Caribbean blue and coral. Her comforter and pillow shams were softer shades of coral and blue with flecks of green tossed through them. She did the walls in the area at the top of the stairs in a peach hue. The window seat cushions were yellow, peach and sky blue. Simple white sheers covered the windows.

"Aunt Maggie, it's beyond beautiful. I can't believe it's the same attic you showed me when you first moved in."

"I know." Maggie gushed. "I sleep here every night and I still can't believe it."

Charlie's bark travelled up the stairs and Maggie noticed the time. She told Bree to freshen up because they had to meet Luke at Murphy's for dinner.

CHAPTER 71

Bree had been to Murphy's twice. Once on St. Paddy's Day and once before she left for college. She liked the tavern. Not because Murph had no qualms about offering a beer to an 18-year-old who was there with her parents. Bree didn't care for the taste of beer, although she would never say that to him. What she liked, was how you felt when you walked in. It was as if no matter who you were or where you were from, this was a place you could belong.

While they waited for their food, Bree looked around and recognized a couple of people she'd met last summer. One of the barbacks recognized her and she thought he might've tried to flirt with her at last year's concert. She waved, but didn't want to encourage him so she started to tell Luke and Maggie about the London opportunity. She ended it with telling them she thought she could raise the money if she worked two days at the bakery, one day at the diner and one day at Tradewinds. "So? What do you think?" She asked hopefully.

Luke and Maggie looked at each other. Luke took a long drink of beer, then shook his head. "No," he said.

Bree was shocked. "No? But Luke, this is such a great opportunity."

Luke stopped her. "What I mean by no is that no, you will not work all those hours."

Bree protested again. "But Luke, this is the only way I can afford to go."

Luke shook his head again. "You don't need to raise the money. Your aunt and I can pay your way." Bree started to argue but Maggie agreed with Luke.

"But why?" Bree stammered. "Why would you do this?"

Luke looked at Bree the way he might his own daughter. "I can afford it," he said simply. "And it's an incredible opportunity." He then told her the money was conditional.

Bree raised her eyebrows, while Luke continued. "You can work two days at the bakery and one day at the diner. The other four days you're to act like a kid home from college for summer vacation."

Bree looked at Maggie for support, but Maggie was with Luke on this one.

"I told you I hate it when he's right. But he's right." She reminded Bree that this would be the last summer she would be able to goof off. "You've been a grown up since you were twelve years old. Please Bree," she said and clasped her hands together in prayer. "For once in your life, just be a carefree teenager with no worries in the world."

Sulking, Bree said she would try. Maggie signaled the waitress for another round of drinks. "Yes. Please. Try not to be so responsible for once in your life."

Over the next couple of weeks, Bree worked her day jobs, and acted like a teenager at night. It was so easy to reconnect with Kathleen, and Scott's band had actual paying gigs every weekend all summer long. They went as far south as Sea Isle City, and as far north as Seaside Heights. So, she spent her weekends as a groupie. Her summer turned out to be a lot more fun than she thought it could be.

One day, Maggie came home to find her kitchen torn apart with flour, sugar, chocolate, measuring cups and spoons. "What is all of this?" She asked at what she saw as a big mess.

Bree didn't look up. She was too focused on her notes. All she would say was that Mr. Bagliotti challenged her to come up with something original.

"Wow." Was all Maggie could think to say.

"He's right," Bree confirmed. "If I want to open my own pastry shop, then I need to experiment and go beyond the normal cookies and cakes." A heavy sigh escaped Bree. She told Maggie she was stumped. She'd combed through her nana's recipes for inspiration, but nothing came to her.

Maggie assured her it would happen. "Take a break. Maybe if you walk away, something will pop."

Then she reminded Bree that she and Luke would be spending the night in Philly. Bree asked if she thought he might propose. Maggie didn't think so, but for a moment, fantasized that he might. After they left, Bree decided to order a pizza, clean up, and take the break Maggie suggested.

Curled up on the couch, she thought about Maggie and Luke and how great they were together. Bree knew there had been some issues in the beginning, but Maggie didn't give up, even when Luke really hurt her feelings.

"How could she be sure? And how could she risk her heart again after what happened to Uncle Jase?" She asked the dogs who sat at her feet and hoped she would share some pizza. She peeled off two pieces of pepperoni, tossed one to each, then told them to go lay down.

As she got ready for bed, she thought of how her aunt was so certain that one day Bree would meet someone too and she needed to be open to it when it happened. Under the covers, she asked Tink her opinion. At the mention of her name, the cat stretched, meowed and curled back up to sleep.

"You're right, it's time for bed." Bree reminded herself that no matter what her parents did, *she* was not them and one day maybe someone could love her who wouldn't desert her. "If I say that enough, even *I'll* start to believe it." She muttered as she drifted off to sleep.

CHAPTER 72

On the drive up to the city, Maggie noticed that Luke was unusually quiet. When she asked him if he was okay, he told her he was, but he had a lot on his mind. Maggie nodded and was silent for a moment.

Then she looked at him. "Like what?" She asked.

Luke snorted because he knew she wouldn't let it go. At first, he said nothing. Then he told Maggie he had thought a lot about them, and where they were headed.

"We're headed to Philly." She responded.

He kissed her hand. "I'm being serious." Then he saw the look on her face and promised this was not a proposal. "At least not yet. But I think maybe we should move in together." He let that last sentence hang in the air and waited for her response.

None came. For a couple of minutes, Maggie stared out the window and watched mile markers rush by. But then, she smiled. She smiled that deep down in her soul smile Nell promised her she would one day, and she squeezed Luke's hand. "Who's house?" Was all she asked.

Luke hadn't realized how nervous he was until he released his breath in a loud whoosh. "After all the work I did at your house, I think we should live there."

Maggie reminded him that she didn't have a fireplace. He told her that was okay, he'd been looking at wood burning stoves and thought he could install one.

"Wow, you have thought about this for a while." Maggie said. To her amazement, the idea didn't terrify her.

By the time they checked into their hotel, it was late

afternoon. As much as Maggie loved small town life, she could fully appreciate everything a big city had to offer. Before dinner, she and Luke decided to take a stroll. They took in the architecture, aromas from street vendors and the noise of buses, cars and occasional clang of a trolley. Summertime in Philadelphia could be oppressive. This evening was no exception. The air was heavy with humidity; but that didn't stop people from stepping out into the city's night life.

Each time a door opened on a bar, live music echoed down an alley, while people stood in long lines as they waited to get inside. After about forty-five minutes, Maggie was painfully aware that the boy from Western Pennsylvania did not share her fondness for the city experience. When she suggested they go back to the hotel, he practically jumped at the idea. They had just enough time to shower before their reservations in the lounge at the top of the hotel.

While Maggie unpacked, the idea of living with Luke excited her. She giggled like a nervous teenager as she undressed and stepped into the shower to surprise him. Luke could only stare as the shower steam surrounded them. Without a word, Luke pulled her to him and kissed her hard.

With her hand on his heart, Maggie felt his pulse beat through her palm and connect with her own. His mouth moved to the base of her neck and his hands moved up her sides. He brushed his thumbs across her hard nipples. As the moan escaped Maggie's throat, Luke slowly kneeled down in front of Maggie. Tasting her wetness caused a shock to explode in the deepest parts of her. Slowly, Luke rose and lifted Maggie off her feet. She wrapped her legs around his hips. Together they rode the waves until there was nothing left inside them.

As their heartbeats returned to a normal rhythm, Maggie leaned her forehead against his chest. Luke picked up the soap and began to rub her back in soft, easy strokes.

A gasp escaped her throat as she looked into Luke's eyes. "If we don't stop now, we'll never make our reservations."

Luke didn't say a word. Instead, he picked her up and stepped out of the shower stall. Together, they tumbled onto the king-size bed and he told her that's why they have room service.

CHAPTER 73

Bree hadn't slept well. The thought of the challenge for an original recipe haunted her dreams. Mr. Bagliotti had been so good to her that she was desperate to wow him. At lunchtime, Bree found him in his office. He looked up from some paperwork as she took a seat opposite his desk.

"Everything okay Bree?" He asked.

She did not want to disappoint this man, but she had to be honest. "No," was all she could say. Then, she confessed that she struggled to come up with an original recipe and maybe she wasn't cut out for the world of pastries and cakes.

Mr. Bagliotti put down his pen and folded his hands on the desk. In the past two years she'd worked for him, he came to think of her as a granddaughter. He hadn't been blessed with children of his own. She had a natural talent, and she was eager to learn everything she could about the business. *Unfortunately though*, he thought, *she rarely believed that what she did was good enough. Probably because of her parents.* He told her not to overthink it.

"You're trying to bake from here," he said and tapped a finger to his temple. "You need to bake from here." He said and patted his heart. "If you can't come up with an original recipe right now, give an old one an original twist."

He walked her to the door, told her to go home and think about flavor combinations that she liked, then to take it from there. Bree stood up and promised to try. Before she left, she asked if he would teach her how to pull sugar next week.

As she disappeared down the street, he looked up at the

sky. "That one will go far Marie," he told his long-gone wife. He went back inside and locked up.

Since she had the afternoon off, she thought she could start to play with those flavor combinations. Then she heard her aunt's voice tell her to relax and be a teenager. After she let the dogs out, she decided to take Maggie's advice. She spent the rest of the day on the beach and hung out like a normal teenager.

CHAPTER 74

Maggie and Luke never made it to the roof top lounge. Instead, they cranked up the AC, cuddled up in the plush robes provided by the hotel and ordered in. For Maggie, it was a perfect night. She woke up the next morning to discover they had slept all night holding hands. The warmth of pleasure still coursed through her body. As Luke stirred beside her, she climbed on top of him and slowly used her mouth to wake him up.

Luke and Maggie had come to the city to have brunch with his daughter Kaitlyn and her husband. The first time Maggie and Kaitlyn met, they hit it off instantly. It took a little longer for Emily to warm up to Maggie, but eventually she saw how happy Maggie made her dad.

Kaitlyn and her husband lived in the historic neighborhood of Queen Village. It's bordered on one side by the waterfront and on the other by Headhouse Square. In between, its walkable narrow streets are filled with brick townhouses, restaurants, shopping and local nightlife. The one problem with neighborhoods like this, is parking. Luckily, they were able to find a spot about two blocks away.

They walked hand-in-hand along Kaitlyn's street. Maggie took note of the brightly painted shutters that all the houses boasted. Before she could say anything, Luke asked her what color she wanted for her own shutters. Maggie elbowed his side. They knocked on Kaitlyn's front door and were surprised when it was Emily who opened it.

Luke hugged her tight and wondered what she was doing

there. After she hugged Maggie, she explained that Kaitlyn had invited her too. Tony came in from the kitchen as he called up the stairs to let Kaitlyn know they were there.

Maggie loved the inside of their home, but was surprised at how modern it was compared to the historical look of the neighborhood. It was an open concept with hardwood flooring throughout. From the front door, you could see straight through to the back door which opened onto a small brick-enclosed yard. All the appliances were stainless steel and there was a small cook-top island in the center of the kitchen. The lines were clean, and white subway tile created the backsplash. They had kept the walls a soft cream color to create the illusion of a larger space. All the furniture was Scandinavian design that worked well in the narrow rooms. When Kaitlyn came downstairs, there were more hugs and she invited everyone into the dining room.

There was a buffet table that held fruit, bagels and danish. Tony had a breakfast casserole in the oven and offered everyone mimosas. As he poured the champagne, Maggie noticed that he had skipped Kaitlyn. She drank plain orange juice. When their eyes met, Maggie raised her eyebrows in a silent question. Kaitlyn couldn't contain her joy. Luke looked at Maggie, looking at Kaitlyn and wanted to know what was going on. Tony stood beside Kaitlyn and squeezed her hand.

"Go ahead." He nudged her. Before anyone could ask any more, Kaitlyn told them she was pregnant. Luke froze, Maggie teared up and Emily screamed. After another round of hugs and congratulations, everyone started to talk at once. Questions flew about due dates, how did she feel, did they know yet if it was a boy or a girl; or would they wait to find out. Kaitlyn told them all to make plates, sit down and then she would answer all their questions.

As they ate, Kaitlyn told them that they were due in December and they did not want to find out the baby's sex because they wanted to be surprised. They waited until they got through the first trimester. They hadn't wanted to say anything to jinx it. She admitted that she had some rough days with morning sickness, but that seems to have subsided.

"But I don't know why they call it morning sickness if it comes on at any time of the day." She asked Emily to be godmother, and then asked Luke if he would build some of the baby's furniture.

"Some?" He asked. "I'll build it all." Then he pulled out his phone and called his parents to let them know their first great-grandchild was expected in December. Everyone could hear his mother's screams through the phone. Luke told her that they would have to come East for Christmas this year. By the time Maggie and Luke got on the road to drive home, it was already late afternoon.

"Well, poppop," Maggie said as they crossed over the Ben Franklin Bridge, "how do you feel?"

Luke thought for a moment, then snorted. "Old."

"Yes, but you're beaming." Then she peppered him with questions about the furniture. How long did he think it would take? How would he squeeze it in between jobs? Did he have the room at his house to make it?

Before he answered, Luke squeezed her hand. "Actually, this opens up the door to what I wanted to talk to you about." With a sideways glance, he told her he'd have mentioned it at dinner last night but she distracted him. Maggie savored the memory and waited to hear what was on his mind.

"It started with that picture I bought at the Art Festival," he began with a faraway look. How it got him to think about the dreams he once had and how life somehow got in the way. He knew Maggie understood. "Then last Christmas I watched you do what you love and you looked so content."

Maggie wasn't sure what this was, but she could hear his excitement. "And?" She prompted.

Luke went on to tell her how he hadn't taken on any more jobs, and that little by little he'd been wrapping up the jobs he did have. He assured her that he was financially secure, so he didn't need to work as much. When they got to Lantern Light Cove, Luke turned on Oyster Road that led back toward the bay. He stopped in front of a warehouse that was for sale.

Maggie looked around. "Why are we here?" She asked unsure of what his answer could be.

"I put a bid in on this place. I want to build furniture. It's what I've always loved to do." Maggie was stunned. And Luke wasn't sure how to take her silence.

"Build furniture? To sell?" When Luke told her that was the plan, Maggie hugged him. "I think that's a wonderful idea. How did I not know about this?"

Luke told her he had wanted to surprise her with a rocking chair. But between his jobs, the work at her house and then Maeve's, things got away from him.

As they left Oyster Road, he said that if everything worked out, he could be in there by September and he wanted her rocking chair to be his first piece. Once they parked, Maggie shook her head no.

"The baby's furniture comes first. You can make rocking

chairs for our porch after that. As Bree opened the door to let the dogs out, Luke grabbed her.

"You said *our* porch." Luke emphasized.

Maggie kissed him. "Yes I did."

CHAPTER 75

By the end of Summer, Luke moved in to Maggie's and started to get his house ready to sell. Although, that would have to wait until after Kaitlyn's baby was born. On Bree's last day at the bakery, she made a cake for Mr. Bagliotti – it was a twist on her nana's coconut cake. He tasted it and beamed with pride. Then he sliced it down, set out free samples and asked customers for their opinion. He let Bree know that at least six different people wanted to order the cake. "They were very disappointed to learn it wasn't, and wouldn't be, available to buy any time soon."

Tears glistened Bree's cheeks. He knew what she was thinking and told her it was okay. "This is likely the last day *you* will ever work for *me*. Next summer you'll be in London and the summer after that you'll be scooped up by some big restaurant or fancy hotel."

Bree's voice trembled with fear. "I know that's what I'm supposed to want to happen, but this," she said and spread her arms out to encompass the small bakery.

"This was where you got your start." He finished for her. "One day, you may come back home. But for now, there's a whole world out there waiting to see what Sabrina Tacarini is gonna do." He handed her a bag filled with custom made piping tips.

"Mr. B, you've already given me so much. I can't take these."

He hugged them into her hands and told her she could and she would. Then he had to shove her out the door before he broke down in tears.

Later that night, Maggie found Bree in her room staring off at nothing. "What's wrong?" She asked and climbed into bed beside her.

Bree wiped away a tear. "Today was the last day that I'll ever work at Mr. Bagliotti's. Monday was my last day at the diner. And," she said with a look around her bedroom, "I don't know how many more nights I'll be able to call this my room."

Maggie squeezed Bree's hand and kissed the top of her head. "Being a grown-up sucks. Doesn't it?"

Bree agreed. Maggie assured her that even if it wasn't her bedroom, this was always her home. And that no matter where Bree went, or for how long, she could always come back. "This small town is my dream. You need to find yours. Yes, you are comfortable here, and that's great. But you have a gift. Follow your heart. If it leads you back here, then that door will always open for you." She stopped on her way out and tapped the packed boxes they'd take back to school in a couple of days. "Part of the reason you chose Boston was to get away from that small town you felt trapped in."

Bree wanted to argue, but she couldn't. Her aunt was right. She was feeling sentimental, and lonely. All of her other friends had gone back to school early. Those that were still here had boyfriends. Rather than dwell on the fact she didn't have a boyfriend, Bree pulled out her nana's leather-bound book. She held it close to her chest and whispered, "I guess it's time for me to start my own recipe book." As if in answer, Tink stood, arched her back and meowed.

CHAPTER 76

Sophomore year started much like the year before. Although it was easier because she already knew her roommate. She was excited to see Melissa and hear all about her summer. Melissa's dad had reached out to a friend of his, and both Bree and Mel got jobs at a hotel near Faneuil Hall. Melissa would be in the front office to get management experience. Bree would work in the restaurant with the pastry chef. And it turned out the chef knew Mr. Bagliotti from his days in New York. Between classes and her job, time flew by. Before she knew it, Halloween had come and gone.

The first weekend in November, Danny called to see if Bree had plans that Saturday. "Me, Jimmy, Laura and her friend have tickets for a comedy show. But Laura's friend bailed for her ex-boyfriend. You wanna come?"

Since she needed a break, Bree said she'd love to. Danny told her Jimmy would pick her up at her dorm around seven. The show turned out to be amateur night at a place near Bree's work and a couple of the comedians were pretty funny. Afterwards, Danny and Laura wanted to go to Cheers.

"Yeah, I'm only nineteen Danny." Bree reminded him. She told Jimmy she could catch a cab back to campus if he wanted to go. But he shook his head.

"That's alright. I'll drive you home."

As they drove, Bree felt like something was strange. She couldn't figure it out. She'd driven with Jimmy plenty of times. He was one of Danny's best friends and a nice guy. As he walked her to her dorm, Bree felt the tension build, but she still couldn't figure out what caused it. There was an all-night coffee cart along the path to her building. For another reason she couldn't seem to understand, Bree was happy when Jimmy suggested they stop there. She didn't want the night to end. They chose a bench near the cart but away from the foot traffic. Bree was surprised when he asked her if she was excited about her semester in London.

"Don't let Danny fool you. He's really proud of you and he brags about you. A lot. He loves you like a sister." He blew on his coffee before he took sip. Then he added that he'd deny ever saying that.

Bree nodded and told him his secret was safe. Then she asked Jimmy about his major. "What made you choose chemistry?"

He told her that his mom was scary smart and she had gotten him interested. He seemed to take to it naturally. Bree asked about his dad and any brothers or sisters. At the word dad, Jimmy stiffened. Anger swam in his eyes. All he said was that his dad died several years ago and he had no brothers or sisters. Bree felt there was more to it, but didn't push. If anyone understood about issues with parents, it was her. So, they sat for a while in silence

After Jimmy relaxed again, Bree was surprised at how comfortable she felt. This close, Bree noticed he had freckles that ran cheek to cheek across his nose. His eyes were light brown, with flecks of gold. His hair was cropped short, but that too was a light brown with streaks of gold. Bree was startled to realize that somehow she'd developed a crush on him. And she wasn't sure at all what to do about it.

She forced herself to shake off that thought. She yawned

and looked at her watch. In a panic, she jumped up from the bench and almost knocked Jimmy's coffee out of his hands.

"What's wrong?" He cried and jumped up too. He half expected to see a wild animal approaching him from the way she shifted from foot to foot.

"It's almost four o'clock in the morning." She yelled.

"No. It isn't." He argued back. The guy at the coffee cart called over that it was indeed almost four AM.

"Your cousin is gonna kill me." Jimmy said to Bree.

"How will he even?" Bree asked, then stopped herself. "Oh my god you two share an apartment." Bree forced herself not to laugh, wished Jimmy luck and thanked him for a nice night.

"It was a nice night." He almost whispered. Something in his tone stopped Bree and that tension was back. This time though, they both felt it.

"Good night, Jimmy. Thanks again."

Jimmy watched her get in safely, then turned for home and what he was sure would be an earful from Danny.

CHAPTER 77

Bree waited a day or two. When she didn't hear from Danny, she figured it was safe to call Jimmy. "I wanted to make sure Danny wasn't being a jerk," she told him when he answered the phone.

"Nah. He ragged me for a little bit, but it's all good." Jimmy was glad to hear from her. He'd thought about her a lot since the night of the comedy show. Before he could back out, he asked her if she was free for dinner that weekend. Bree hesitated, then said sure.

Jimmy didn't allow himself time to think. "I mean just you and me," he said before he chickened out. When she didn't answer right away. He apologized. "I'm sorry. Forget I said." But she cut him off.

"No. I'm sorry. I'm surprised. That's all." Her insides had turned to jelly; but outside, she remained calm. She told Jimmy that she would absolutely have dinner with *just* him. An hour later they hung up and Bree was amazed again at how easy it was for her to talk with him.

Friday night came faster than Bree expected. She called Maggie in a panic. "I need help. I have no idea what to wear."

Maggie wanted to know to wear to what. Bree didn't answer right away. "Promise me you won't get all you about it."

Maggie wasn't sure what that meant, but promised and waited for Bree to continue. It took her a couple of seconds, then she simply said, "I have a date."

Maggie wanted to scream for joy, but she kept herself composed. "Tell me about him and where is he taking you?"

Bree told Maggie all about comedy night with Jimmy and how they sat on the bench and talked for a while afterwards. About how she called him to make sure Danny hadn't been an ass to him. And that he asked her out. "It's weird Aunt Mag. He's so easy to talk to."

Maggie was stunned. "And you're just telling me all this now?" Bree bit her lip and reminded Maggie that she promised not to make a big deal.

"Right. Not a big deal." After she talked Bree her through her wardrobe, Maggie told her that she was glad she'd said yes. Before Bree could argue, Maggie stressed that she needed to give this a chance. That whatever may be starting, was based in friendship and that is the best basis for any relationship. "I'm sure he knows all about your parents, and that doesn't seem to faze him. I don't think you're about to start to make wedding plans, but every marriage does start with a first date. Give him a chance. More importantly, give yourself a chance."

Bree didn't say anything at first. "I do like him Aunt Mag. He's cute. He makes me laugh. I can be myself around him."

Maggie silently thanked whatever god or goddess brought them together. Again, she told Bree to have fun, hung up and immediately called Lizzie.

Over the next two weeks, Bree and Jimmy went out several times. One night, they were at Danny and Jimmy's apartment. Danny mentioned that he and Laura would be in Boston over Thanksgiving. When Bree said she had to work that Wednesday so she couldn't go home either, Jimmy suggested they have dinner at their place. They all looked at Bree expectantly.

She reached for a handful of popcorn and looked back at

them. "Should I assume you all want me to cook?" She asked. But before they could respond, Bree had already begun to plan a menu. And she had to admit she was excited about it.

Jimmy knew what she was thinking and decided to encourage it. "Consider it a trial run for when you have your own place. You come up with the menu, how you want the table set, everything. Your call."

Bree got up and started to pace. As she did, she rearranged the furniture in her mind. She found a pad and pen and started to make a list. The movie they'd been watching was forgotten. As Bree wrote, the other three chimed in with suggestions and offers to help however they could. When Bree called her aunt to say she wouldn't be home for the holiday, she was surprised to hear that she was relieved.

"Don't get me wrong Bree, you know I would love to see you. But Luke's parents will be here the Tuesday before Thanksgiving and plan to stay through the New Year. They don't want to miss the birth of their first great-grandchild." She reminded Bree that Kaitlyn was due the first week of December and that instead of just a cradle, Luke had furnished the entire nursery. "And honestly, there aren't words to describe it. I hate to cut this call short, but I'm headed to the warehouse now to take pictures for the website." She added that they wanted to have that ready to launch by December first.

They talked a little more and Bree promised she would be home for Christmas. When Maggie asked if she'd bring Jimmy home for the holidays, Bree told her that they weren't there yet. Maggie started to say something, but Bree said she had to go and hung up.

CHAPTER 78

From the minute Evelyn and John Skala got out of their rental car, Maggie adored them. After almost fifty years of marriage, they were still very much in love. Maggie had no response when Evelyn told her that she'd be in charge of the turkey. "You are more than welcome to help with the sides, but that bird is mine."

Emily came up the steps behind them. She apologized for her Gram in advance. Kaitlyn and Tony would drive down for the day on Thursday. The whole house already hummed with holiday energy. The one downside was that it would be Maggie's first Thanksgiving without Lizzie. But like Lizzie told her, this was her family now and it was her time to start her own traditions. As Luke brought their bags in, he kissed Maggie's cheek and wished her luck.

On Wednesday morning, Maggie was in the kitchen making coffee. Luke had gone to the bakery for cinnamon buns, which his parents loved but struggled to find decent ones in Arizona. Evelyn and John grabbed mugs and sat at the table. Maggie could sense they had something on their minds but she wasn't sure how to start. After she let the dogs out back, she sat down with them.

John marveled at her table and Evelyn asked about the weather. Maggie tried to stop it, but the laugh bubbled up and burst out of her. When they both looked at her with raised eyebrows, she managed to get it under control and became serious. She reached for both their hands and looked at them with affection. "I love him." She said simply. "More than I ever thought I could love someone again, I love him."

John winked at her and raised his mug in her direction. "Good coffee."

Evelyn teared up. "It's just that. He can't get hurt again. I needed to be sure." Maggie squeezed Evelyn's hand.

"I understand. And you can be." Before anything else could be said, Luke came in with pastries and they planned out their day.

By four o'clock, they were back home. Luke's parents had never been to the Cove. He took great pride in showing them around. Maggie and Emily broke off to do some shopping, but they all met up at his warehouse. When he showed them the baby's furniture, Evelyn and Emily cried. John boasted a reminder that he'd taught Luke everything he knew.

In addition to the cradle, Luke had managed to build a crib that would convert into a single bed, the changing table and a rocking chair. It was done in pine, and stained traditional cherry. Maggie had watched the progress of the furniture, and she was still amazed at how beautiful it had turned out.

Once they were back, Maggie gave full range of the kitchen to Evelyn. She and Emily decided to set the table and polish the silver. Luke and John studied plans for the wood burning stove that Luke was determined to install. Charlie and Molly went from person to person in search of a treat; and every once in a while, Tink would make an appearance. When a light snow began to fall, Maggie thought it was an absolutely perfect start to the holiday weekend.

CHAPTER 79

When Bree got out of work Wednesday night, she was a little nervous about the drive home. There was already an inch of snow on the ground and the weatherman promised there'd be at least five more before morning. The wind had picked up and Bree worried about blizzard conditions as she tried to make her way. She walked with her head down. The icy air burned her throat with each step she took. Bree looked up to see how close she was to her car. She stopped when she saw a man leaned up against it. Not sure what to do, she started to pull out her phone. Then she heard Jimmy call her name. With relief, she walked over to him. "What're you doing here?" She asked.

"Hello to you too." He said as he leaned in to kiss her. Bree was still trying to adjust to the fact that she had a boyfriend. His hug warmed her, and she asked again why he was there.

"Don't like the weather, or you driving in it." He took her keys and opened the passenger door. "Biggest party night of the year," he reminded her. She wondered at the sanity of a group of college kids that appeared to be on a pub crawl. In the driver's seat, he started the engine and let the heat run for a couple of minutes.

"Danny and I figure it'd be better if you spent the night at our place. Laura is already there. We're gonna swing by the dorm so you can pack a bag."

Bree looked at him. "Do I?" She started to ask when Jimmy cut her off.

"No. You don't get a say in this one." When Bree's mouth dropped open, Jimmy chuckled. "Danny said you'd ask that."

By the time they got back to the apartment, there was more than two inches of snow on the ground, and it seemed to be falling harder. Bree eyed Danny in disbelief when he came out of his room in shorts and a t-shirt.

"Are you crazy? It's like the arctic out there!" She pulled off her parka and kicked off her Uggs. Danny told her to get used to it.

"Last winter here was mild. This," he said with a nod to the window, "is normal."

Laura told Bree it was pointless to argue with him. "He's hopeless," she added and helped Bree with the bags she'd brought in.

Bree muttered under her breath as she followed Jimmy into his room and dumped her overnight bag on his bed. She gratefully took the hoodie he offered her and tried not to look anxious. She and Jimmy had just started dating, and while he hadn't pressured her into sex, she knew they'd be sharing a bed tonight.

As if he read her mind, Jimmy pulled her close and told her he didn't expect sex. Then he stepped back. "Unless you're offering?" He asked hopefully.

Bree released a nervous laugh. "Not tonight," she replied and walked back out to the living room.

"Tomorrow?" He asked as he followed her.

Bree ignored him and started to think about where to start to have everything ready for the next day. She declined offers of help and zoned everything else out.

She checked the turkey and found it was still partially frozen. Remembering a trick she learned from her nana, she told Jimmy to put it in the sink breast side down and cover it with cold water. Danny and Jimmy had arranged the furniture the way she asked them to, so she started there.

From the bags she'd brought with her, she took out a tablecloth, napkins, glasses and serving platters. Danny picked up one of the green wine goblets. "Fancy." He said but put it back down when Bree slapped his hand.

Laura told Bree that she had to work on a paper in Danny's room but to holler if she needed any help. Danny and Jimmy made popcorn, grabbed a couple of beers and jumped on the couch for a college football game. Bree pictured Nana T, then clasped her hands. *Alright Bree*, she thought to herself, *let's see what you got.*

CHAPTER 80

For the next two hours, Bree meticulously set the table. She'd found a cream-colored table cloth trimmed in burnt orange, with cloth napkins in the same burnt hue. It wasn't fine china, but she did find dinner and dessert plates in a pretty goldenrod color. Bree had also found antiqued candle holders and dark green tapers. Once she added the green water goblets and silverware, Bree took a step back and almost jumped for joy. The table *looked* like Thanksgiving.

Bree blushed when she heard Laura exclaim how beautiful it all was. This brought Danny and Jimmy to their feet. "Wait. How'd you?" Danny stammered while Jimmy kissed her cheek.

"It's beautiful." He whispered. "Like you."

Bree forced the tears not to come as she thought *this must be what love feels like.* Bree let the feeling linger, then pushed them all away.

"Time to make the pies," she told them.

"Pies?" Laura asked. "As in more than one?"

Bree pulled individual pie pans out of her bag and washed them. "You," she said to Laura, "like apple. Jimmy likes pumpkin and Danny loves cheesecake."

Laura asked Bree what she liked. "Ice cream." She said with a laugh. "So, I'll make a personal ice-cream pie for me."

Laura squeezed Bree's shoulder and told her how impressed she was. Only half joking, she said "I'm lucky I can boil water for pasta."

Bree dismissed the praise. "Yeah, but I don't have your people skills. Which is why you will be an excellent counselor."

The two girls shared a smile, then Laura returned to her paper and Bree started on the pies. Danny and Jimmy were already back on the couch focused the game.

Once the baked pies were on cooling racks, Bree pulled out sugar, butter and heavy cream and began to make caramel sauce. She hadn't noticed that Danny had gone to bed or that the TV was off. She didn't hear the radio that played softly or take note of the fact that Jimmy laid on the couch and watched her. She hadn't noticed that the winds had quieted and now there was only an occasional flurry that floated past the window. Bree was in her world doing what she loved.

Jimmy was impressed with how she turned their kitchen table into something you'd find in a fancy restaurant. He was in awe of the fact that she whipped out three individual pies with homemade crusts like it was nothing. He was a little confused when she placed an empty metal bowl into the freezer, but was certain she had her reasons. *And now she's making homemade caramel sauce.* He thought to himself. Jimmy had watched her make it before and knew it was better than any you could find in a store.

"She's amazing," he whispered to himself. He smiled at the way she pushed strand of hair behind her ear, knowing it wouldn't stay there. She couldn't carry a tune to save her life, but he loved the way she sang out loud when she thought no one could hear her. He knew her all-time favorite movie was ET, and she cried whenever she watched it.

"I'll be damned," he whispered and slowly sat up. "I think I'm in love."

He knew about her parents. Danny had told him the whole story. After which, he threatened Jimmy with severe bodily harm if he ever hurt Bree. Because of them, he knew he'd have to take things slowly. There were times when they were alone that Bree looked like a scared rabbit and all he wanted to do was protect her. But he also knew that she was fiercely independent. She'd had to be.

"Yeah. I have to tread real careful here." Bree startled him when she asked him what he'd said. Before he could answer, he noticed she looked around in surprise.

"What time is it? Where are Danny and Laura?"

Jimmy stood up and stretched. Between yawns, he told her it was after midnight and that Danny and Laura went to bed about an hour ago. He pulled open the freezer and pointed at the bowl. "Why," he asked.

Bree took the bowl out and instructed him that if he was ever going to make whipped cream, chill the bowl first.

"Of course," he mumbled and dipped a finger into the caramel sauce. "That's delicious. You ready for bed?"

Bree had already poured cream, some sugar and vanilla into the frozen bowl and whisked vigorously. She gave Jimmy a quick kiss, and told him as soon as she finished the cream and cleaned up, she'd be ready. He waited with her. They cleaned up together and were asleep before their heads hit the pillows.

CHAPTER 81

Thursday morning was chaotic. Maggie wanted to be done all her chores before noon. Her Eagles were playing Detroit. John was a die-hard Steelers fan, but agreed to cheer for Philly. "Just for today," he winked. Evelyn walked from the kitchen to the front door every ten minutes to see if Kaitlyn and Tony were there yet. Once they finally arrived, Evelyn didn't let either granddaughter out of her sight. Although she reluctantly allowed Kaitlyn and Tony to drive to the warehouse to see the furniture, which Luke promised to deliver on Saturday.

Thanksgiving morning, Bree opened her eyes not sure where she was at first. Then the weight of Jimmy's arm around her waist reminded her that she'd spent the night in his bed. Snuggled deeper into his arms, she thought about Jimmy and how natural it felt to be around him. Then she murmured happily. "I guess Aunt Mag knew what she was talking about. You do know when it's right."

Jimmy stirred and mumbled. "Hmmm?" Bree told Jimmy to go back to sleep. She slipped out of bed, gave him a light kiss then followed the scent of coffee.

"Good morning," Laura greeted her.

Bree grabbed a mug, filled it and inhaled deeply. Laura lifted her own mug in a toast and said that coffee was the one kitchen thing she could do right. When the toaster popped, Laura pulled out a bagel and offered Bree half.

They didn't want to mess up the table, so they sat together on the couch. Bree enjoyed this time with Laura. She'd always wanted a sister, but a cousin-in-law would have to do. Bree knew that Danny was serious about her and would be surprised if he didn't propose by graduation. When they heard movement from both bedrooms, Bree figured it was time to start the turkey and everything else that would go along with it.

Dinner was ready by three o'clock. Once everyone was seated, Danny toasted Bree. "I knew you were good cous, but this," he said and looked all around the table, "is amazing Bree. You should be proud of yourself."

Bree felt her cheeks flush when Jimmy and Laura joined in. Deep down, she was thrilled. She'd done everything from shopping, to setting the table, to preparing the meal. All of it reinforced her desire. More than that, she finally believed that she really could do it. Although, she was also certain that she only wanted to work with pastries and desserts.

After dinner, she asked Jimmy to sit with her to try and figure out how much it would cost her to go to London for classes. As much as she appreciated the offer from Luke, she wanted to pay for as much as she could on her own. She was able to estimate how many hours she'd need to work. With that in mind, she rearranged her classes for the Spring semester. When she was done, she thought she had a good plan in place. Until she ran it by Danny.

"I think it's great Bree, but how do you think my mom and Aunt Mag will react when you don't go home for Christmas?"

Bree thought about that for a minute. "To be honest Danny, I think it'll be okay. Aunt Maggie will be busy with Luke's family are in town for Kaitlyn. I'll go down for a weekend after the baby is born, but other than that, I'll be in the way." With a charming but sly smile, she added, "as for Aunt Lizzie, she'll only be upset with me until you tell her you plan to stay in

Boston after you graduate."

Danny started to say something, but stopped. Bree was right. His mom was gonna flip.

CHAPTER 82

The second week of December, Kaitlyn and Tony welcomed a beautiful, healthy little girl into the world. Anna Maria weighed in at seven pounds, three ounces, was twenty inches long and had a full head of black hair. Bree waited til they were home before she made the trip to Philadelphia to see them. She was thrilled when Kaitlyn introduced her as Aunt Sabrina. As much as she wished she could stay longer, she reminded Kaitlyn that she was having an early Christmas with Maggie and Luke.

"And my grandparents," Kaitlyn added with a laugh. "But please call me when you can talk. I'm dying to hear all about Jimmy."

Bree promised she would call once she got back to Boston, and Kaitlyn was a little more rested. On the drive to Lantern Light Cove, it occurred to Bree that Kaitlyn and Emily, like Laura, had become like sisters to her. It surprised Bree to see just how good her life had become.

After dinner, Bree and Maggie took the dogs for a walk. For a while, they talked about the baby, Luke's furniture and how wonderful his parents seem to be. Maggie then asked Bree about Jimmy.

Bree hesitated before she answered. "He's different than any guy I've ever met Aunt Mag. It's wierd. I know we've only dated for a little over a month, but I can't seem to remember a time he wasn't in my life."

Maggie knew that feeling well. That's how things had been first with Jase, then again with Luke. Sometimes, she felt guilty knowing the love of two good men. The way Bree talked about Jimmy, she knew that Bree had found real love, and hoped her niece knew it too.

Back at the house, Bree braced herself for the lecture she knew was coming. She busied herself with trying to show Evelyn how to crop photos on her phone and then how to send them in a group text. It gave her an excuse to ignore Maggie the first time she brought up the holidays.

"You can pretend to ignore me all you want Sabrina, but I know you."

Evelyn looked at Bree and grimaced. "She used your full name. I don't think that's a good sign."

Bree waited until her aunt poured herself a glass of wine, then she asked for one. "I'll be twenty in two months. And I'll be in Europe for most of the summer. I'm pretty sure I'll be able to have a glass of wine with dinner while I'm there."

Luke and John joined them at the table. Maggie set out glasses for everyone and grabbed a second bottle of wine. Once she poured, Bree tried to get them to understand.

"First, Luke, thank you for the offer to pay for my trip. I cannot tell you how much it means to me. And before you say anything, I'm not saying that I won't accept your offer. If I work through the holidays, yes, it will help me financially. But," she stopped to take a sip of wine, "that's not all." She stressed that it was more for the experience than the money.

"Thanksgiving proved to me that I absolutely want to open my pastry shop. And while it was fun to prepare the whole dinner, it was desserts that made me happy. I got lost in homemade pie crusts, fillings, whipped cream and caramel sauce. It was as if I'd found pure joy. I want to play with cookie doughs and cake recipes. I know that I will get that experience in London; but real-life experience is so much more worthwhile."

Bree stopped to look at Maggie, then Luke, then back at Maggie. "This is my dream. And I need to follow it the best way I know how."

She looked at Maggie. "You taught me that." Then she pulled out the ace she had up her sleeve. "Besides, these holidays should be all about Anna Maria," she added with an innocent smile.

Evelyn spoke first as she raised her glass to Bree. "Well played Bree. Well played."
Maggie narrowed her eyes and said it was more like a low blow using the baby as leverage.

Luke raised an eyebrow in appreciation. "Bree, you're right." Then he stopped Maggie before she could interrupt. "Mag, you know that experience is what counts. And let's face it, we are all about the baby right now." With a salute to his mom, he told Bree that it was well played indeed.

John spoke for the first time to tell Maggie she was outnumbered. Then he told Bree that if she wanted to play with recipes while she was there, he'd be more than happy to taste them for her.

"You got it. Make me a list of your favorite desserts." She looked at her aunt expectantly.

A storm brewed in Maggie's head and everyone could see it on her face. But she knew she was beaten and threw her hands up in defeat. "Fine. You win. I just hoped to finally meet Jimmy."

Bree said that wouldn't have happened anyway because

he'd be in South Carolina at his grandparents. By the end of December, Bree had aced her finals. While at work, she learned how to perfect buttercream rosettes as she helped decorate a wedding cake.

CHAPTER 83

The first week in February Jimmy asked Bree if he could take her away overnight for Valentine's weekend.

"Have you slept with him yet?" Melissa asked as they made their way to the library.

"No. Not yet."

Melissa looked at her surprised. "You guys spend so much time together, I assumed."

Bree agreed. "I know. But I wasn't ready, and he hasn't pushed."

Melissa stopped and grabbed Bree by the arm when she tried to keep walking. "If that guy, who is adorable by the way, respects you that much. You grab onto him and never let go." Then she snickered. "If you don't, I'll grab him myself."

Bree thought that he definitely was one of the good ones.

When Mel asked if Bree was still a virgin, Bree got a faraway look in her eye. "No," she admitted, "not since Junior year in high school. I wasn't in love or anything. My friend Gary and I talked about it one day. We liked each other, trusted each other, and decided to just get it over with."

Melissa was shocked. "Get it over with?"

Bree smiled. She explained that she never had a boyfriend in high school and they both agreed it was better that way. "We're still good friends. We have absolutely no regrets about it. And yeah, we hung out for a while, 'cause let's face it. Once you have sex, you wanna have it again."

Both girls laughed.

"But then my nana got sick and my plans changed. He

took off for California to pursue acting, and I'm here."

"Well that sounds a lot more mature than my first time." As they left the library, Melissa told Bree how it been the August before she started Junior year in high school. She was certain she was in love and would eventually marry the guy. He proceeded to break her heart about six months later. When Bree started to say how sorry she was, Mel stopped her.

"Oh please. That was four years ago. Last I heard he had a shotgun wedding and was miserable." In the bond that girlfriends shared, they both thought that was Karma. Then Mel told Bree they absolutely had to shop for her overnight with Jimmy.

Since where they were going was a secret, Bree wasn't sure what to pack, or shop for. Melissa insisted she needed a dress and heels. Even if they were low heels she added when Bree started to protest. Bree didn't want to wear red. "I'm sure everyone will be in red."

Melissa told Bree that since every woman should have a little black dress in her closet, that was the way they'd go. "Besides," she whispered, "you can save red for the lingerie."

Melissa dragged Bree to a boutique that seemed to have everything she would need. She tried on several dresses and was frustrated because none of them seemed right. Finally, she tried one on that brought tears to her eyes.

It was black knit with capped sleeves and a neckline that formed a low-cut vee. It hung just below her knees. The dress was ruched and hugged every curve she had, and created curves that never existed before. When she stepped out of the dressing room, Mel clapped in delight.

"It's perfect." She gushed and handed Bree a pair of low-heeled black pumps. They found tear-drop garnet earrings with a necklace that matched to complete the outfit. Before they left, Bree found lacy red lingerie and told Melissa to shut up when she added it to the purchase.

CHAPTER 84

Jimmy picked her up, but still wouldn't say where they were going. Bree noted they drove South, but it wasn't until they passed through Connecticut that she guessed New York. Jimmy confirmed they were going to Manhattan, for dinner, a show and a hotel in Times Square. By the time they stopped for lunch, found their way to the hotel and checked in, it was already four o'clock.

While Jimmy jumped into the shower, Bree unpacked their clothes. Outside the window, she watched as every color neon imaginable lit up the night sky.

"No wonder you're the city that never sleeps. How could you with all that light?"

Jimmy came out of the bathroom. He had a towel wrapped around his waist and his skin glistened with dampness. He sat beside her, pointed to the high-rise buildings and asked if she would ever consider living here.

"No." She said without a moment to even think about it. "And I hope you're not asking that because you've found a job here."

She started to move toward the bathroom, but Jimmy pulled her back to sit on his lap. "I would not take a job here. I wouldn't even apply for a job here." Then, nibbling on her ear he told her he liked that she was concerned about the possibility.

Bree laid her head on his shoulder and was again amazed at how comfortable she was with him. When he kissed her, Bree's fears were replaced with hunger. Greedily she kissed him back, it took all her willpower to pull away.

"You promised me dinner and a show." She said and climbed off his lap. Then with a light kiss, she told him she had to get her shower and he should get dressed.

Once she closed the bathroom door, Jimmy let out a loud huff. "Yeah," he said. "It's gonna take a minute or two before I can stand up."

As Bree put on her makeup and did her hair, Jimmy tapped on the door. In order to give her some privacy, he told her to meet him in the lobby bar when she was dressed. Bree rode down in the elevator. She could barely contain herself. She never thought of herself as beautiful, but tonight she thought she looked the part. The sideways glances she got from the two men on the elevator with her confirmed it.

Bree stopped before she got to the lobby. She felt like Julia Roberts in *Pretty Woman*. She knew that once she walked into the bar, she would cross the point of no return with Jimmy. Bree had to force herself not to run into that bar.

Jimmy watched Bree walk toward him. He was blown away. *She has no idea the effect she has on men.* If he wasn't certain before, he was now. He would be as patient as he needed to be, but he was determined that he'd spend the rest of his life with her.

Jimmy's reaction caused heat to rise through Bree. When she kissed him, he had to laugh as he watched men turn back to their drinks and conversations disappointed that Bree was spoken for. *She really has no idea,* he thought again and handed her the glass of wine he'd ordered.

When they got to the theater, Bree almost screamed with excitement. "Les Mis?" She asked. "I can't believe you remembered."

Jimmy told her he remembered everything she says. After the show, they took a cab to Little Italy. He'd made reservations at a small restaurant complete with red and white checked tablecloths, chianti bottles that substituted for candle holders and an owner with a broken accent.

To Bree, it was absolutely the most perfect night. *And it isn't over yet*, she thought with a wicked grin.

CHAPTER 85

One dreary day in March, Unalii approached Maggie about buying the shop.

"Wait. What?" Maggie asked in disbelief.

Her friend went on to say that she wanted to spend more time with her grandchildren and she wanted to get back to her easel and watercolors.

Maggie assured her she understood and was definitely interested. "But I'd like to talk to Luke first. We've got so much going on. Between his warehouse, my work, the grandbaby." Maggie stopped when she noticed the way Unalii smiled at her.

"What's that look for?" She asked.

"It's nice to hear you talk about Luke that way." Unalii answered

Maggie huffed at her friend. "Yes. Yes. Luke and I are in love. Let it go." But she couldn't contain the smile that crept up whenever she thought of Luke. Before leaving, she promised to have an answer for Unalii by the end of the week.

At dinner, she and Luke started to see the possibilities. Maggie suggested they break open the second floor and turn that into a studio that would better showcase paintings and photographs. This would free up space on the first floor to display some of Luke's smaller pieces. Which in turn would allow them to direct customers to his website for custom-made furniture. The more they talked about it, the more they thought it could work. All they needed to do was figure out the numbers. By the first week in April, they had a plan in place and were ready to move forward.

True to her word, Bree came to the Cove for Spring break. Maggie was disappointed that again, she wouldn't be able to meet Jimmy. He and Danny had taken off for Florida.

Bree apologized. "I do plan for you to meet him before the end of the year. You'd meet him at graduation if you could make it."

Unfortunately, that was the weekend of Anna Maria's christening. "I miss you. That's why I'm whining so much. You're a young woman building a life for yourself. Or one with the boy you're in love with, and I miss you."

Bree reminded Maggie that she was a big part of the reason she had the confidence to build this life. "Now you're just being mean." Maggie replied as they went shopping for what Bree would need for London.

By June, Anna Maria was baptized; Danny and Laura had graduated; and Maggie and Luke had settled on the shop. They decided to wait until the winter to renovate. This would give them time to design the store in a way to highlight their current artists, while still provide space for Luke.

And although Jimmy completed his bachelor's degree in chemistry, he decided to stay in school and get his teaching certificate. He thought teaching high school science would be more rewarding than a job in a pharmaceutical company. Bree was thrilled with his decision.

CHAPTER 86

London opened up a whole new world for Bree and she brimmed with ideas. Most of which revolved around how to finish school early and get started on her own pastry shop. She'd already spoken to her boss about more independence in the kitchen. She was grateful that he agreed to work something out with her. Bree had a long list of things she wanted to at least research before school started. When she reached out to Mr. Bagliotti about a business plan, he'd told her he was happy to help her.

"First though," he told her, "you need to have a clear idea of exactly what you want your shop to be. Décor. Seating. Specialty cakes vs standard pastries. You need to know what it is you want before you can figure out how to get it."

Bree promised she would work on it. On her flight home she filled a notebook with her wishes and must-haves. Once through customs, all those plans and ideas flew out of her mind as she caught sight of Jimmy.

She took off in a run. As she got close, Bree dropped her backpack and jumped into his arms. If Jimmy hadn't seen it coming, she would've knocked them both over. He swung her around, kissed her hard then lowered her to her feet so he could hug her tight.

"Missed you too. Wait. What's wrong?" He asked as her eyes filled with tears.

"I'm sorry." She stammered wiped the tears away. "It's just that. I wasn't sure." Bree looked at the other reunions going on around them. She took a deep breath. Then kissed him again. More softly, she whispered that she was so happy to see him.

"I'm not going anywhere, Bree." Jimmy said as he picked up her bag and took her hand. "In fact, there's something I want to talk to you about."

In the car, Jimmy brought up Bree's dorm situation. "I know. When Mel said she was going to spend this semester abroad, I didn't think about it." Bree pursed her lips. "I have no idea who I'll be stuck with this year. I totally messed up with my paperwork."

Jimmy let her ramble. Then teased her about how organized she usually is. When she blamed the time difference between here and England, Jimmy didn't comment. Instead of going to campus, he pulled up to the apartment he used to share with Danny. Bree stopped mid-sentence when they parked. Confused, she asked why they were there.

"Did you know that Danny and Laura had gotten their own place near Cambridge?" He asked as he turned in his seat to face her. When she nodded, Jimmy then said he'd decided to keep this place because of its location. "And, of course, all my stuff is here."

Bree thought it would be a good idea for him to be where his stuff was.

"I know you Bree," he said. "If your new roommate is not as committed or as driven as you are, you'll be miserable."

Bree was confused until it hit her. "Oh my god. You want us to live together?"

Jimmy told her he'd thought about it the whole time she was gone. To him it made perfect sense. "I wanna spend the rest of my life with you."

Bree whipped her head around and looked at his hands. It took Jimmy a minute before he figured out what she was thinking.

"This isn't a marriage proposal." He held up his hands to prove he didn't have a ring for her. "One day. Some day. We'll shop for a ring. Today, I just want you to think about us living together."

Bree stared at him before she said anything. She did think that it would *probably* be better than whoever they stuck her with in the dorm.

"Probably." He responded.

"And I do like the neighborhood." She added as she noticed some kids walk into the corner ice cream parlor.

"Yeah. It's a good neighborhood."

Bree started to see that it was the right choice. "Okay. Let's live together."

Jimmy was speechless. "Just like that?"

Bree asked if he was trying to get her to change her mind.

"No!" He yelled and kissed her. "I promise Bree, one day, we'll shop for that ring."

Bree stopped him. "You don't have to shop for a ring. Just talk to my Aunt Maggie." Then she told Jimmy about the sapphire engagement ring her aunt had promised to Bree. "When you're ready, all you have to do is ask her."

CHAPTER 87

During the Fall semester, Bree took extra credits which would allow her to graduate a semester early. The pastry chef at the hotel had given her more freedom, and Bree was earning a good reputation as a cake decorator. Every night, she went home to Jimmy and things couldn't be better.

Bree never imagined she would meet someone she could love. She certainly never expected to meet someone she could trust. Once again, she was amazed how blessed her life had become. As happy as she was, when he asked her to go home with him for Christmas to meet his mom, Bree was nervous.

"Actually, Aunt Maggie, I'm terrified. What if she doesn't think I'm good enough?"

Maggie told her niece that she most definitely was not good enough! "It's an Irish mother and her son."

"Not helping." Bree cried into the phone.

Maggie tried to calm her niece down. "His mom will be tough on you. At first. But you'll win her over with your baking." Then she suggested that Jimmy find out what his mom's favorite dessert was so Bree could make that for Christmas dinner.

"Aunt Maggie you're a genius. I love you."

Maggie joked that maybe she'd finally meet Jimmy on their wedding day. When Bree didn't respond, Maggie asked her if there was something she hadn't said.

"No. We're not engaged. But we have talked about it." Bree hesitated then asked her aunt if she thought it was all too soon.

Maggie asked Bree if *she* thought it was too soon.

"Yes. No. I don't know. I know I love him. More than that, I trust him. Sometimes I feel like I've known him forever, then I remind myself that it's only been a couple of years. And I've never had any other serious relationship. But I don't even notice other men."

Maggie reminded Bree that her Aunt Liz and Uncle George have been together since high school. "It's the only boyfriend your aunt has ever known. At least you waited until college. Honestly Bree, listen to your heart. If this is the one for you, it's your heart that'll let you know."

"I do know Aunt Mag. He's the one you always told me I'd find." Then she reminded Maggie that she had promised her the sapphire ring. "I hope it's okay, but I told Jimmy about it. It truly is the only ring that I will ever want."

All Maggie could say was wow. "You have talked about it. And, of course the ring is yours." Happily, she told Bree to have Jimmy call her when he's ready. Maggie heard Bree's sigh of relief. "Better yet, have him come see me so I can actually meet him."

Bree promised it would happen before the wedding day. Then hung up before Maggie could respond.

For a couple of minutes, Maggie stood by the kitchen island. At first, she was hurt that Bree had chosen Jimmy's family over her own for the holidays that year. Then she felt guilty. She reminded herself that Bree was simply following her own path. Charlie pawed at Maggie's leg. She looked down and noticed the white that had seeped into his face.

"You're getting old my handsome boy." She said and knelt beside him to hug him close. She couldn't stop the tear that escaped down her cheek as she thought about Bree not coming home for Christmas and how she and Jimmy had talked about marriage. "I guess we're all getting older," she told him.

CHAPTER 88

Maggie paced the porch. Every couple of seconds she looked up the street and almost willed Bree's car to turn the corner. "Um, Mag," Luke said. "I thought you were gonna help me get things secured ahead of the storm."

Maggie had her back to Luke but didn't answer him. "What time is it? You don't think they got into an accident? Do you?" She wondered.

Luke puffed heavily. "Maggie." He called her name twice. When she didn't turn around, he grabbed her by the shoulders to force her to face him.

"She said they'd be here by one, and it's almost two."

Luke cupped her chin and softly kissed her. Maggie pulled back and asked him if that was his way of shutting her up.

With patience, he reminded her that Bree said they would try to be here by one. "Key word is *try*. Maybe there's traffic. Maybe they stopped to get something to eat. Maybe. And I might be on to something with this one. Maybe she's not in any rush because she thinks you might embarrass her when they finally do get here."

Maggie wanted to deny that, but she knew she was acting a little crazy. It wasn't entirely her fault. She was going to meet the boy Bree wants to spend the rest of her life with. *That's huge,* she thought to herself.

"Okay. You're right. Let's finish this and then I'll go check on the soup." Maggie shivered against the damp. It was early March and a nor'easter had turned back toward the coast. Lantern Light Cove was in its path.

Fifteen minutes later, Maggie watched a small red Dodge drive past, make a U-turn and pull up to park behind Luke's truck. They watched as a young man got out of the driver side and walked around to open the passenger door. Bree jumped out.

Luke whispered in Maggie's ear. "He opened the door for her. I like him already."

Maggie elbowed him in the stomach then ran down the steps to hug her niece. When Jimmy reached out a hand, Maggie felt a twinge of recognition. But she shook it off and hugged him.

"I warned ya. She's a hugger," Bree said as Luke swept her up and spun her around.

A giggle escaped as she told him to put her down. Luke shook Jimmy's hand but promised he wouldn't hug him til he got to know him better. Jimmy thanked him for that. Maggie and Bree shook their heads. When the dogs began to bark from the back yard, Bree ran to the gate to let them out.

"Jimmy," she yelled over her shoulder. "Come meet Charlie and Molly." Jimmy walked over and the labs bounced back and forth. First they jumped on Bree then they jumped on Jimmy. They wagged their tails and barked for attention.

Luke whispered in Maggie's ear again. "The dogs like him too. So, I like him even more."

Again, she elbowed his stomach. It dawned on Luke that Maggie still hadn't said anything. He grew serious and asked if she was okay.

"Mm?" She answered vaguely. Yeah." She said with a nod.

Luke hesitated, then told her that she didn't act like everything is okay.

263

"No. It is. It's just that when I first met Jimmy, I felt like I knew him."

Bree and Jimmy walked back with the dogs at their heels. "He gets that all the time, Aunt Mag. Everywhere we go, somebody thinks they know Jimmy from somewhere."

Maggie agreed and said he must have one of those faces. When a chill danced up her spine, Maggie couldn't be certain it was from the cold. She suggested they all go inside.

CHAPTER 89

Jimmy felt less nervous, but something bothered him. He hadn't said anything, but he thought he recognized Bree's aunt when they first met. Initially, he chalked it up to how much Bree talked about her, and the pictures she showed him. Now, he couldn't be sure.

"Get a grip Jim," he told himself. "It's your nerves. That's all."

Maggie told Bree that she had set up her old bedroom and there were clean towels in the bathroom. Jimmy took their bags upstairs. When he came back down, Jimmy told Maggie and Luke that Bree was on the phone with her Aunt Liz and then she wanted to take a shower. With a straight face he added, "she thinks you want to talk to me alone and find out what my intentions are."

There was a moment of silence before Luke burst out laughing. He offered Jimmy a beer and raised his own in Maggie's direction. "I believe he's talking to you."

Maggie bit her bottom lip and rolled her eyes. "Oh shut up and pour me a glass of wine." Jimmy relaxed for the first time since he got there. Since Bree was in the shower, Jimmy took opportunity to ask Maggie and Luke if he could talk with them.

"Sure." Maggie said. "Do we need to sit down?"

Jimmy shook his head no. "But I'll take another beer if you're offering."

Luke and Maggie exchanged a look. He grabbed two more beers and topped off Maggie's wine. With a look at Jimmy he said, "the floor is all yours."

Jimmy fidgeted from foot to foot. He struggled to put his feelings into words. Yes, he loved Bree, but it was more than that. More than he ever imagined. She was also his best friend and he wanted to build a life with her. When he brought up Bree's parents, Maggie noticed Jimmy's eyes went dark. But he shook it off and kept talking. He told them that he'd already asked Lizzie and George for their blessing, but he would like Luke and Maggie's blessing as well. He wanted to ask Bree to marry him, and he was certain she'd say yes.

Maggie smiled at him. "With or without our blessing. She'd say yes."

"That's true," Jimmy said then looked at Luke. "She loves you and she respects you. What you think matters to her." He shrugged and added, "so it matters to me too."

Luke looked at Maggie. "What are you thinking?"

She took a sip of wine, then answered. "That I'm going to kill my sister for keeping this from me." Before she could say anything else, the oven timer went off. She took fresh baked bread out of the oven then looked at Jimmy.

"Bree loves you. And it's obvious you love her. That's good enough for me." She then asked him if he had a ring picked out.

"I don't. Bree does." Maggie knew what he was about to say. But she still wasn't prepared for it.

Jimmy cleared his throat before he asked Maggie about the ring she had promised to Bree. "It's the only one she wants."

Maggie had to force herself not to cry. She asked him if he knew the ring was a sapphire surrounded by diamonds and not a traditional engagement ring. Jimmy nodded and said it didn't matter whether or not it was traditional. He repeated that Bree had her heart set on that particular ring. Maggie knew he was right. She told him the ring was his if he wanted it.

What Jimmy wanted to do was jump up and hug her, but he heard Bree on the stairs. Not sure how to change the subject, Luke came to his rescue. As Bree came into the kitchen, she heard Luke ask Jimmy to help him secure the patio furniture. They went outside, and Maggie asked Bree to set the table.

Bree got out bowls and wondered what Maggie thought of Jimmy.

"He seems nice. Luke's convinced that since the dogs like him, he must be a good guy." Maggie added that all that matters is that Bree is happy.

"I am, Aunt Mag. Never thought I would fall in love, but I did." Bree hugged Maggie with tears in her eyes. Then she whispered, "thank you for pushing me to never give up on finding someone."

Maggie whispered back. "Thank you for listening to me." Before Bree could respond, Luke and Jimmy came back in and claimed they were starving.

While they ate, Bree talked about early graduation and how she was lead cake decorator at the hotel. "Last summer at le Cordon Bleu really paid off." She told them about her business plan and was anxious to show them the drawings she'd done of her pastry shop. Jimmy had been student teaching and did seem to connect with the kids he worked with.

Maggie listened to them talk and couldn't help but smile. As she and Luke cleaned up, Luke whispered to Maggie that he thought she worried for nothing.

"He loves her Mag." Then he kissed her. "Like I love you," he whispered. With a smirk he added that later he would show her how much he loved her.

Luke and Maggie lay in bed that night and talked softly. "You don't have to give them the ring Mag. I'm sure they'd understand. It means a lot to you."

Maggie looked at Luke with so much love, she had to turn away. *He has so much faith in us, that he's okay if I keep the ring another man gave me*, she thought. Maggie kissed him with pure love. "That ring was a promise of a better life with a good man. Jase kept that promise when he led me here. To you. And now, that same ring can be Bree's promise of a better life. Because I believe Jimmy is a good man."

She shifted her weight and climbed on top of him. She leaned in to nibble on his ear, and whispered, "I believe you promised to show me how much you love me." Luke rolled her over on her back and reminded her that he never broke a promise.

CHAPTER 90

The next morning, Maggie woke up to gray skies and dog breath. As soon as she opened her eyes, both dogs licked her face. The clock radio told her it was just past six in the morning. Stretching, she asked the dogs if their dad had gotten an early start. They didn't answer, but since the house was quiet, she assumed he was already gone.

Whenever a nor'easter was forecasted, the residents of the Cove always got together to board up windows and secure anything that might blow away. As bad as these storms could be, they always brought out the best in this town and it's one of the reasons Maggie knew she'd never leave it. With the exception of the diner, which Joe insisted he keep open for the emergency crews, all the other businesses would shut down by late afternoon. As she started to make the bed, Maggie made a mental note of what she'd need to have in the house to ride out the storm.

Before she headed downstairs, she stopped in front of her dresser and opened the top drawer. Her fingers shook when she picked up the ring box. She stood there for a while and let memories wash over her. Through her. Finally, she opened it. The sapphire and diamonds gleamed. She held it in her hand and marveled again at its beauty. Brushing away a tear, she pressed the ring to her heart. "Bree," she whispered, "I hope this ring brings you all the love and happiness it brought me."

Maggie put the box in the pocket of the hoodie she'd thrown on. She hoped she could somehow slip it to Jimmy. As luck would have it, she ran into him in the hallway.

"Bree wants to take me to the diner for breakfast if you'd like to join us," he told her.

Without a word, Maggie handed the ring box to him. When he opened it, he was speechless. He told her he would never have found a ring like that in a million years.

"I was stunned the first time I saw it too." Jimmy had no idea how he could ever thank her. On impulse, he hugged her and promised that he would always take care of Bree.

Once again, Maggie felt a strange sensation stir in the pit of her stomach. When Bree called up from the kitchen, Jimmy quickly put the box in his backpack. Bree came up to see what was taking Jimmy so long. When she saw Maggie, Bree asked if she wanted to come to the diner.

"Thanks, but Jimmy already asked." Back downstairs, she told them her plans for the day. "I need to make sure the store is boarded up, and then I want to run to the market. I'm sure we're well stocked, but you never know."

Bree insisted that she show Jimmy as much of the Cove as she could before the storm hit. "I want him to meet Mr. Bagliotti, and of course, Joe and Angie. I might try to stop in at Oyster Bed to say hello to the O'Roarkes since Saturday supper is out tonight."

Maggie told them to have fun, but reminded Bree how the storms could sweep in without warning. "Please be home before the shops start to close." She stopped on the stairs and turned back around. "Ooh, if Mr. Bagliotti has any cannoli, please get some."

CHAPTER 91

Bree and Jimmy started at the diner. When they walked in, Joe nearly jumped over the counter to scoop Bree up in a bear hug. "Angie, get out here," he called to his wife. Several of the patrons called out to welcome Bree home and nod to Jimmy. Angie appeared in the same grease-stained apron she'd worn for years.

"There's my best sous chef," she cried and pulled Bree close. She turned to Jimmy and asked, "are you the young man who's been keeping her from us."

Jimmy tried to protest that it wasn't his fault when Angie reached out her arms.

"Another hugger," Bree whispered.

She told him she was happy to finally meet him. "And if Joe gives you a hard time, ignore him." She said loud enough for her husband to hear. Joe snorted, but Jimmy knew Joe was sizing him up and trying to decide if he was good enough for Bree.

They took a booth and ordered breakfast. Bree told Jimmy how Maggie had landed there five years ago. That she had come into the diner, spent the weekend at a B&B and decided to make this place home. Joe put coffee down in front of them, and added that Maggie, and Bree, were family. "And we look after family." He said directly to Jimmy. Joe's smile was more menacing then friendly. He left them to check on their food.

Jimmy heard Joe's veiled threat. "He's a little scary," he whispered to Bree.

"He's a big teddy bear who's all talk," she yelled loud

enough for Joe to hear.

"Ya got that right girl," Angie hollered out from the kitchen. Some of the regulars raised their cups in agreement. Joe shook his head.

After breakfast, Bree and Jimmy walked the three blocks to the bakery. People stopped them now and then to say hi to Bree and ask her about school.

"I remember when you moved here after your nana passed. It's nice to know that you were able to make this place your home." Jimmy said as they walked into Bagliotti's.

Bree told him it wasn't hard to make Lantern Light home. "Actually, Aunt Maggie made it home. They more or less adopted me."

Once inside, Jimmy watched as Bree transformed into another being. It happened any time she was in a bakery, pastry or coffee shop. She picked up scents that any other person would miss. If someone walked past with a box, she could instinctively tell you what was in it. Not based on anything but the person who carried it.

She could look at a customer and tell you if they preferred strawberry shortcake or carrot cake. She knew if they would order cinnamon buns with or without nuts. And she was one hundred percent accurate on picking out anyone's favorite donut. This was her world and she was never happier than when she was able to tweak an old recipe or create something brand new.

"Is that my Bree?" A man called out. Bree turned as Mr. Bagliotti came from behind the counter. With a tear in his eye, he hugged her close. Bree wiped away her own tear before she took a step back. She wanted him to know that they were just home for the weekend. Since she wasn't sure what would happen with the storm, she made sure she stopped in today.

"And who exactly is this *we*?" He asked with raised eyebrows.

Bree held Jimmy's hand. "Mr. Bagliotti, this is Jimmy." Bree turned to Jimmy and explained that while her nana taught her to bake, it was Mr. Bagliotti who taught her how to decorate.

"He encouraged me to experiment with different flavors and piping tips. Basically, Nana T taught me the science of baking and Mr. B taught me the art of it."

The old baker brushed off the compliment. "You are the granddaughter I never had. And I am so proud of you." Before either of them got too emotional, Mr. Bagliotti called for everyone's attention. He proceeded to brag about his protégé who had gone to London for summer classes at Le Cordon Bleu. The last part said with his best French accent. His customers clapped and Bree blushed. She remembered the cannoli for her aunt, and ordered half dozen mixed. She added a box of petit fours for the O'Roarkes. Before she left, Bree promised to stop back the next day if the storm wasn't too bad.

Outside, Bree had to sit down on the sidewalk bench. "You okay?" Jimmy asked and sat beside her.

Bree didn't answer right away, she sat there and looked up and down Main Street. "These people," she said and extended her arms. "They have been so incredible to me." She looked back over her shoulder at the diner and thought about her first day with Angie. "I was such a klutz when I started there," she smiled with nostalgia. "But Angie was so gracious with me. And even though my heart is in baking, my shifts at the diner taught me time management in the kitchen."

Then she stared in the window of the bakery. "That man in there, is why I have been as successful as I am. He's the reason I was able to succeed in those classes in Europe. And, I don't know. Seeing them all today, I'm overwhelmed with." Bree stopped. She struggled for the right word. "I'm grateful for these people. And if things work out the way we have planned, you and I will stay in Massachusetts."

Bree held up her hand and reminded him she hadn't told her aunt that yet and wasn't sure how she would take it. But she knew, that this would be the last time, for a long time, that she would be back here. They sat a little while longer before Bree stood up and kissed Jimmy's cheek. "I am so glad I finally got to share this place with you."

CHAPTER 92

By noon, Bree had introduced Jimmy to all the people she wanted him to meet. They had made it out to the peninsula and were back on Main Street in and out of whatever shops hadn't yet closed. They stopped in front of This 'n That. She told him how her aunt had come to own it. Then they went into The Clothes Horse. Bree insisted she needed leggings, although Jimmy couldn't imagine how. Since it's all she wore and she had about a hundred pairs.

An hour later, they walked out with three bags filled with leggings, warm socks and several shirts for Jimmy he didn't remember buying. A light rain had started to fall and the air developed that cold raw feel to it only people who lived on the northeastern coast could recognize. Bree wanted to check out a couple more places, but Jimmy reminded her that they promised Maggie they'd be home before the shops started to close. And most of them were already locked down tight.

As Bree and Jimmy walked in the house, the winds started to pick up. They stood and shook off the damp. Luke had started a fire in the wood burning stove that he promised would make the entire downstairs feel warm and toasty. One end of the dining room table looked like an aisle in Wally's Hardware. It was lined with flashlights, batteries, candles, lighters and a battery-operated radio. Something in the crockpot had Jimmy's mouth salivating and his stomach growling.

Maggie hoped he liked chicken and dumplings. Jimmy sat the box of cannoli on the counter and asked if the dogs needed to go out before the storm hit. As if on cue, lights flickered. Bree walked to the back door to try to coax Charlie and Molly out.

"They won't go any further than the patio in this weather," she told Jimmy. Sure enough, the dogs ran out, did their business and came right back in. Bree gave him a told you so look and took their bags upstairs while Luke and Jimmy did one more property check.

Bree sorted out the bags, and put all of Jimmy's shirts into one. Then she picked up his duffel bag, emptied it and rearranged his clothes to fit the bag in there. As she turned back to the door, she caught sight of the ring box that had fallen onto the bed. Her hands trembled as she picked it up and opened the box. She started to cry.

"Oh," she whispered. "He must have asked permission." Bree didn't want to ruin his surprise, but she stood there transfixed on the sapphire unable to put the box back. She didn't hear Jimmy in the doorway until he coughed.

Startled, she jumped. "I'm sor. Jimmy I wasn't snoop." Bree stopped talking. "I just wanted to put your shirts in here. The box caught my eye and I couldn't help myself."

Jimmy walked over to hug her. "Look," he said. "Yes, I want to marry you. But I also want to propose properly."

Bree sniffed back tears. She looked up at him with love and said she would like that too.

"Okay. Then think of this," he said and closed the box, "as a promise." Because she didn't trust herself to speak, Bree simply nodded. Before she could kiss him, the lights flickered to remind them that a storm was brewing.

CHAPTER 93

Maggie bolted up in bed. The rain still pelted the roof and windows, but at least the winds had died down. *What was that?* She wondered. Luke stirred beside her.

"Whas wron?" He mumbled. Maggie leaned over to kiss his forehead.

"I thought I heard the front door open and close." Luke rubbed his eyes and asked if it might've been the wind. "I don't think so. But I'll go check."

Luke mumbled again and Maggie assured that he was indeed the man of the house. "But since I'm already awake," she let her words trail off as she got out of bed, pulled on socks and grabbed a flannel shirt off the back of the door.

On the second floor, she passed Bree's door and heard crying. Charlie and Molly ran ahead of Maggie. *If someone is in the house*, she thought, *they'll let me know.* Instead, she knocked on her niece's door.

"Bree, are you okay." At first, Bree didn't answer. Then she opened the door and fell into her aunt's arms.

"Jimma. Jimma. Jimmy is gone." She stuttered.

Maggie was stunned. "What do you mean gone?" She asked as she looked around the bedroom for any sign of him. Bree caught her breath. Maggie hollered up the stairs for Luke. Then she pulled Bree into the bedroom and sat her on the bed.

"Bree." She said and tried to soothe her niece. "What happened?" But Bree didn't answer. She sat there numb. Finally, she found her voice.

"I don't know," was all she could manage. Luke stood in

the doorway confused. When he started to ask what was going on, Maggie held up her hand. Softer than before, she asked Bree again what had happened.

Bree told Maggie that she'd found the ring box by accident, and they had sat up talking. They were happy and had begun to make long-term plans. He'd said they weren't officially engaged yet, but they would be. "Then I started to tell him about the ring. About Uncle Jase and how he died." All of a sudden, Jimmy had gone silent.

"He looked like he'd seen a ghost. He started to tremble. He shook his head and said this couldn't be real. That if he knew who my aunt was, he never would have gotten involved with me."

Maggie interrupted. "Wait. Why would being related to me stop him from getting involved with you? That doesn't make any sense."

Bree nodded her head and blew her nose. "I know. And then he started to ramble on about how if you knew who is brother was, and his dad." Bree stood up and started to pace. "I didn't even know he had a brother. I mean, Aunt Mag, if I don't know that what else don't I? But Bree stopped.

Maggie had gone as white as a ghost and looked like she was about to pass out. "Oh my god. Oh my god." She repeated over and over.

"Aunt Maggie. Are you okay?" Maggie didn't answer. Instead, she hugged Bree tight and kissed the top of her head.

"Oh Bree. I am so. I." She turned to Luke, and told him he needed to find Jimmy and bring him back.

Bree jumped up. "No. If he's gonna run out for some stupid reason."

But Maggie cut her off. "Bree. Stop. Jimmy has very good reasons to think we would not welcome him." Again, she asked Luke to find Jimmy and bring him back. Then she turned to Bree and told her to splash some water on her face and come downstairs. When the phone rang, Luke ran down to the kitchen to answer it. Maggie started to follow.

She stopped in the doorway and looked back at her niece. "I promise you Bree, I will tell you everything. Please don't ask questions right now. You have to trust me."

Downstairs, Luke had hung up the phone. "That was Joe. You know he keeps the diner open during storms for the emergency workers. Jimmy went in hoping to catch a ride to the bus station. I told Joe to keep him there." Maggie went to Luke and hugged him. He pulled her tight, and kissed her forehead.

"Got a lot of questions Mag," he started to say.

"I know." She looked up at him and asked him to trust her.

"You know I do. But this kid hurt Bree, and I don't."

Maggie cut him off. "I promise. It will all make sense. But I have to talk to Jimmy." She told Luke to be careful, watched him slip into boots, pull on a coat and head out the door. Maggie stood in the kitchen and relived a horrible moment in time that she had worked so hard to let go.

Charlie brought her back to the present and she let him and Molly out into the yard. Since they wouldn't be long, Maggie stood in the open doorway. She was numb inside and didn't even feel the cold that had begun to seep into her skin. An old CCR song came to mind. Bree had come into the kitchen to hear her aunt sing soft and low. She didn't know the words; but she knew the tune.

With the dogs back inside, Maggie closed the door, turned

and almost knocked into Bree. "Sorry sweetie, I didn't know you were there," Maggie said as she brushed away a tear.

"What song were you singing?" Bree asked, frightened by Maggie's vacant stare.

With a wave toward the window, Maggie told her it was Who'll Stop the Rain. Before she could say anything further, the front door blew open.

CHAPTER 94

Luke and Jimmy stood there. They shook with cold and wet. Jimmy kept his head down too afraid to make eye contact with anyone. He didn't want to see the hurt he knew he caused Bree. As steady as possible, Maggie told them to go up, take warm showers and to leave their clothes outside the doors so she could throw them in the dryer. When Jimmy started to protest, she stopped him.

"Jimmy, I promise you we will talk. We need to talk. But right now, you are dripping all over my floor."

Maggie pointed to the puddle that had begun to form. "If you've ever cared about Bree," Maggie stopped when Jimmy's head snapped up. The look in his eyes told Maggie everything she needed to know.

Jimmy still couldn't bring himself to look at Bree. Resigned, he followed Luke upstairs. Maggie got towels to mop up the water, and suggested Bree make breakfast. When Bree started to argue, Maggie reminded her that was her go to stress reliever.

"And while you're at the stove, how 'bout a pot of coffee?" Maggie asked.

Bree mumbled that her aunt was impossible, but started to grab things from the refrigerator to make omelets.

After his shower, Luke came downstairs and found Maggie curled up in a corner of the couch. She stared out the window, but he could tell she was somewhere far away from Lantern Light Cove. He poured coffee for both of them and went to sit with her. She laid her head on his shoulder.

"I never, in a million years, could've seen this, could've imagined," she whispered. Maggie wanted to tell him everything privately, but knew she could only go through this once. Maggie asked Luke to be patient while they waited for Jimmy. Once breakfast was ready, she told everyone to sit at the table, and asked Luke and Bree to be patient while she and Jimmy spoke.

"Don't interrupt. Don't ask questions. Just listen." Maggie looked at Jimmy who sat across from her. "Tommy Chason is your brother. Half-brother," she said with a nod. "You're Kevin's son. But you changed your name." Jimmy didn't say anything.

Those names clicked somewhere in the back of Luke's brain. Then it crashed down on him. "Oh Mag," he started. Maggie squeezed his hand to stop him.

"Jimmy," Maggie said in a firm but gentle voice. "Please look at me."

It took a minute, but when Jimmy finally raised his head, his eyes were filled with tears. "I'm so sorry," he whispered.

Bree had enough. She slammed her hands on the table. "Could somebody please tell me what is going on?" She demanded.

Maggie didn't take her eyes off Jimmy, but asked Bree what she remembered about the night Jase died.

"Not much. I think I was about thirteen. My nana told me that there had been a horrible accident." Bree answered still not sure what her uncle's death had to do with Jimmy.

With tenderness, Maggie looked at Bree, then back at Jimmy. "That's exactly what it was. A horrible accident." When Jimmy started to speak, Maggie reminded Jimmy that it was an accident he had absolutely nothing to do with.

"Jimmy. Why do you think you had something to do with Uncle Jase's death?" Bree wanted to know.

Maggie told Jimmy it was up to him, but one of them had to tell Bree everything. He couldn't speak at first, when he did, his voice was shaky. But he held Bree's hand as he told her his story. Tommy, the one who was driving the car, was Jimmy's half-brother. He told her that his father had been a cop at the time and tried to cover it up.

"But your last name is Macnamara." Bree said between tears.

"I was born William James Chason," Jimmy said quietly. "After Tommy killed your uncle and my dad well, did what he did, I wanted nothing to do with either of them. So, I changed my name legally and told them both that they were dead to me. I am so sorry Bree. I never said anything about them because they don't matter. In my world they don't exist."

Bree started to shudder. "I don't even know what. None of this makes any sen." She looked at Maggie. As tears spilled down her cheeks, she pleaded. "What am I supposed to do with this?"

Jimmy jumped up from the table and started to pace. "This is why I took off. I never want to hurt you Bree, but, but." He stopped for a minute and rubbed his hands together. "I never imagined that your aunt was. Is." He moved toward the door. He told Bree that it would be better if he left before things went any further.

Bree snapped. "Better for who?" She yelled. "No. You know what Jimmy? William? Or whoever you are. Go ahead. Run. Bail. I'm used to it. My parents were champs. I don't care what you do."

Bree got up from the table and headed toward the stairs. Jimmy almost ran to the door.

Luke felt helpless. The pain in Maggie's eyes shattered his heart but he didn't have a clue what to do. Apparently, she did.

CHAPTER 95

Maggie slammed her own hands on the table and stood up. "Enough!" She demanded in a tone that caused both Bree and Jimmy to stop in their tracks. "You two." She pointed at them. "Sit. Down. Now." The defiant look on Bree's face lasted exactly two seconds before she walked back and sat down. Jimmy followed.

Maggie turned to Luke. She felt deflated. "It looks like the rain stopped. Why don't you take our kids," she gestured to the dogs, "down to your house? They aren't used to yelling and I'm sure they feel the tension." Before he could argue, she reminded him that they'd need to check for any storm damage because settlement was next week.

"And, as always, by us checking, I do mean you," she said with a weak smile. "I'll be down soon and then we can drive around and see if any of our friends need help." Her eyes told him she was okay, or at least she would be.

He whistled for the dogs. Maggie walked them to the door where Luke hugged her and whispered, "I love you." With a wink, she whispered back. "I like when you prove that to me."

Maggie ran up to Bree's room, grabbed the ring box off the dresser and went back down. She took a seat at one end of the table and asked Bree and Jimmy to sit on either side of her. It took a minute before either of them moved. She set the ring box on the table in front of her.

"Look," she began. "This," she said and made a circle with her hands, "is beyond anything anyone could've imagined. But here we are."

Bree tried to interrupt, but Maggie stopped her. "Again. Please. Just listen." Maggie looked away and spied the glass seahorse she'd bought at This 'n That a lifetime ago. She turned first to Jimmy, and covered his hand with hers. With a calm she finally started to feel, she told him that he needed to forgive his brother and father.

Jimmy felt a lot of things. Anger. Sadness. Embarrassment. Not forgiveness. The look he gave Maggie showed all of it.

"Jimmy, forgiving them isn't for their benefit. It's for yours. Otherwise, you will spend the rest of your life carrying a weight that was never yours to bear."

As she squeezed his hand she added, "I've forgiven your brother. He made a horrible mistake. I've even forgiven your father, although what he did was intentional. But I get that too."

Jimmy shook his head. "How could you forgive him?" He couldn't help the anger that rose in his voice.

Maggie responded as tenderly as she could. "He wanted to protect his child. It was wrong. But if you are ever lucky enough to have a child of your own one day, maybe you'll understand."

She looked at Bree and added that Jimmy was right to be concerned about how any of them would react. "True, he didn't handle it well, but I am pretty sure he was scared. And that fear was overwhelming because he loves you. Now that you know this truth, can you accept it?"

Bree didn't say answer. Couldn't answer. Maggie squeezed both their hands before she stood up. She tapped the ring box. "If you love each other and truly want to build a life together, then that is all that matters." Outside, she saw the sun had broken through the clouds. She hoped it was a good sign.

"You two need to talk. And you two need to listen. Go take a nice long walk on the beach. Don't let what anyone else may think, feel or say influence what you decide to do. Listen to your hearts. At the end of the day, it's always the best advice you'll ever get."

Maggie leaned over and kissed the top of Bree's head. Then she grabbed her coat and went to find Luke.

For a while, they both sat at the table in silence lost in their own thoughts. Jimmy spoke first. "Bree, if you want me to."

She cut him off. She walked into the kitchen and started to pull out flour, sugar, eggs and whatever spices she could find. She reminded Jimmy that baking was the best way she knew how to deal with a problem. "Aunt Maggie walks the beach. I bake."

Jimmy knew this. And in the two years they'd been together, he learned the hard way not to interrupt her. He got up and walked over to the back door. The storm had carpeted the yard in wet leaves. "And it threw in some large branches and twigs for good measure" he said to no one in particular. He found trash bags, grabbed his hoodie and went outside to clean up.

CHAPTER 96

By the time Maggie and Luke turned onto their street, it was late afternoon. Maggie noticed large piles of leaves and branches out by the curb up and down the sidewalk. As they got out of the truck, their neighbor across the street called out. "Hey Mag, thank Bree's boyfriend for us. He did a heck of a job to help everyone clean up today."

Maggie couldn't reply. She turned to Luke. "If he came out here to help, they apparently didn't go for a walk. Do you think they talked at all?"

Luke squeezed her hand. "Whatever they decided, we support them. It's their decision, Mag." He kissed her, then pulled her toward the house.

As she opened the front door, the smell of fresh baked chocolate chips, coupled with something cinnamonny filled the air. At the kitchen table she stopped. There were three large trays filled with about seven different types of cookies.

Luke didn't hesitate to unwrap the tray with the chocolate chips. He took a bite and almost purred in delight. It was crispy on the outside and soft and gooey on the inside. Before Maggie could stop him, he inhaled that one and popped another into his mouth.

Maggie looked around not sure what to think. The house was quiet and she couldn't remember if she'd seen Bree's car out front. She was about to go look when Charlie and Molly ran to the back door. She walked over but stopped. She could hear muffled voices in the yard. Luke came up behind her and asked if she planned to let the kids out.

Maggie held up her hand. "Bree and Jimmy are out there," she whispered. "I'm not sure what I should do."

Luke looked out the window and saw them at the fire pit. "I think they're making s'mores." Then he asked Maggie, what drinks go with 'smores.

"Wh-what?" She stammered still unsure if she should open the door or not.

Luke ignored her. He opened the refrigerator and pulled out the bottle of champagne Maggie always kept in for mimosas.

"Champagne does not go with s'mores." She said emphatically.

"No. But it does go with celebrations. And I am pretty sure we have something to celebrate."

It took a full second for the realization to set in before Maggie turned and yanked open the back door. By the light of the fire, she could see the sparkle of sapphire on Bree's left hand.